To my agent, Jim McCarthy. Six books in and counting!

PROLOGUE

A drop of sweat trickled down the soldier's neck. It settled briefly atop her sun-warmed shoulder before a vigorous swing of her arm jostled it loose. She raised her staff. Kicked the air. Jumped. And brought her staff down with a yell.

A hundred quarterstaffs thudded on the dirt. A hundred voices shouted. The soldier smiled at their bright timbre, the lack of baritone and bass notes.

The women around her were red with exertion and covered in dust. Their braids hung damp and dark with sweat. Still, they blocked, punched and kicked as one. Not a single soldier lowered her kicks or softened her blows as the sun climbed higher, its rays blazing hotter. On their tunics, the soldiers had embroidered names of women long gone – generals, soldiers, wrestlers, fencers. It was an homage to those heroes, and perhaps an attempt to summon their spirits, if the embroiderer herself proved worthy.

Their leader stood in front, shouting commands in a clear voice. Mulan, war hero of China, barely recognisable from the girl who'd run off a few years ago to join the army in her father's stead. Looking at Mulan, the soldier felt pride, but also compassion. Mulan had mastered the art of war, but there remained obstacles ahead, dangers more nuanced than a simple exchange of swords. She was close to fulfilling her destiny, but first, she'd have to learn the way of the spirits, to use their strength as her own. And she would know pain. Because the fenghuang, the phoenix, that guardian of imperial harmony, does not grant its blessing to everyone. Only the most honest, loyal and selfless. The one who is brave against encroaching darkness.

CHAPTER ONE

The chessboard in front of Mulan was clearly made for men. The carved, rounded stones were slightly too large for a woman's hand to hold comfortably, slightly too heavy for Mulan to balance easily on her fingers. This awkwardness was familiar to Mulan from her days in the army – sword pommels that were too wide, saddles that were just a bit too long. It brought a strong sense of déjà vu.

She moved her cannon forwards on the board. The piece had its name carved on its rounded top, and she ran her thumb across the imprint before putting it down. Mulan looked at her hand. Though her palms and fingers were calloused by years of sword and staff training, her bone structure was still too fine for a man's. She'd got out of the habit of hiding her hands from view. Silently chiding herself, she curled her fingers under her palm and lowered her fists into her lap.

Thankfully, her opponent was too engrossed in the game to notice. He was an older man, well dressed. There was a bit of white in his moustache, though he still sat straight and his shoulders were sturdy with muscle. He had a scar over his right eye, and another one from his nose to the left edge of his face. Rich silk sleeves covered his arms, but once in a while, they rode up, and Mulan saw more scars in various stages of healing. If she peeked beneath the table, she'd see the sword he wore at his waist. Weapons of any kind weren't allowed in this chess teahouse, but Yang Dafan did what he wished.

Dafan finally moved, capturing one of her pawns with his elephant. "You're losing quite a few of your soldiers, young Master Chen," said Dafan. "Is this some new strategy I'm unfamiliar with?"

"I'm not a very skilled chess player, I'm sorry to say." She spoke from the bottom of her diaphragm to accentuate the lower registers of her voice.

"Why step foot into a chess house, then?"

"I used to play half-board chess with my father. I was feeling nostalgic on the road."

"Half-board chess?"

"Perhaps you call it blind chess. When you start with the pieces facedown and flip them, one by one."

"A child's variation."

"I did mention I played it with my father."

Dafan pushed the cuticle at the base of his thumbnail.

Mulan noticed that the little fingernail on his left hand was groomed elegantly long. She wondered how he protected it when he fought.

"At some point," said Dafan, "one does have to grow up."

"I know," said Mulan. "But the children's version appeals to me. I like the idea of keeping your soldiers disguised until they are right next to your enemy."

In fact, both Mulan and her chess partner were well practised in hiding from the enemy. Just five days ago, Yang Dafan and his men had waylaid a travelling caravan. They'd killed half the guards and disappeared with a fortune in fine silk.

Dafan and his team of brigands had been the scourge of Mulan's region for close to a year. He was also very careful, much to the area magistrate's chagrin. Dafan stayed hidden most of the time. When he did move in public, usually to indulge in music, chess or tea, he took bodyguards with him. He posted men to watch the roads whenever he entered a building, and his near-supernatural ability to disappear at the first sign of pursuit had stymied the magistrate on more than one occasion. After several failed attempts, the magistrate had scaled back his attempts to catch the criminal. Mulan suspected it was because he could no longer handle the humiliation.

Both Mulan and Dafan glanced up as a woman came by to refill their tea. Mulan nodded a thanks, though the woman barely glanced at her. Instead, she gazed up at Dafan in adoring invitation.

Liwen was exceptionally beautiful, with full lips, long lashes, a proud nose and smooth olive skin. She was young, about the same age as Mulan, and deadly with just about any weapon known to man. Mulan had seen her split one arrow with another and disarm full-fledged soldiers with nothing but a scarf. But until today, she'd never seen Liwen flirt.

She was pretty good. At least, it seemed so to Mulan, the way her eyes flitted to sneak glances at Dafan, the amusing but decidedly effective sway in her hips as she circled the room. The swordsmen Dafan had stationed at the corners of the teahouse now spent their time watching Liwen instead of scanning for threats, though Mulan guessed they'd snap out if it quickly enough if a fight broke out. Unfortunately for Liwen, however, the target of her attentions seemed far more interested in his chessboard than in her.

Mulan cast another glance around the room. Besides the men in corners with forbidden swords, Dafan had other bandits scattered here and there, drinking tea and enjoying their own chess matches. Mulan counted at least ten. And though she had her own women spread throughout the shop – tea girls with daggers tucked in their sashes, kitchen maids with short swords stashed among the pots – she would rather it not come to an all-out fight. It would be better if Liwen could lure Dafan out into one of the upstairs rooms, as they had planned. Capture the general, win the game. Just like in chess.

Mulan moved her cannon across the river, forcing Dafan to retreat one of his horses.

"Where do you travel from here?" Dafan asked.

"West a few days," said Mulan. "My father is looking to buy land suitable for vineyards. Our wine business has been growing steadily."

"I don't drink grape wine myself," said Dafan. "Is it any good?"

"You'll find it sweeter than rice wine," said Mulan. "We've had the honour of shipping several barrels to the emperor."

Dafan raised his eyebrows, a movement that pulled at his facial scars. "Really? That is a great honour indeed."

Mulan nodded modestly. "A bit of good fortune."

Liwen came again to refill their cups, though neither Mulan nor Dafan had taken a sip. "Master Yang," she said, laying a hand lightly on his shoulder. "You are such a skilled chess strategist."

Dafan coughed low in his throat and waved her away. Liwen gave Mulan an exasperated glance over his shoulder as she retreated.

Mulan worked hard to suppress her smile. Liwen was usually so good at everything she did that it would have been amusing to see her struggle if the stakes hadn't been so high. Mulan watched her go, and then made a quick decision.

"Master Yang," she said. "Perhaps I may redeem myself from being such a poor adversary in our chess game today. I have several jugs from our winery in my room upstairs. I'd be honoured if you would have a taste yourself."

Dafan raised his head. "I would, indeed. Have the staff fetch some for us."

"I don't trust any of the staff with this batch," said Mulan. "It's a new blend of grapes from several different vineyards. I formulated it myself and wouldn't want to see it sold to our competitors. What of this? I clearly have no hope of victory in our game today. Perhaps you can spare me the shame of actually living out my defeat and come upstairs with me."

The bandit lord studied the chessboard, then shrugged and pushed his chair back. Mulan remembered to grab her cane as she stood, and to walk favouring her right leg. The robe she wore, suitably fine for a rich merchant's son, reached her ankles and was gathered at the waist with a jade-inlaid belt. Though the robe was loose enough that she might have tried hiding a sword under its folds, she'd deemed it too much of a risk. A cane was the second-best option. At least she had something other than her limbs with which to stop a sharp edge.

The bell sleeves of Mulan's robe flapped distractingly as she waved at Liwen. "Bring some fresh wine cups to my room."

Dafan walked towards the stairs, motioning for his swordsmen to follow. Mulan fought down her frustration as one henchman ran up the stairs ahead of them, and no less than three fell in step behind.

"I'm afraid I can't offer a drink to your men," she said.

"Pay no attention to them," he said. "They're a necessary precaution in my line of work, but they do not expect to be treated to a sample."

"You have not yet told me your line of work," said Mulan. She allowed a hint of suspicion to enter her voice. Though the rich young traveller she impersonated was new to the area, he wasn't naive enough to be oblivious in the face of five prohibited swords.

"I'm a businessman," said Dafan. "But I don't conduct business in my places of relaxation."

The henchman who had gone ahead reappeared at the top of the stairs as Mulan and Dafan approached. He gave a quick nod and took his place behind the bandit lord.

The hallway upstairs was narrow, with closed doors to the establishment's few guest rooms lining each wall. The group's footsteps echoed on the wooden floor, more heavily than they should have. Everyone was weighed down with metal and armour. That knowledge wound Mulan's nerves even tighter.

Mulan stopped at the first door and opened it wide enough for Dafan to see inside. It was a sparsely furnished room, with a small bed and a table equipped with pen and ink sticks. Two packed bags and a large clay jar lay on the ground next to the bed.

"As you can see," she said. "There is nothing threatening inside my room. I must insist that your men stay outside."

Dafan nodded. The swordsmen stayed put as the bandit lord followed Mulan in. Mulan bent over the jar, which was as tall as her thigh, and untied the burlap cloth over the top.

"It's a freshly sealed jar," she said, moving aside for Dafan to see the fibre plug. She rummaged through her bag for a knife and brought one out without any reaction from Dafan. He had no reason to be worried. It wasn't as if she was going to fence him with it.

As she pried at the plug, footsteps shuffled in the hallway. Dafan tensed ever so slightly and moved his hand towards his sword. The swordsmen outside exchanged puzzled glances.

"Cups for Master Chen," came Liwen's voice. She and three other serving women edged their way in with polite smiles and apologetic shrugs. She carried cups and napkins, while the next woman held plates, and two others brought trays containing an assortment of dried fruits, nuts, dried fish and roasted seeds.

Dafan lowered his hand.

"Thank you," said Mulan. She took the cups from Liwen, meeting her eye but not giving any kind of signal as she weighed her options. She'd hoped to get Dafan up here alone, or at most with one or two guards. Instead, there were four guards here, and four of her own women. She supposed Liwen could not have brought more maidservants without raising suspicions. As it was, Mulan was impressed that her second-in-command had thought of so many plausible refreshments to offer.

It would be an even fight then, five against five. Mulan was confident in her own skills, and Liwen was peerless with a sword. But could the other three take on seasoned bandits? Two of the girls had trained with Mulan for close to a year. They were good students, but they'd never seen real combat. The last one, Zhonglin, was a new recruit who'd spent a few months with them at most. In fact, she wasn't even supposed to be here. Mulan had assigned her to a backup post at the end of the road to cut off any escaping bandits.

Two veterans, two skilled but green fighters and a new recruit, against five seasoned criminals. Liwen and Mulan could cover for the others to some extent, but Mulan still didn't like the odds. She hated the idea of aborting their mission when they were so close, but she didn't want these women's blood on her hands.

Zhonglin placed her tray down on the table. Her eyes widened, and she clutched at her dress. There was a clattering as a short sword landed at her feet. Mulan's heart landed on the floor with it.

"What's this?" Dafan asked. He crossed the room in two steps and snatched up the sword. "Why would a maid carry this?"

Zhonglin's already-pale face turned completely white.

Her rosebud lips quivered.

Mulan exchanged a panicked glance with Liwen. "She's just a maid. They cut things in the kitchens."

"Search the others," Dafan commanded his swordsmen. The first to enter grabbed Liwen by the arm, oblivious to the icy warning in the false maid's gaze.

It looked like Mulan had no choice.

"Yang Dafan, you're under arrest," she said. "Under order of the magistrate." She really wished she'd had a chance to get her sword.

Dafan stared at the maids, puzzling them out. "Armed women?" he said. And then he took a closer look at Mulan. "You're not what you said you were."

"No, sir," said Mulan, and she didn't bother to lower her voice. "I am not."

Liwen delivered a vicious kick to the kneecap of the swordsman holding her. He crumpled, screaming in pain, as a long dagger materialised in Liwen's hand.

"Watch out!" Liwen shouted.

Mulan raised her cane just in time to keep Dafan's sword from splitting her skull. The bandit lord's face was red, his eyes wild, and he attacked with a ferocity that was hard to counter. Each of his blows vibrated down her cane, numbing her hands and arms. Mulan backed up slowly, uncomfortably aware that the wall was coming up fast behind her.

She saw an opening and thrust the end of her cane into

Dafan's solar plexus. As he bent over, wheezing, Mulan took another step backwards. Her heel knocked against the bag by her bedside. She took a quick gamble and dropped her cane, tearing open the bag and pulling out a sword and a knife. She threw the knife to Zhonglin, who was backed against a wall, unarmed. The sword Mulan kept for herself. Screams and shouts sounded from downstairs. Her women had barricaded the stairway.

Dafan was no longer wheezing. He held his sword at the ready, though his other hand clutched his ribs. His eyes flicked from the doorway, to the injured swordsman on the ground, to his three remaining fighters, still locked in combat with Mulan's women.

"We have the stairs blocked and more soldiers coming in," said Mulan. "Surrender now and we'll bring you before the magistrate unharmed."

Shouts drifted in from outside. Through the window, Mulan saw women running for the entrance of the teahouse – more members of her militia, dressed as farmers and peasants. It gave her some satisfaction to know that Dafan had walked right past them on his way here and not realised what they were.

Dafan stared at them for a moment. Then he sheathed his sword and hoisted himself out the window.

Mulan suppressed a few choice words. She really should have seen that coming. Sticking her own sword through her belt, she followed him out. There was a creaky covered walkway on the other side, its carved floral railing dry with age. Dafan sprinted down its length and, when he reached the end, jumped up onto the balustrade and swung onto the roof.

This time, Mulan did curse. Gritting her teeth, she climbed onto the railing, grabbing on to a wooden column for balance. A bunch of persimmons, strung out to dry, hit her in the face. The roof stretched out above her, overhanging the balcony by one arm's length and supported by a crossbeam. Mulan was shorter than Dafan. The crossbeam was considerably more of a leap for her.

She jumped for it, catching the dry wood with her fingertips. The railing swung beneath her, as did the ground below. Funny how clearly she could see the jagged edge of every rock, the sharp ends of every tree branch. Mulan lifted her eyes. Swinging hand over hand, she worked her way to the end, and then swung her arm over the edge of the upturned black-tiled roof.

By the time Mulan clambered over the brittle tile, Dafan was running along the slanted roof, slipping and sliding, but somehow not falling off. Tiles knocked loose by his footfalls clattered down the slope, and Mulan hoped there was nobody standing below. The very end of their building abutted a grove of trees, and the bandit lord sprinted directly towards it.

Mulan stood, waving her arms for balance. Her shoes gave

her some traction but not enough for peace of mind. The trick, she found after a while, was to put the next foot down quickly enough so that it didn't matter if the last one slipped.

Dafan stumbled and fell flat against the roof with a great crash. He threw his arms and legs out, sliding down spread-eagled, until his foot hit the lip of the roof. Mulan redoubled her speed and drew her sword.

He regained his footing just as she reached him. Somehow he'd managed to hold on to his sword, and as she neared, he charged her. Mulan skidded to a stop to avoid splitting herself on his sword, shifting her weight to parry his incoming blow. Tiles crumbled under her feet, shattering on the distant ground below. Out of the corner of her eye, she could see a crowd gathering, their rapt faces distracting impressions she tried to ignore. This was dangerous. She needed to end things soon.

Dafan swung at her face. Instead of blocking this time, Mulan ducked and kicked out her leg, knocking his feet out from under him. The bandit landed on his side with a thud. His sword slid off the edge of the roof, and he clawed at the roof tiles to keep from following it over. Mulan slammed one foot down on his wrist and held the point of her sword to Dafan's throat.

"Enough. The magistrate's expecting you."

...

Mulan didn't dare lower her guard as she tied Dafan up. Even unarmed, he was an extremely dangerous man, and the raw hate in his eyes was frightening. Add to that the fact that they were one slip away from breaking their necks... By the time Mulan had Dafan seated on the roof with his hands secured in front of him, every muscle in her body ached from tension.

She stepped away from the bandit lord. With her sword pointed at Dafan's back, Mulan finally allowed herself to look down at the courtyard. The fighting had slowed, and the few remaining of Dafan's men were outnumbered by Mulan's forces.

"Mulan!" Liwen called to her from below. The ribbons in her carefully braided hair hung ragged. "Are you safe?"

"Bring me a ladder!" Mulan said.

A recent recruit ran up with a ladder balanced on her shoulder. Mulan worried that Dafan might throw himself off the roof rather than be captured, but he climbed carefully down, gripping the rungs with his bound hands. Three women with swords waited at the bottom. As soon as the bandit's foot touched the ground, they pushed him against the wall, patted him down and chained his feet together.

Mulan followed him down, accepting Liwen's hand as she jumped off the third-to-last rung. The fighting had stopped completely now, and prisoners were lined up against one side of the courtyard. Dafan's men ranged from mere boys to greying men. Some looked defeated while others looked as if they required a close eye. Mulan scanned the groups, her gut tightening when she saw the handful of bodies strewn across the courtyard's flagstone pathways.

She braced herself. "Casualties?" she asked.

"None of those are ours," said Liwen, following Mulan's gaze. "We have several with cuts being treated. Jiayi has a broken arm." Liwen pursed her lips. "Fu Ning has a bad cut on her leg."

The knot in Mulan's stomach unfurled but not completely. Liwen would not refer to a cut as *bad* unless it was very serious.

"Take me to her," said Mulan.

The main room of the chess house was unrecognisable as the room Mulan had left just a half hour earlier. Elegant lacquered tables were overturned. Chairs lay shattered. A large clay statue of a horseman had been toppled and broken in two. Chess-piece-sized dents marred the fine latticework of the windows, and blood darkened portions of the stone floor. Mulan's heart sank when she remembered the elderly husband and wife who owned the establishment. They'd shown immense trust in Mulan, first in coming to her about Dafan's activities, and then allowing her to spring this ambush. She'd have to think about how to make up for their loss.

A portion of the floor had been cleared in the centre of the room, where a cluster of women crouched around a supine figure. Mulan took a moment to gather herself, suppressing her own dismay and bringing up strength the others needed to see. Only then did she approach.

Fu Ning was one of Mulan's younger soldiers, a hard worker who never complained through even the most gruelling of drills. Now her face was pale, almost green, and a sheen of sweat covered her forehead. She gritted her teeth as another woman bound the gash across her thigh, but she didn't cry out.

The crowd parted for Mulan. Ning's expression became almost apologetic when she saw her leader. "I didn't keep my guard up," she said with an earnestness that broke Mulan's heart. "He got past my sword, just like you warned me about."

Mulan took Ning's hand, stopping her words with a squeeze. "You did well. None of us fight our best in the heat of battle. That's why we train so hard. You fought, and you stayed alive. You handled yourself far better than you would have if I'd sent you here a year ago."

Ning smiled. Six months ago, she hadn't known the difference between a sword and an axe. "Sometimes I wonder if I'm just meant to be a farmer's daughter."

"There's no shame in being a farmer's daughter. And no one says a farmer can't wield a sword. But don't let anyone tell you that just because you were born a farmer, that is the only thing you can be. Do you know you share a surname with a great warrior?"

Ning turned to look at her, curiosity unclouding her gaze.

"Her name was Fu Hao," said Mulan. "She was a great general, and she led an army of three thousand."

Ning's eyes brightened. "A woman?"

Mulan nodded. "Greatness runs in your blood. Don't let anyone tell you otherwise."

One of the village herbal woman came with a bitter-smelling brew. "To help her sleep," she said.

Mulan nodded, suppressing an irrational urge to send the herbal woman away and care for Fu Ning herself. "Take good care of her."

Neither Mulan nor Liwen said anything until they were well out of earshot.

"Do you think she can keep the leg?" Mulan finally asked. Even the act of asking threatened to invite misfortune, but she couldn't help herself.

"Maybe her ancestors will intercede for her," said Liwen.

"Have you seen Ning at the festivals?" said Mulan. "She's an exuberant dancer." Mulan had a distinct memory of Fu Ning spinning to a quick drumbeat, her face radiant, a feathered fan in each hand.

"Let's not give up hope yet."

There wasn't much more to say beyond that, and they both fell silent. Outside, the courtyard was a bustle of activity. Women rushed back and forth along the stone path, tying up prisoners, lifting statues into place, rinsing off the flagstone with bucketfuls of water. A few clasped their hands and bowed to Mulan before returning to their tasks.

There was another concern pulling at Mulan, and it took her a moment to realise what it was. "Zhonglin wasn't supposed to be with you."

Liwen's lips tightened, and she gave a terse nod. "She was assigned to watch the roads. I didn't see her until I'd led the women upstairs and it was too late to send her down. I don't know how she managed to tail us like that. I'm sorry."

Mulan frowned, rubbing at a patch of dirt on her arm. It wasn't the first time they'd had trouble with Zhonglin. The girl was skilled – the fact that she'd slipped past Liwen's watch was evidence enough of that – but she didn't listen to orders. "I would have called off the raid if she hadn't dropped that knife. We salvaged the situation, but it could well have ended in disaster."

"Do you want me to discipline her?" said Liwen. "I mind these things much less than you do."

It was true. Mulan liked to call Liwen the most disciplined rebel she knew. The woman professed no respect for self-proclaimed authority, be it the nuns who raised her or the local governor. But as second-in-command of Mulan's militia, she ran a tighter ship than Mulan suspected any nun or governor would. Liwen saw no contradiction.

As tempting as Liwen's offer was, Mulan shook her head. "Thank you, but it's my responsibility. I'll speak with her tomorrow."

Finally, all the prisoners were bound, and Mulan led the long march back to the village proper. They must have made quite a sight — a crowd of dishevelled, bloody and jubilant women helping their limping comrades down the road as their prisoners, roped together two by two, marched between them.

The magistrate was at the door of his whitewashed brick hut when they arrived. Mulan supposed her group's approach was hard to miss.

"Lady Fa," he said, his voice as stiff as his long, trailing moustache.

Mulan joined her hands in front of her and bowed in greeting. "Magistrate Fong, I hope you are well." Conversations with him were always slightly awkward. Mulan didn't get the impression that Fong actively disliked her, but he always seemed slightly nervous when she was around. Perhaps she was too unpredictable for his taste. "We have Yang Dafan," she told him. "Along with fifteen of his men."

The magistrate, who'd been eyeing the prisoners behind her, did a double take. "I shouldn't have doubted you, Lady Fa. How did you capture him?"

His face was turned towards the prisoners, and Mulan wished she had a better view of his expression. What she had done was embarrassing for the magistrate, but she hoped he'd be big enough not to let that interfere with his duty.

"It was a matter of getting armed soldiers near him without his knowledge. I sent my women with hidden weapons."

"Very clever, Lady Fa. Shall the bounty be delivered to your father's house?"

"You can give the bounty to the proprietors of the Bamboo River Chess House. They'll be needing considerable repairs."

"Will you be available, should I have any questions?"

"I'm here every morning in the outer fields. Training my soldiers."

...

The women gathered before dawn the next day, as usual. No one complained outright, because any complaints would have meant extra laps around the untilled field they used as a training ground, but Mulan caught the occasional grimace as her soldiers stretched and yawned in the predawn chill. She was feeling the effects of the battle herself. Her legs and arms ached from climbing and rooftop running, and bruises bloomed across every single one of her limbs. Still, she put on her commander's face and took her place at the head of the field, surreptitiously rubbing a sore spot on her back and glaring at Liwen when she smirked.

"Take formation!" Mulan called. Her voice carried clearly across the cold. The women hurried into place, standing with feet shoulder width apart, hands clasped behind them.

"You fought well yesterday," said Mulan. "You brought

down a group of bandits that terrorised our region for close to a year. You succeeded where the magistrate failed."

The women stood straighter.

Mulan continued. "But wars don't end because you fight well for a day. Wars are won because you keep fighting, day after day, through pain, through hunger, through bone-crushing exhaustion, until the work is done." She took a moment to let the words sink in. "So we shall train as if we are at war. Give me a horse stance."

Foreheads wrinkled in consternation, but everybody dropped into a low crouch. Mulan didn't make them hold it very long before she launched them into their first drill. As her company kicked, punched and jumped, Mulan walked through the lines, occasionally correcting someone's form.

"Men would have us think that we're not suited for battle, that swordsmanship and kung fu are their domain." A flock of crows took flight, and Mulan waited for their wingbeats to fade before speaking again. "But nothing could be further from the truth. In fact, it was a woman who gave us the foundation for swordsmanship. The Yue maiden taught herself to fence and wrote the first treatise on sword fighting. She forged a short sword to suit her needs, one that was sharp yet pliant, with a flexible core that responded to her commands.

"Many more women have followed in her footsteps. Generals, pirates, archers, horsewomen, wrestlers, fencers.

We embroider their names on our tunics so we remember their bravery. We train every day so our descendants can sew our names onto their tunics when the day comes."

The women moved valiantly. Mulan watched them push through their soreness and discomfort, and she felt a deep pride well up within her. Despite her fancy words about persisting through pain, she ended their training a half hour early, pretending not to notice their relieved groans and sighs.

"Zhonglin," she said. "I want to speak to you afterwards."

Zhonglin was sitting on the ground, alternating gulps from her water skin with bites of a rice ball. She'd tossed another rice ball in front of her for two sparrows to peck at and was currently coaxing a third to come near. She didn't look surprised to be called, and her comrades, who showed no surprise either, quickly cleared out. Zhonglin put down her water skin and dusted herself off before coming to stand in front of Mulan.

Mulan drew a deep breath. Might as well get it over with. "Zhonglin, what was your assigned post yesterday?"

Zhonglin looked Mulan in the eye. "To watch the roads, Commander."

"Why, then, were you in the teahouse?"

"I wanted to be in the middle of the fighting."

Mulan looked for signs of remorse or shame in the girl's large eyes and found none. "I assign posts for a reason, soldier. You're a new recruit. You're still learning how to use a sword.

You don't yet have the skill to be an asset on the front lines."

Zhonglin's chin lifted the slightest bit. "I disarmed a bandit."

"One defeated enemy means nothing. People win fights by luck all the time. An untrained soldier is not only ineffective, she's a danger to her comrades. Have you forgotten that your dropped blade was what betrayed our hand in the first place?"

The girl's eyes flashed. "We won, didn't we?"

"Because your comrades salvaged the situation. They bore the cost of it too. Fu Ning may never walk again."

Zhonglin's face fell at Ning's name. For a moment, she cast her gaze down, uncertain, but then she marshalled her features back into a combative mask. "Why do you even call us soldiers? You tell us how strong we are, and then you do everything in your power to keep us from fighting. Would a general of the emperor's army treat his soldiers this way?"

"Don't lecture me about the imperial army," snapped Mulan. "Only one of us has served within its ranks, and it's not you. For disobeying orders yesterday, you'll help the village herb woman for the next month instead of attending practices. See if you can make up for the suffering you caused your comrades. And for your insolence this morning, you'll clean the practice armour."

Zhonglin's jaw tightened and her eyes sparked defiance. Mulan met her gaze with equal force, her own anger rising. For a moment, she wondered if Zhonglin would go so far as to disobey an order while Mulan was right there. But then Zhonglin turned away. Mulan watched the girl's back as she took a long breath, then slowly and deliberately picked up a set of practice armour. As Zhonglin piled two more sets into her arms, Mulan walked off the field, nerves tingling.

Liwen met her at the edge. "Talk didn't go well?"

Mulan glanced over her shoulder at Zhonglin, who was gathering the practice armour into a pile. She couldn't remember any soldier being this openly defiant, even in the imperial army. "She needs to learn discipline. I can't keep a soldier who doesn't listen to orders."

"She reminds me of when I was young," said Liwen. "I never took well to rules."

"Is that why the nuns kicked you out?"

"They didn't kick me out. I left."

"And you've been braiding your hair ever since."

Liwen ran a hand over her elaborate coiffure. Today she'd wound braids on either side of her head into two buns, then looped two smaller braids underneath. "You would take care of your hair too, if you had to go without it for so much of your childhood."

Mulan thought about her own days in the army, when she'd cut her hair short to blend in with the men. She hadn't really missed it. If anything, she'd found the new length much easier to take care of. But then, there was a big difference between trimming one's hair and shaving it off completely.

"Do you think I'm overprotective of the women?" Mulan asked abruptly.

Liwen's talent for quick rejoinders made the ensuing pause even more noticeable. "It's hard to know, from drills, how prepared a soldier is for battle."

"That was neither a yes nor a no," said Mulan.

Liwen shrugged. "If I wanted the headaches of being a commander, I would have started my own militia. But I joined yours."

The manner in which Liwen had joined Mulan's militia had been pure Liwen. Some local bandits had been harrying a farmer in Mulan's village, and Mulan had volunteered to patrol the lands with some of her senior fighters. Sure enough, a gang of five rogues showed up a few days later. They were in the midst of giving Mulan a healthy brawl when a stranger leapt into the fray.

She was a woman. Her clothing was tattered, but her sword was sharp. The stranger disarmed one bandit as easily as if she were performing a fencing exercise, then moved on to the next. When the dust settled, Mulan opened her mouth to speak, but Liwen beat her to it.

"You're Fa Mulan?" she asked with the same efficiency as her sword strokes.

"Yes," Mulan answered, taken aback.

"You lead a female militia?"

"I do."

With that, Liwen nodded and walked away.

The next morning, she showed up a quarter hour into morning practice and watched quietly from the side of the field. Liwen observed them an entire week, always arriving after they started and leaving right before they finished. Then she'd approached Mulan to offer her sword.

"I can't guarantee how long I'll stay," she said. "But I'll give you my best while I'm here."

Mulan had her doubts about this aloof swordswoman, but Liwen proved true to her word, dedicating herself to the militia with the same single-mindedness with which she'd approached that first fight. Over time, Mulan learned more of Liwen's past – her childhood as an orphan in a convent, how she left eventually to travel the country as an itinerant swordswoman. Despite Liwen's frequent reminders that she wouldn't stay for long, she seemed at home here. Mulan had given her more and more responsibilities, until Liwen became her de facto second-in-command.

Liwen dusted off her hands. "I'm finished here. Do you want to—" She squinted down the road. "Why are they coming back?"

Mulan followed Liwen's gaze to where six women from the militia were sprinting towards the practice field. Mulan would have worried if not for their gleeful smiles.

Wenling, one of her younger recruits, windmilled her arms as she came to a stop. "Mulan, there's a rider coming down the road. He's from the Imperial City." She wiggled her eyebrows while the two women behind her giggled in a decidedly unsoldierly manner.

"I see. Why do you come to me?" Though Mulan had a guess, and the possibility kicked off a flip-flop in her chest.

Wenling took her hand, pulling her away from an amused Liwen. "Come on!"

Mulan ran to keep up with the girls, weaving through streets of latticed windows and pitched-tile roofs, kicking up dirt from the paths in their madcap rush. A dumpling vendor yanked his cart out of their way, and a stray dog darted out of a corner to howl after them. Finally, breathless, they reached the imperial road leading out of the village. A handful of others had gathered as well, and all had their eyes on a quickly approaching rider.

Mulan walked in front of the crowd to get a closer look. The rider had broad shoulders, and his ease and posture showed him to be an expert horseman. He wore the polished iron-mail overcoat of a highly ranked military officer. As he rode closer, Mulan saw his high cheekbones and the strong line of his chin, the expressive mouth that so easily split into a grin. But by then she already knew who he was. Li Shang had come to her village.

CHAPTER TWO

He dismounted a good distance from the village, moving with the same quick grace – uncanny in a man of his size – that Mulan remembered from their time in the army. Mulan waved in greeting, wishing that she'd had time to wash up after training. Which was a silly thought. Shang had seen her tired and sweaty many times before. As he led his horse closer, he caught Mulan's eye and smiled.

The last time Mulan had seen Shang, he'd been in a convalescent bed, pale from a deep sword wound. His regiment had been sent to meet a Balhae incursion in the Shanhai Pass, and she'd lent them her sword. Somehow, she and Shang became separated from the rest of the troops, trapped in a mountain crevice as enemy soldiers combed the surrounding area. They'd stayed hidden for a day, but their water ran out, and they decided to attempt escape before they weakened from thirst.

Balhae soldiers found them almost immediately. Shang broke through them, but three soldiers cut off Mulan's path and surrounded her. She'd yelled at Shang to leave her, but he'd run right back, cutting two men down to get to her side. She'd never forget that exhausting battle, fighting back-to-back as every fallen foe was replaced by a new soldier, nor could she forget her utter horror when Shang cried out and fell. She'd shouted his name, and that long terrifying moment before his pained reply had lasted a lifetime in itself.

Somehow, she'd got him on an enemy's horse. Somehow, they'd lost their pursuers. And somehow, she'd kept him alive and awake the entire gruelling ride back to the imperial camp. She'd paced outside the physician's tent until the doctor assured her that Shang was stitched up and resting, and only after he woke the next day did she find peace again.

By the time Mulan had to leave for home, Shang was well enough to speak and eat but not yet allowed to get out of bed. Mulan brought a bowl of broth to his bedside to say her goodbyes. Shang sipped appreciatively while Mulan tried to figure out whether she imagined the greenish cast to his skin, or if his hand shook when lifting the bowl to his lips.

"You could have avoided all this if you hadn't come back for me," she said. "For all we knew, there might have been fifty more invaders over the next hill. You should have run for it when you had the chance."

31

Shang put down his bowl. His hand was steady as ever, and his dark eyes deep and expressive. "You know I couldn't have done that."

There was some undercurrent of emotion in his voice that Mulan felt deeply in her being. Something that made her mind linger over the conversation as she rode home that day, that made her read and reread his letters in the months after, weighing the meaning behind his well-wishes and every professed desire to see her soon. They'd intended to visit each other when they had the chance, but things got busier. Shang was promoted to general and rode out on new campaigns. Mulan's duties with her militia piled up. They exchanged letters when they had the chance, though Mulan stopped herself from analysing his words quite so obsessively. Surely, in all his travels around China, Shang would be meeting scores of interesting people. Mulan needed to remember and make peace with that.

Wenling's giggle ended in a squeak, snapping Mulan back into the present.

"Why do you think he's here?" asked Ruolan. Ruolan was an older recruit with a four-year-old son. Mulan wouldn't have expected her to be part of this gaggle. Actually, she was surprised that any of these women would remember, much less recognise, Shang. He'd only dropped by her village a few times after the end of the war. Though Mulan supposed Shang was the type to leave an impression.

"Maybe he's on an errand for the emperor," said Mulan. She thought she sounded mature in delivering her explanation. Appropriately dignified.

"Maybe he just wanted to see you," said Wenling.

Mulan wondered what kind of stories had been circulating behind her back. "Don't be ridiculous. He's wearing official livery."

"He wears it well," said a sly voice behind her. There was a slight scuffle, as if the speaker had been elbowed in the ribs, but she continued. "And I bet he's happy to see you regardless."

"I'm happy to see him too," said Mulan. "It's always nice to meet up with old comrades-in-arms."

Out of the corner of her eye, she saw the girls exchange knowing looks.

"That's enough," Mulan said. "Off with you."

To her surprise, they actually obeyed, though their leaving didn't quiet the butterflies in Mulan's stomach. Shang's growing proximity didn't help. He was almost within speaking distance now, approaching with an easy stride. His arms and shoulders were well muscled, perhaps more so than the last time Mulan had seen him. His armour was definitely fancier, as befit his new rank. The metal scales of his armour were polished and set in blue and green rows, and his silk overskirt was embroidered with lions and tigers in combat.

He was still as distractingly handsome as he'd been the day they'd met.

"Shang." A curtsy didn't feel like the right way to greet a fellow soldier, and a bow felt too formal for someone she'd dragged injured through the mountains. "I didn't know you were coming."

"Mulan." The warmth in his eyes kindled a reciprocating glow that spread from her chest to her fingertips. "I'm sorry not to send notice. The orders came unexpectedly." For a moment, neither of them said anything, and then his mouth curved into a grin. "I hope it doesn't ruin your day too much."

Mulan laughed, and the awkwardness between them fell away. "I'll try to salvage it as best I can," she said. "Who do you need to see?"

The crowd was starting to disperse, with the more polite individuals returning to their homes while others found convenient tasks to do just within earshot. A handful of children stayed to gawk openly at the new visitor. Shang waved at them, sending a toddler with hair tied atop her head running for her mother.

"The message is for you actually," said Shang. "The emperor requires your presence at the Imperial City."

"The emperor?" Mulan was aware of ears pricking up all around them. She started down the road, away from eavesdroppers, as Shang fell in step beside her.

"I don't know why. All he said was that he wants you at the capital, and he'd like you to leave as soon as you can."

Mulan slowed in her walk. After the war, the emperor had

offered Mulan an official position in the palace, but she'd asked to go home instead. Since then, she'd seen the emperor a few times when visiting the Imperial City, but he'd never expressly sent for her before. "Has something happened?" Was there a war she didn't know about?

Shang shook his head. "Not that I know of. Can you leave tomorrow?"

This was progressing rather quickly. Mulan ran through the next days in her mind. "I suppose I don't have anything keeping me here. Liwen can take over the militia training for a few weeks. She'll complain about the responsibility, but she'll be fine. I'll let Mama and Baba know tonight."

"Good," said Shang. And he smiled. "I'm glad to see you, Mulan."

The morning sun warmed her face as she smiled back. "I'm glad to see you, too."

•••

Mulan's mother fussed over Shang. Despite such short notice, she slaughtered one of the chickens and whipped up a feast of chive dumplings, sweet potato leaves and soup. Mama Fa clucked her tongue at how skinny Shang had become and insisted he eat his fill. Mulan eyed Shang's massive bicep and decided not to comment.

"Congratulations on your promotion to general, Shang," said Mulan's father. "Quite an accomplishment at such a young age."

"Thank you, Commander Fa." Mulan was amused to see Shang flush at her father's praise. He was in awe of Fa Hsu, which surprised Mulan because Shang's own father had been a general.

"Mulan follows news of you closely," continued Mulan's father. "Every single time we have visitors from the Imperial City, she makes sure to ask them for news of you."

Mulan ducked her head, mortified. She was already self-conscious enough around Shang. The last thing she needed was for him to know just how often she thought about him.

"Speaking of the Imperial City," Mulan cut in hurriedly. "Any news from there?"

Mama Fa brought out the soup just then, and the steaming aroma of mountain mushrooms filled the air. Mulan busied herself ladling the soup into bowls.

"Good news and bad," said Shang, taking an appreciative whiff of the rising steam. "It's peaceful for the most part, now that the war is over. But there's some unrest. Some people have lost faith in the country's leaders after they allowed the Huns to launch an attack inside the capital. There have been a few rebellious tracts written and distributed around the city."

"About the emperor?" Mulan asked, surprised. She couldn't imagine an emperor more beloved by the people.

"The emperor still has the people's loyalty, but there's a lot of talk against the ministers."

"And what do the ministers say?"

"To be honest," said Shang, "they seem too distracted among themselves to really react. The emperor is getting old, and he's held off on naming an heir. He must do it soon, it seems, and everyone is jockeying to catch his favour. Though I'm not sure why anyone would work so hard to get such a thankless job."

"Really, Shang?" asked Fa Hsu. "It doesn't tempt you?"

Shang wiped his mouth, carefully folding the napkin before answering. "A general reports to his emperor, but the emperor is beholden to the heavens and to the people. I find the responsibilities of a general to be enough."

Mulan's mother spooned more soup into Shang's bowl. "And what of things besides politics? Do you have plans to marry soon?"

Mulan choked on a chicken bone. Tears filled her eyes as she coughed and gagged.

"Not yet, Mama Fa." There was a smile in Shang's voice, though Mulan couldn't see well enough to know for sure.

"Are you not looking? A handsome young man like you should have no problem finding a bride."

"I do hope I find the right bride soon."

Mulan thought she saw Shang's gaze flicker in her direction. But then, he also looked to Mulan like he was completely underwater right now. And that chicken bone was sure taking its time working its way down her throat. Mulan wiped her eyes and pushed back from the table. It took several attempts to speak before actual sound came out of her mouth. "I should go pack my things for tomorrow. Please excuse me."

Mulan's father asked Shang a question about army supply trains as she fled.

Packing went more quickly than she expected. Funny how much clearer her mind became when Shang wasn't in the room. Mulan preferred to travel light, so she brought only a few sets of men's travel clothes and some simple dresses. The good thing about being Fa Mulan was that nobody expected her to appear at court swathed in silk, with a catty of precious stones hanging off her hair and neck. Mulan rolled everything into a small bag, then set it by her bed. When she stuck her head out of her room, talk had died down. The rest of the table must have finished dinner. Everyone would probably take an early night. Mulan wanted to as well, but there was one last thing she had to do.

The soft pit-pat of her footfalls echoed through dark hallways as she tiptoed towards the courtyard. Outside, the evening air was crisp. The fragrance of sweet osmanthus wafted across her path as crickets chirped near the burbling stream. Mulan followed a stone walkway over a bridge and under a round archway that took her out of their inner yard. A small red pagoda sat atop the hill beyond.

The Fa family ancestral temple had always been a sacred space, hallowed ground where the spirits of her forebears rested. But ever since Mulan's grandmother passed on, the place had taken on new meaning. It was still sacred, but now it also felt like home. Perhaps Mulan imagined it, but she felt a warmth beckoning her whenever she passed.

The stone steps were smooth under her feet. Mulan lit an incense stick and sat down quietly. A slight breeze lifted the hair at her temples, in the same way Mulan's grandmother had brushed her hair away from her eyes so many times before.

From up here she had a clear view of the garden below. Just next to the wall was the worn bench where Mulan had so often sat with Grandmother, helping her sort vegetables as Nai Nai told fantastic stories of the monkey king, the zodiac animals, the thunder god's wife and the woman on the moon. When Mulan expressed awe at those adventures, Grandmother told her about the adventures in store for her.

"See how wide your forehead is?" Grandmother would say. "That means you'll travel far and bring back good fortune."

"I will?" Mulan responded, rapt.

"Yes, but it won't always be easy," Nai Nai said, and she'd point to a scar on Mulan's temple from a childhood fall. "That scar means you'll struggle and face hardship, but if you persevere, you will overcome it."

How right Grandmother been. During long cold nights in the army, when the ground sent icicles through her hopes,

Mulan had clung to Grandmother's words.

She turned to face Grandmother's spirit tablet. "I'm going away for a few days," she said, softly but clearly. "Shang arrived today from the Imperial City. He says the emperor's summoning me. It's a long trip, but I'm excited. It'll be nice to see the capital again." And nice to travel there with Shang.

Though she didn't hear any reply, the air felt full, as if someone, or many people, was listening.

"I do miss you, Nai Nai," she said.

There was a scuffling sound outside, and a pebble skittered along the ground. Mulan straightened her skirts as her father came down the garden path.

His eyes crinkled as he spotted her. "I thought I might find you here. Saying your goodbyes?"

"Just updating her on how things have been. I've been so busy with the militia that I haven't come by as much as I should."

As her father came up the steps, Mulan noticed with a pang that he leaned harder on his cane than he used to. Time was catching up to him, as it had with her grandmother. He sat down with her, and the two of them watched the smoke curl up from the glowing incense sticks. There was a playfulness to the way the wisps danced. Mulan could imagine Grandmother directing them into whimsical patterns.

"She would have been proud to see what you've done these past years," said Baba. "Your grandmother always knew you could change the course of rivers."

Mulan smiled and felt a familiar tingle at the back of her eye. "Streams become rivers because there are tributaries to feed them. If I've shifted anything, it's only because you, Mama and Nai Nai lent me your strength."

As Mulan let out a long breath, a spark leapt from one of the incense sticks. As it floated downwards, it seemed inexplicably to multiply, over and over until there were hundreds of sparks floating in the air of the temple.

"Baba," Mulan whispered.

The sparks rearranged themselves, clustering, expanding and re-forming, until they became a dragon that soared through the air. Next to it, a fiery bird flapped its wings. They cavorted together, chasing each other in dizzying circles, until, suddenly, they scattered again into ash. The glowing sparks floated slowly to the ground and winked out one by one.

For a moment, the air inside the temple had an added dimension to it, as if thousands of years existed at one time in this space. And then a cricket chirped, and the wind began to flow again.

"What was that?" Mulan asked.

Baba stood and straightened his robe, gazing down at her with pride. "Travel in peace, Mulan. Your ancestors watch over you."

...

Mulan and Shang were up the next morning before the sun cleared the horizon. They prepared their horses in relative quiet, walking past each other as they fetched bags and tied saddles. The process reminded her of their days together in the army. As their ragged band of recruits transformed into a cohesive unit, everyone grew so familiar with each other's routines that they didn't have to communicate as they packed up in the mornings, instead silently keeping tabs on one another's progress, picking up tasks and adjusting their pace as necessary.

Mulan loaded her last bag onto her stallion Khan's back and looked up to see Shang finishing up as well. Mama handed her a bundle of sweet buns.

"These are easy to eat when you're riding," she said.

Mulan popped one into her mouth. The lotus-paste filling was piping hot and just the right amount of sweet. "They're easy to eat right now," she said with a wink. She bowed to her mother, and then her father in turn. "Take care of yourselves, Baba and Mama. I'll be back soon."

The clip-clop of their horses' hooves echoed in the predawn stillness. They rode at a steady pace – not so fast as to tire the horses, but fast enough so that conversation was inconvenient. Their silence was a companionable one, though, and Mulan found herself enjoying the ride. It felt natural to be travelling with Shang, riding and hunting instead of poring over his letters or avoiding awkward questions from parents.

They stopped occasionally for water and once for food. Mulan shared her mother's bao with Shang after an appropriate amount of begging. A little after noon, Shang shot a rabbit from the road. Not to be outdone, Mulan brought down a quail just before sundown. Their spoils promised a satisfying dinner, and they set up camp for the night at the base of two tall cliffs.

"It's fitting for us to make camp here," said Shang as he skinned his rabbit.

Mulan raised her head from stoking their fire. "Oh?"

"Two centuries ago, a general by the name of Wu set up an ambush here."

Mulan looked at the rock walls around her. Though most of their trip had been through flat farmland, the terrain on this stretch of road was growing steadily hillier. Here, sandstone cliffs came together to form a corridor wide enough for fifty men to walk abreast. Further on, the walls widened again. "It's not a bad place to hide an army."

"And it offers good shelter from the wind, if you pick the right nook. The general sent smoke signals over the top of the cliffs. From there, they could be seen from a great distance," said Shang.

They set up their bedrolls. As the fire died down to embers, Shang stretched out on one side and Mulan on the other. The stars were bright overhead. "I really should sleep outside more often," she said, gazing up at them.

Shang chuckled. "Spoken like a soldier who's forgotten what it's like to bed down in the mud."

Mulan grinned into the darkness. "Fair point. I guess I forget about the dirt and fleas and lack of soap."

Shang's voice took on a wondering tone. "That seems so long ago, doesn't it? And now we're travelling together once more, against all odds."

That was a strange way to put it. "Were the odds really all that steep?"

There was a silence, and she could sense him gathering his thoughts. "We've been through a lot. There are many things over the years that might have ended our friendship."

"I suppose the day you almost had me executed was a low point." She meant it as a joke, but Shang grew quiet.

It was a twist of fate in the darkest days of the war that had finally revealed the unassuming foot soldier Ping to be Mulan, a woman in disguise. An inconveniently located injury was all it had taken to unravel months of careful deception. Mulan had been discharged from the army in disgrace. And though she'd later redeemed herself in the eyes of the country by saving the emperor's life, it was still many months before she regained Shang's trust. The other men in their regiment had recovered more quickly, but the stakes were higher with Shang. He'd been her commanding officer, and it was his reputation, his life even, that she'd put on the line when she lied about who she was.

And it wasn't simply the blow to his reputation that had hurt him. Truth was, Ping and Shang had been friends, sharing stories with each other at the campfire, confiding in each other on midnight watch. Both Ping and Shang had fathers with decorated military pasts, fathers they loved dearly, and both had been terrified they wouldn't measure up. After Mulan's true identity came to light, she tried to tell Shang that everything she'd said in those conversations had been true. She'd simply substituted 'son' for 'daughter' at the relevant times. Mustering up the courage to say those things to Shang had been difficult. It was even harder for Shang to get to the point where he believed her.

The punishment for Mulan's crimes had been clear-cut. It was Shang's duty as an army captain to uphold the laws of the country, and Mulan had flouted one of its most sacred. She'd lied about who she was, passed herself off as a man and made a mockery of the emperor's war effort. In that fateful moment, kneeling in the snow before Shang, Mulan had felt the weight of her failure, the bitter disappointment of all her plans gone to ruin. She remembered bracing for the bite of Shang's sword on her neck, feeling perversely grateful that death would, at the very least, bring an end to her shame. But instead of cutting her down, Shang had spared her. *A life for a life. My debt is repaid.*

And he'd left her on that mountain top.

"I shouldn't have abandoned you," said Shang. And Mulan

knew the same scene was playing in his mind.

"I prefer it to being beheaded, in retrospect."

"Leaving you there could easily have been a death sentence. You'd saved us so many times on the battlefield, and yet that was how I repaid you."

"I also committed treason," she pointed out. "I lied to the army, and by extension, the emperor. I might very well have dishonoured my family, if things had turned out differently."

"You wouldn't have dishonoured anyone. You would have kept trying until you claimed victory. I know that now. I think I knew it even then. I just wasn't brave enough to act on it."

Mulan turned his words around in her mind. Shang wasn't looking for words of forgiveness, and it wouldn't have felt right to absolve him lightly. Still, it was comforting to know that the day weighed on his conscience.

"I did deserve better than you gave me," she said. "But the past is a good teacher. You're a general now. Maybe what you've learned will make you a better one."

A shadow passed overhead, an owl in search of its evening meal.

"What does it mean to be a better general?" asked Shang. "Kill more of the enemy? Protect the lives of my troops? When I think back to everything we saw during the war, it seems it'd be better to live in times where we don't need generals."

At Shang's words, Mulan felt the ache of dead comrades, the hollowness of loss, even in victory. Even now, years after the war, the scent of their dying campfire conjured up images of villages burned to the ground, a ragged doll abandoned in the dirt.

"Perhaps," she said, "if a woman can learn to fight in battle, a general can learn to work for peace."

A crack sounded from the dying embers. Mulan watched as an arc of light brightened and dimmed.

"What you've done with your women's militia," said Shang, "it's truly impressive. We hear about it even in the Imperial City. Your father and mother must be proud of you."

Mulan groaned at the mention of her parents. "I'm so sorry my mother badgered you about marriage. It's the way of mothers, I suppose. I don't know why I expected her to be any less mortifying."

She expected a chuckle from Shang, but instead he shifted onto his side. Mulan could feel his eyes on her in the darkness. "And what do you think?"

"About what?"

"Marriage. Settling down."

Mulan froze, a rabbit caught in a carrot patch. "Settling down?"

"Well, perhaps not settling down exactly, but... being married." He spoke in a rush. "Just whether you might have room in your life for a husband when you're not saving the country."

His question sent a rush of embarrassment through

Mulan. Truth was, she had thought about marriage from time to time, and it usually involved dramatic and saccharine declarations from the man currently on the other side of the campfire, proposals that would send Mulan forever into hiding if their imagined speaker ever actually learned of them. "Well, I don't know. Husbands take up a lot of space. And don't always smell the best..."

A shift in the air made her stop, some inexplicable sense that she'd said something wrong.

Shang didn't speak.

"Shang, I'm joking," said Mulan, uncertain now.

"I know." Shang turned so his back was towards her. "We should get to sleep. We have an early morning tomorrow."

She could tell, by the rhythm of Shang's breathing on the other side of the fire, that it was a while before he fell asleep. Sleep eluded Mulan as well, and she couldn't help wondering as she drifted off if she should have answered differently. They'd joked about marriage plenty of times before, traded jabs about the other's prospects. It had all seemed so distant. Shang was a general now, no doubt surrounded by adoring, beautiful women who put jewels in their hair and wrapped perfectly symmetrical dumplings. Shang was Mulan's good friend, her comrade-in-arms. She knew that, and she'd made her peace with that. Now, though, she wondered if she might have been mistaken.

•••

On the surface, everything seemed the same the next morning. Mulan and Shang woke and packed their things quietly, rolling up their blankets and saddling their horses. They didn't speak, other than Shang's word of thanks when Mulan divided up the last sweet bun.

Still, tension hung in everything they did, the way they studiously avoided meeting each other's gaze, how they subtly altered their walking paths so they'd be further apart. It didn't make sense. Why would a simple joke from Mulan, something they'd teased each other about so many times before, suddenly change things? She wanted to say something, but what? *I'm sorry I said that men smelled bad. I think you smell fine. Better than fine, in fact. I think you smell wonderful, and I've been in love with you ever since you stood in front of us at basic training.* She cringed.

Finally, the horses were ready to go. As Mulan prepared to mount, Shang finally spoke.

"Mulan, wait."

Something in his voice sent a shiver across her skin.

Shang came over. He was agitated, his eyes darting from one thing to another, his fingers pulling at a non-existent wrinkle on his tunic. "I have to… I wanted to… before we reach the capital…"

It was impossible not to be infected by his nerves. Mulan forced herself to stay still as he deliberately took a moment to gather himself. She was afraid to hope, and yet…

He looked her in the eye.

"I know you have no use for a husband now, but I hope…" He let out a breath, and finally he steadied. "I hope that when you're ready, you'll consider the proposal of someone who's done quite a few stupid things. Someone who's made many, many mistakes, but who respects and cares for you. Very much." The raw vulnerability in his eyes was terrifying.

Shang's words left Mulan frozen. She was aware that her mouth was open, and that she should say something, but she seemed to have been struck dumb. As her shock faded, something else welled up. Joy. Elation.

"Shang, I…"

He backed away, putting his palms up. "Not now, of course. I don't mean to make things awkward between us, I—"

Mulan closed the distance between them and took his hands, slowly lowering them down between them, countering his nerves with her newfound calm. "You misunderstand." She looked in his eyes, and spoke deliberately and gently. "I would be honoured."

He smiled then, his entire countenance brightening. For a long time, they beamed at each other.

•••

Riding over the next days, Mulan felt she was skimming the clouds. The two travelled no differently from the way they always had. They rode at the same pace, and they didn't speak often. But Mulan felt as if a glow surrounded them.

They made quick time, occasionally racing their horses on remote stretches of road. As the city grew closer, they passed more houses and farms. When they were less than an hour from the Imperial City, they stopped one last time at a creek for water. Before they mounted again, Shang spoke.

"Mulan, wait."

She stopped, one hand on Khan's bridle. "Mmm?"

"One more thing. Before we get to the city. I wanted to…"

The new surge of nervous energy from him, and the way he looked at her, made her stomach do a somersault.

"Wanted to what?" And her voice faded away, because he'd reached out to brush her arm with the tips of his fingers. How strange it was, that she could feel him even through the coarse travel tunic, that one touch could travel all the way to the bottoms of her feet.

"May I…?" he asked.

Mulan was already leaning in before he finished his sentence. Their lips touched gently. It was warm. Delicate. Perfect.

She opened her eyes to see Shang gazing at her with a tender expression she'd never seen before. "It's been a good trip," he said quietly.

Mulan gazed up at him. Her friend, her comrade-in-arms. Her love.

"Indeed, it has."

CHAPTER THREE

The Imperial City was just as crowded and bustling as Mulan remembered. Travellers streamed in and out through the city gates. The guards stationed there saluted Shang, and as Mulan followed him through, she thought she saw one guard nudge the other. She felt their eyes following her long after she passed.

The streets were narrow and packed. Men and women gathered below rooftops that swept up at the corners, exchanging the day's gossip and cheering street performers on. Merchants shouted above the noise of the crowd, hawking their latest wares. As Mulan and Shang navigated between densely packed houses and shops, the crowds grew steadily thicker. Men, women and children squeezed in close, and many called Mulan's name. At times, she and Shang could hardly move forward because of the crush of people. Mulan found herself deeply grateful that neither of their horses startled easily in crowds.

"The city's really grown," she shouted over the fray.

Shang laughed. "It's no different from before. It's just that word spread that you'd come."

"Me? Surely not." Mulan hid her confusion by waving at a group of young girls, who promptly hugged each other in excitement and ran away.

"Don't you realise you're a hero?" said Shang. "Your legend grows by the year. Fa Mulan, fearless warrior and saviour of China. The one who buried Shan Yu's armies under a mountain of ice."

"It was just a well-aimed rocket." Mulan remembered the crack of ice, the avalanche cascading down.

"The warrior who came to the emperor's aid when Shan Yu took him hostage. Who fought and defeated Shan Yu in mortal combat atop a palace roof, saving the emperor and restoring China to its rightful ruler. All while wearing a dress."

That night came back now, too, the dizzying fight on the rooftops, the sea of faces looking on. "The way I remember it, it was a team effort, and I was really lucky not to end up skewered. Besides, that was years ago. I've hardly been in the Imperial City since the war."

"That, if anything, has made you even more larger-than-life. At least once a month, I see a little girl waving a stick and shouting for the Huns to release the emperor."

Now that Shang mentioned it, it did seem like the crowds were thickest around her. "They have the wrong idea," said Mulan. "I'm sure anyone in my position would have done the same…"

"They feel differently," Shang said.

The crowds didn't thin until Mulan and Shang reached the imposing red gates of the imperial palace. Uniformed soldiers waved them into a vast square paved with cut stone, where they were set upon immediately by a crowd of eunuchs and servants. Grooms took their horses as a high-ranking eunuch in a long blue robe greeted them.

"Greetings and welcome, General Li and Commander Fa." The ribbons dangling from the black fu tou on his head didn't wobble an iota when he bowed. "His Imperial Majesty requests that Commander Fa go straight to an audience with him."

Mulan glanced down at her dusty travel cloak. "I should make myself more presentable."

"The emperor stressed you come as soon as possible, Commander." The eunuch had a way of speaking that was exceedingly polite yet brooked no disagreement.

Mulan exchanged a glance with Shang, who shrugged his ignorance. "All right, then. Take me to the grand hall."

"Not the grand hall, Commander. The emperor has already held court for the day. He'll see you in the imperial apartments."

Once again, Mulan looked to Shang. He'd turned away completely from the groom taking his horse and was now staring at the eunuch, his brow knit in confusion. The emperor always received guests in the grand hall. The imperial apartments were his private retreat, not a place for commoners to set foot.

"Is something wrong?" asked Mulan.

"There's no immediate danger," replied the eunuch.

That wasn't exactly comforting. Mulan took her leave of Shang, her nerves buzzing as the eunuch led her through parts of the palace she'd never seen before. She had met with the emperor a few times after the Hun invasion, but it had always been in the ceremonial sections of the palace. What could be so urgent now?

The imperial apartments were set apart from the rest of the palace. While the throne room and ceremonial courts were grand in scale, the buildings Mulan now passed were more modestly proportioned, though no less intricately constructed. The posts supporting the covered walkway were elegantly carved from dark wood. Intricate geometric latticework lined the windows, and statues of lions and dragons kept watch at steady intervals. The building where the eunuch finally stopped was laid out like a normal courtyard house, though it had the same red walls and swooping tiled roofs as the rest of the palace. Two soldiers opened a door carved with flying dragons to reveal the emperor at a small wooden table, wearing a gown of gold silk and writing on a scroll.

"Commander Fa Mulan," announced the eunuch.

Mulan entered and dropped to her knees, touching her forehead to the ground.

There was a swish of cloth as the emperor turned to acknowledge her presence. "Stand up. There is no longer any need for you to bow this low."

Mulan puzzled over the emperor's words.

The emperor waved his hand. "Leave us." The eunuch bowed and left. Footsteps sounded from the corners of the room, and four guards whom Mulan had not noticed also took their leave.

"Sit, sit." The emperor perched his brush on an inkstone at the edge of his desk and pushed his scroll to the side. An exquisite blue floral teapot sat on the table alongside two cups, and the emperor reached for it.

"Your Majesty," said Mulan, shocked.

"Let me," he said.

Mulan watched the emperor pour tea for her, fully aware people had been executed for doing less. Now that Mulan had a better view of the emperor, she thought he looked older than the last time she saw him. He still had the long white moustache, beard, and kind eyes, but the wrinkles in his face were more pronounced. Dark circles lined his eyes, and he seemed thinner. There was a slight tremor in his hands as he poured.

"Now," said the emperor, "I trust your trip back here was smooth?"

"We encountered no problems, Your Majesty." She couldn't get past the idea that she was drinking tea with the emperor in muddy travel clothes, making polite conversation. What kind of bizarre dreamworld had she landed in? She half expected the emperor to sprout wings in front of her eyes, or change into a camel.

The emperor, on the other hand, acted as if nothing was out of the ordinary. "I hear you've stayed busy in your home village."

"I've had plenty to keep me occupied," she said truthfully.

"Such as?"

"Most of my time has been spent training my militia."

"Ah yes, an all-female army, is it not?"

Mulan nodded, her nerves falling away as enthusiasm took over. "It started with just a few women watching me doing my morning exercises. They wanted to learn to defend themselves, so I began teaching them the basics. From there, more and more women came on. They all have families and obligations, so we train in the early morning before they get to their chores. I convinced some of the wealthier villagers to contribute money for training equipment and weapons, and we now have enough soldiers to field patrols on a regular basis."

"Has it made a difference?"

"I believe so, Your Majesty," she said, hoping she wasn't being too boastful. "The farmers feel much safer."

"And not just that," said the emperor. "The resulting peace and security have increased prosperity in your village. Tax revenue has gone up by fifteen percent in the district due to increased farm yields. You've also used your influence to establish a school in your county, where all students are welcome to attend regardless of their gender or family wealth."

"I… I'm humbled that Your Majesty has taken such close notice."

"It's all very impressive," he said. "And a pity that more of China does not get to benefit from your leadership. I still feel the loss of you from my court, Mulan. You would have made a very good minister."

Mulan bowed her head. "Your Majesty is very kind, and it was a great honour to be offered a place in the palace. But I wished to be with my father and mother after being separated from them during the war."

"Of course. We already knew you were a filial daughter. But many things have changed since the end of the war. Perhaps I can convince you now to reside in the capital."

Mulan put her cup down, unsure of what to say. The bustling Imperial City was no more appealing now than it had been after the war, but how many times could one really say no to the emperor? "I am quite fond of my home," she replied carefully, "but if Your Majesty wishes so strongly for me to become a minister, I can speak with my parents."

The emperor smiled. "Ah, Mulan, I don't want you to be a minister. I want you to be my heir."

Mulan dropped her teacup.

"Oh!" she cried as scalding liquid flowed across the table. She cast around for a towel, but there was none. In a fit of desperation, she yanked off her cloak and threw it over the rapidly spreading puddle before it flowed into the emperor's lap.

"I'm so—I'm so sorry, Your Majesty... I just..."

"You were surprised." He looked faintly amused.

"Yes, Your Majesty. I was surprised. I—" She balled up her soaked cloak and succumbed to the absurdity of the situation. "Your heir? You can't be serious."

The emperor reacted to Mulan's criminal impertinence with mild amusement. "There is no obvious successor to my throne. Surely you know that. My three daughters gave up claim to their throne when they married commoners, and there is no one else in line save some distant cousins who are unqualified to rule."

Unqualified to rule? As if Mulan were some veteran of government bureaucracy. "But surely there are others. Your Majesty has a cabinet full of ministers, people who have lived their lives in service to the country."

"The people have lost faith in my ministers, and though it shames me to say this, they've lost confidence in me as well. We let the Huns come to our very doorstep. We would have lost the country entirely if someone" – he looked meaningfully at Mulan – "had not risked her life to intervene. It is imperative that the next emperor inspires the full confidence and devotion of the people."

Mulan wrung her hands. "Your Majesty, I'm just a girl from the countryside. I know nothing of the court."

"You are the hero whose quick thinking saved our country. You are the warrior who risked great personal loss and dishonour to protect your family and, by extension, all of China."

It was absurd, the disconnect between the emperor's words and Mulan's own conception of herself. Yes, she supposed she had done these things, but she was also just Mulan, Fa Hsu's daughter, who tripped over chickens and stole sweet buns from the kitchen.

The emperor continued. "Court customs can be learned. Laws can be looked up in books. What is much harder to acquire is character, bravery, selflessness. The devotion of the people."

"But, Your Majesty—"

He raised a hand. "You think I hardly know you, but you're wrong. I've had eyes and ears in your village since the day you left the Imperial City. I know everything you've done, from the number of new recruits in your militia to the size of the crowd that greeted you and Li Shang when you rode in this afternoon."

Mulan fell silent.

"You will have advisers, of course. Li Shang shall be your head general. You will also have the counsel of my current ministers. They have made mistakes, but together, they still possess a large amount of collective experience."

The emperor stopped talking then, and his silence was more disorienting than his words. Because it meant now that Mulan had to reply. But how could she possibly, for something like this? He might as well have asked her if she was agreeable to becoming the thunder god's wife.

"I—I'm honoured. Your Majesty. I just— Forgive me. I wasn't expecting this. I can't—"

For the first time, there entered a note of sternness to the emperor's voice. His kind eyes took on a new focus. "Fa Mulan, I've spent many months mulling over this decision. I have made what I believe is the best choice, but I will not force it on you. An emperor or empress cannot be coerced to lead. But I will ask you now. Will you try, at least, to take my place? Stay in the capital. Attend meetings with the ministers and act as my heir. Speak with me daily, and learn what is needed to rule. Will you do that, for China?"

Mulan bowed her head, trying to wrap her head around

the idea of herself as empress when just a few days ago, she'd been shovelling manure out of the hen house. She tried to imagine herself ascending the throne, taking on that much power and responsibility. A whirlwind of images flashed through her mind – state dinners, visiting dignitaries, all the people of China bowing down before her. It was seductive, terrifying and overwhelming.

"Will you do it?" the emperor said again.

Mulan let the moment stretch as long as she dared.

"Yes, Your Majesty."

Was that her voice speaking? She'd just dived off a cliff, and she had no idea when she'd reach the bottom, or if there even was a bottom at all.

The emperor inclined his head, and a faint smile formed beneath his moustache. "Good. The next step will be to announce this to the court. We will speak more tomorrow morning. But until then, tell no one about what we have discussed."

CHAPTER FOUR

The same eunuch who escorted Mulan to the emperor met her when she stepped outside.

"Your bags have been taken to your room, Commander Fa. Would you like to be shown there now?"

Mulan looked at the man, blinked, and looked at him again. It seemed inexplicable that he would ask such a mundane question when the world had just tilted onto its side.

"Yes, please. Take me there."

Empress. Heir. Mulan put one foot in front of the other, mechanically following the eunuch's quick footsteps. Servants and staff passed them. A few bowed to her, but others didn't even seem to notice her presence. Why should they?

"Your quarters, Commander." The eunuch had unlocked a door.

Mulan snapped out of her thoughts. "Thank you."

The guest room was sensible by palace standards. The walls were still of the finest lacquered wood, as was the furniture, but they were not carved with nearly as much ornamentation. A curtained bed sat against the back wall and a desk lined the wall to its right. In the centre was a giant tub of water with steam rising off the top. Mulan rushed towards it, eager to dip her hands in the water, but a piece of paper on the desk caught her eye. It was written in simple script – Shang's handwriting. *I hope your conversation with the emperor went well. Meet me for tea before bed?*

Mulan held the note between her fingertips, wondering at the thought of Shang in his apartments outside the palace, completely unaware of what had just transpired. What would he say? What would he think of the emperor's decision? Mulan turned towards the door, bursting with the need to talk to him. She needed his counsel, needed to talk out her shock.

But the emperor had commanded her to tell no one.

There was no way she could see Shang and keep this secret. He would take one look at her and know that something was deeply wrong. Mulan stood frozen before finally picking up a blank piece of paper from her desk. She dripped some water from her bath onto an inkstone and rubbed her ink stick into it. Then she dipped a brush and thought.

I'm exhausted. Let's rest tonight and we can speak tomorrow. She blew on the ink until it dried. Carefully, she folded the paper and opened the door to the outdoor walkway. A palace maid stood outside, staring out into the garden. She was young and skinny, with a long face and upturned nose. Her simple dress hung off her body's sharp angles. The maid jumped to attention and curtsied when Mulan opened the door.

"Comman—Commander Fa Mulan," she yelped, her eyes wide as a deer's.

"Please have this brought to General Shang," said Mulan. She wondered if guilt showed through in handwriting.

The maid curtsied several more times, as if multiple frantic curtsies could make up for a proper one. "Yes, of course."

As Mulan returned to her room, she realised she hadn't lied about being exhausted. She could hardly lift her arms and legs to get out of her travel clothes and into the bath. Still, after she finally dried herself off and settled herself in bed, Mulan found that exhaustion and sleep didn't go hand in hand. Though her body wanted nothing more than to sink into slumber, her mind continued to run in circles, and she tossed and turned long into the night.

•••

"Commander Fa? Commander Fa?"

Mulan opened her eyes to find the maid from yesterday standing nervously over her bed. It was really bright inside the room.

"Forgive me, Commander." The maid wrung her

hands. "The emperor has called an audience in his private apartments and you're to attend. It begins in a quarter hour. I didn't know when you preferred—"

"A quarter hour?" Mulan jumped out of bed, nearly tripping herself in a tangle of sheets. She cast around for her belongings. Her bags were in the corner. She'd done a little unpacking...

"Water for washing?" The maid held out a basin and curtsied cautiously, eyeing Mulan as one might watch a runaway tornado.

"Uh, yes, thank you." Mulan splashed her face and riffled through her bag for clothes. She'd only brought two linen dresses, and they were wrinkled from the journey.

The maid took a tentative step towards her. "Perhaps I could iron—"

"How much longer do I have?" Mulan asked.

The maid glanced at a water clock in the corner. "The audience will start in six minutes."

"How long does it take to get there?"

"Eight minutes if you walk quickly."

Mulan threw the dress over her head and ran out the door. She'd reached the end of the walkway when she realised she no longer remembered how to get to the emperor's apartments. She cast around helplessly, fantasising about scaling the palace walls and fleeing into the hills.

"Commander, I can take you there if you'd like." The

maid had followed her.

"Yes, please."

The young woman looked surer of herself as she led Mulan through the palace's maze of corridors and courtyards. This time, Mulan took careful note of the turns and passageways.

"I'm sorry," said Mulan. "I didn't ask your name last night."

"Oh." The maid blushed. "I'm Ting. At your service." She paused for a moment and then continued in a rush. "I've heard all about your great deeds, Commander. How you fought the barbarians on these very rooftops. And is it true that you've started a militia for women?"

The young maid's enthusiasm took the edge off Mulan's panic. Mulan smiled despite herself. "I did. They're very good soldiers by now."

Ting's eyes opened wide, as if she were seeing Mulan's militia for herself. Just then, the two of them turned the corner to the emperor's apartments. Mulan slowed, her nerves returning with a vengeance.

"This is it, Commander," said Ting. She stopped a few steps from the threshold.

Guards once again opened the door for Mulan. She went in alone.

The sitting room from the night before was empty, though Mulan heard voices further inside. A eunuch stationed just inside the entrance bowed to her, catching her off guard and scaring her half to death. He gestured towards an open door down the hall, and Mulan hurried through, bursting into what looked like a miniature audience chamber. The emperor sat in a high-backed chair, his feet resting on a low wooden pedestal. Wall panels painted with images of trees in bloom hung over a crowd of ministers and servants. A thick red-and-gold rug muffled everyone's footsteps and voices. When the eunuch, who'd apparently followed Mulan to the room, announced her name, everyone turned to look at her.

The emperor smiled. "Ah, Mulan. Come in."

A dozen sets of eyes took in her appearance, and a dozen pairs of eyebrows wrinkled in consternation. Mulan's cheeks grew hot, and she suppressed the urge to smooth down her hopelessly wrinkled dress. She caught sight of Shang standing to the side. He had traded in his mail for ceremonial armour. Gold silk padding embroidered with red, blue and green clouds protected his chest instead of the usual chain mail. He stood easier without that extra weight, and he looked well rested. His mouth curved upwards as he nodded a greeting. Mulan gave him a nervous smile, wishing she knew what was to come.

The emperor cleared his throat. "I know you have all been eagerly awaiting the announcement of my heir. I've come to a decision."

Silence hung for three heartbeats, and then the ministers came to life.

An older man with a round face and sparse moustache

stepped forward. "That is good news, Your Majesty," he said cautiously.

"The country is eager to know," simpered a minister with a mole on his face.

The emperor acknowledged their words with a nod. "I considered many factors: character, wisdom, ability to inspire the people. Because of this, I have decided not to place any of my distant relations on the throne."

No one spoke, but a palpable excitement filled the room at the emperor's words. Mulan realised, with dread, that they were all hoping to be the chosen. She sneaked another look at Shang, who was listening calmly, a hint of curiosity in his stance.

The emperor, as well, surveyed the faces around him before continuing. "Today, I officially name Fa Mulan as my heir."

Breaths hissed out. Mouths gaped open in shock. If Mulan thought all eyes were on her before, it was nothing compared to now. Mulan looked over at Shang. He stared wide-eyed, just like the others.

She caught his gaze. *I'm sorry I didn't tell you.* Shang's expression didn't change. Mulan willed him to react, to show happiness or anger or confusion. The moment stretched on, and then Shang broke his gaze away, dropped to one knee and bowed his head. "All hail Crown Princess Mulan. May she live ten times ten thousand years." He spoke loudly, with the commanding voice she knew from the battlefield. But was she imagining the strain behind his words?

Now everyone stared at Shang, who remained motionless, his head bowed. If not for the heavy rise and fall of his chest, he might have been a statue, bent low in a posture of supplication that Mulan had only seen him direct towards the emperor himself. *But he's not bowing to the emperor. He's bowing to me.* Mulan recoiled at the wrongness of it.

There was a rustle of cloth and a soft thud. A servant had followed suit, followed by a frail-looking old minister. One by one, people fell to their knees until Mulan and the emperor were the only two people not bowing.

"Please, stand up," she finally said. "Everyone, stand up."

The room came to life in a flutter of rustling finery. A minister with owl-like eyes was the first to his feet. He bowed to the emperor. "Your Majesty has made a good and wise choice."

"Yes," said the frail-looking minister, the one who'd bowed after the servant. "Empress Mulan will no doubt lead China to new prosperity."

One by one, each official spoke words of congratulation and approval. Mulan stood numbly, absorbing praise from men who minutes before had hoped to be in her place. Could it really be this easy? She had no time to think, because the ministers were coming at her now. Pigeons to breadcrumbs they were, bobbing their heads, bowing and wishing blessings on her.

"Heaven smiles on China today."

"What good fortune, to have an empress as wise as she is beautiful."

"May your reign last tens of thousands of years."

Their words clung like spiderwebs on her skin. She resisted the urge to rub her arms.

"Thank you," she murmured, looking away. "What great fortune to... have you in my court..."

Her attention strayed to the other side of the room, where Shang still stood. The minister with owl-like eyes said something to her about dams and the importance of keeping them in good repair. Mulan nodded politely and tried her best to catch Shang's eye, but her new conversation partner stepped in front of her, blocking her view. By the time he moved out of the way, Shang was disappearing through the door.

"The best time to audit their condition is in the winter," the minister said. "Before the spring rains."

Mulan inclined her head and stepped around him. "That's fascinating, Minister. Excuse me, I must—"

She half walked, half ran for the door. By the time Mulan reached it, Shang was halfway to the residence's front entrance.

"Shang!"

He looked back, his expression guarded.

Mulan caught up to him. "I wanted to—"

A tightening in his jaw made her go abruptly quiet. "This way," he said, jerking his head. She followed him outside into the emperor's private garden. It was small, well kept and empty. Shang led her through giant rock gardens of porous stone and across a small arched bridge. A pagoda stood on the other side, surrounded by long-limbed trees.

Shang swivelled his head, scanning the trees around them, and finally his shoulders relaxed. Mulan had never seen him this cagey before.

He broke his silence. "I take it this is why he summoned you last night."

"Yes. And then he forbade me from telling anyone."

Shang nodded knowingly. "He wanted everyone to hear it from him." Though tension and worry radiated off him, Mulan realised she sensed no surprise from Shang.

"Did you suspect any of this?" she demanded.

"It crossed my mind, but I didn't want to make assumptions. He made a good choice."

His demeanour was so solemn. Mulan scanned his face, trying to figure out if he was sincere. "There's one problem. I don't know anything about leading a country."

Shang's reaction was lightning fast. He grabbed her by the shoulders and whirled her around to face him. "Don't ever let them hear you talking like this. Don't show any signs of weakness. They'll use anything you say against you."

Mulan stared at him, stunned at his vehemence. A moment

passed, in which he seemed to realise he was manhandling the heir to the throne. His fingers sprang apart. "My apologies."

The apology threw her off more than anything else he'd done thus far. Mulan thought of the countless times they'd traded friendly punches on the shoulder or wrestled each other back from the lunch line. If she faced him on the training field now, would he pull his blows?

"Who's looking for reasons to take me down?" she asked.

"Who's looking? The real question is who isn't. You're the heir now. You have what everyone in the palace wanted."

She watched him carefully. "Everyone?"

He returned her gaze, quietly acknowledging her real question. "Not everyone. I know the emperor made a good choice in you. You are the hero of China, and you have my full and undying fealty."

How was it that a pledge of loyalty could sound so much like a rejection? "Fealty?" she asked softly. "Is that all I have?"

Shang looked away.

"What does this mean for us, Shang?" She flung her words like hooks, desperate to pull his gaze back to her, but they didn't catch. Shang's eyes stayed fixed on the tip of a nearby boulder, though Mulan got the impression that he saw nothing at all.

"The country comes first," he said softly. "We knew that when we were sworn into the army."

"What's that supposed to mean?"

"You'll have state visits soon." He didn't exactly speak louder, but his words came deliberately, each one pushed along by the force of the next. "There will be negotiations conducted, invitations made."

Mulan's heart dropped. "Marriage alliances?"

"You'll certainly get offers."

Mulan swallowed, feeling as if she needed to shake a fog out of her head. "There must be other ways to do diplomacy." She searched back through what history she knew. Did empresses marry generals? The empresses from the history books had all been consorts to emperors. Mulan knew of no empresses who took the throne first. The walls around the palace suddenly felt higher, more solid.

Shang drew a breath. "Whatever happens, know that I will always be your most loyal servant," he said.

He hesitated, took one last look at her and then left.

CHAPTER FIVE

M inister Kin of finance suffered from seasonal allergies. He'd had bad congestion the entire week, which resulted in a particularly nasal tone when he talked, interrupted by pauses in which he heroically attempted to inhale through his nose. Mulan found herself getting nervous whenever he spoke a particularly long sentence, bracing herself for him to keel over from lack of air.

"Millet harvests have been down in surrounding provinces," he droned, glancing down at his notes. He, Mulan and the rest of the emperor's cabinet stood in the council room, arrayed around the emperor's chair. "This was projected to lower tax revenue by twenty percent. I recommend raising the grain tax to make up for the shortfall. Otherwise we may not be able to afford planned road improvements."

Mulan racked her brain, trying to remember what last

year's tax revenue was. She'd read it a few nights ago, she was sure. In fact, she might have fallen asleep on top of that exact report. But the numbers eluded her. Though it seemed she spent every waking moment trying to catch up, she still felt hopelessly behind. The other ministers and the emperor followed the endless parade of news and numbers with ease. Even Shang, who'd always preferred practice fields to council rooms, asked astute questions.

"Would the grain farmers be able to afford the tax increase?" asked Mulan.

The minister gave her a quizzical look. "Estimated tax burdens are on the third chart in my report."

"Yes, you're right. I'm sorry," said Mulan.

"Your Highness will pick this all up soon enough," he said. He didn't sound incredibly sincere. These weeks were supposed to be a training period for Mulan, a time for her to learn the nuances of palace life so she could envision herself taking over after the emperor passed on. Sometimes, though, this time seemed less a training period and more a test, and her score on the test kept going down. How long had she been here? Four weeks? Five weeks? Every day, it seemed she knew less instead of more.

There was a table set up in front of the emperor, and Shang approached it, gesturing towards a scroll that lay upon it. When the emperor nodded, he picked it up and handed the report to Mulan. She squinted at the numbers, inked in careful rows across the paper like tiny soldiers. "It looks like five percent of the grain-farming peasants would have trouble feeding their families if the tax is increased."

"The numbers likely look more dire than the reality," said Minister Kin. "Peasants are resourceful."

"Resourceful?" asked Mulan. "Are they going to figure out a way to eat tree roots?"

Minister Kin gave a pained smile. "Your Highness has a pointed sense of humour," he said. "But I assure you—"

The emperor tapped his finger on the table. "I agree with the crown princess that there's no need to put an undue burden on the people," he said. "If necessary, we can delay any road construction projects until next year."

Minister Kin's smile stiffened, but he bowed. "Of course, Emperor."

"General Shang," said the emperor. "Please report on your recruitment and training progress."

Shang bowed. "Recruitment numbers have been down this year, but the trainees proceed on schedule. The new troops have completed basic training and will be assigned to outposts in two weeks."

"Where do you intend to send them?" asked Mulan. Shang's reports, at least, she could always follow. Outpost names and locations were familiar to her, as well as their tactical importance.

"I will send five hundred men each to the main provincial

and border outposts."

"That's fewer than we've been sending in past years," said the emperor.

"Yes, Your Majesty. I'd prefer to send more soldiers, especially up north. There have been rumours of a new leader taking power among the Huns, but a military draft seems unwise in the absence of any solid threat."

"Do you think they'd attack again?" asked the emperor.

"Not imminently," said Shang. "But they're watching us, just as we're watching them. If they sense a weakness, they might well decide to strike."

Mulan wondered if crowning an empress would be seen as a weakness. "Have you spoken with local leaders about their militias? If there are regions with well-established local garrisons, you could divert their imperial troops to the border."

Shang nodded slowly. "That's a good idea, Your Highness." He flashed a grin that buoyed her spirits. "I will send messengers out today."

"Good. It's decided, then. Let us adjourn for this morning," said the emperor. "Mulan and I will continue in my private apartments." The ministers bowed and turned to leave. Shang was the first out the door, as was his habit these days.

A servant approached Mulan, head bowed as he presented a letter on a lacquered tray. "From your mother and father, Your Highness. You requested it be brought to you as soon as we received it."

Mulan snatched the letter, quick as a goose snapping breadcrumbs off the ground. It was all she could do not to rip the paper along with the seal. She'd been waiting for this reply for weeks. After the emperor announced Mulan as heir, she'd written her father and mother immediately with the news. She also invited them to come live with her at the palace.

My dearest daughter. Even the sight of her father's elegant calligraphy lifted her spirits. *This is an honour beyond our wildest dreams. The heavens smile on our family. Our duties here keep us at our village, but we hope to visit the capital soon.*

"News from your mother and father?" asked the emperor.

"Yes, Your Majesty," said Mulan. She turned away, pretending to scan the room for her remaining belongings as she erased the disappointment from her face. She'd known that her parents had responsibilities at home, that they couldn't just pack up and leave, but part of her had hoped.

A maidservant took the emperor's arm to help him up. Mulan noticed how much effort it took him to get out of the chair. His steps were laboured, and even the short walk out the door left him short of breath. This was more than the usual fatigue of old age. The emperor was sick, though he never spoke of it.

"How did you find the meetings today?" the emperor asked. Mulan supported him on one side while the maidservant held his arm on the other. She could feel the emperor's arm bones through the heavy sleeves of his gown.

"Still a little overwhelming," she said, "but I'm starting to follow the reports better."

They entered the emperor's apartments, sitting down as more maids brought a light lunch of dumplings and stir-fried pea shoots. The dumplings were so juicy that Mulan used a spoon to catch the broth that spilled out with the first bite.

The emperor fell silent as they began to eat, and by now Mulan knew to wait. In the past weeks, she'd come to a better understanding of his personality and history, as well as his mannerisms. She could tell that he was thinking now, and she gave him time. They had these lunches every day. The emperor didn't seem to have a set agenda for them, often just speaking what was on his mind.

"You are experiencing first hand now the difficulties of running a country," he said. "Council meetings. Tax calculations. These are far less glamorous than sitting on a throne and receiving the adulation of the people. Many want to rule. Many want the power, but few of those people see the costs."

Mulan thought about Shang, who had been distant since the day she was named heir. She hadn't wanted the power, yet it had come to her anyway.

"You don't want the power," said the emperor, as if reading her mind. "That is one of the reasons I chose you."

He spoke of her reluctance as if it were some rare virtue,

but really she just wanted to go home. Even in her early days in the army, she'd never felt so incompetent. So alone.

The emperor took a long sip of tea and continued. "A ruler cannot simply do anything he wants. The heavens watch. The gods bestow or take away power. If the emperor rules well, they reward the nation with good harvests and prosperity. But a bad ruler will lose the Mandate of Heaven. His country will be beset by misfortune: war, earthquakes, famine, floods, warnings written in the stars."

Mulan tried to think of misfortune that had occurred during the emperor's reign. "The gods seem to approve of you."

"They haven't sent earthquakes or famine, and they delivered a hero to save us from the Huns," he said. "Though I may not be so forward as to claim the gods' approval, I'll hazard to say that they don't disapprove. But that wasn't always the case. And there were sacrifices involved in getting here, not just from me, but from those around me.

"Did you know that I wasn't born to the empress? She never had a son, and I was the firstborn son to my father's concubines. So they took me from my mother to be raised by the empress instead.

"I never wanted to be emperor. From a young age, I was studious and desired nothing but to be left alone with my books. Even after I was crowned, I ignored my responsibilities and reaped the consequences of my negligence. One decision from a ruler can destroy countless lives. Even the lack of action can kill thousands. I learned this, during my early years."

Mulan wondered what he was talking about. Part of her didn't want to know.

"As I grew older, I learned to shoulder my responsibilities. I didn't like it at first, but I also realised that my throne wasn't the prison I thought it would be. I realised I didn't have to forget the scholars and philosophers that so fascinated me in my youth; I could use the wisdom of the sages to guide my reign."

The emperor's voice softened. "Still, there were things I had to give up. As a young man I fell in love with the daughter of the imperial tailor. But emperors didn't marry daughters of tailors. We had unrest in the western provinces back then. The local governors didn't welcome my rule. I needed to bring them onto our side, and marrying one of their daughters was the firmest way to do it. Sometimes a leader must sacrifice his own dreams and desires for the good of the nation, do you understand?"

He raised his gaze to look at her, and as much as Mulan wanted to look away, she couldn't. In the emperor's eyes, she saw decades of responsibility, joy, sacrifice and grief. And she sensed that he saw everything she struggled with, everything she clung to. The emperor knew exactly what he was asking her to give up.

She pressed her hands to the table to keep them from shaking. "I understand."

The emperor nodded, and a faint smile peeked out from beneath his moustache. "I knew you would. That's another reason why I chose you."

...

Mulan could tell that Shang wasn't expecting visitors for the evening. He'd changed out of his ceremonial armour into a simple blue robe that hung loosely off his muscular frame. Mulan charged past him as soon as he opened the door to his apartments, leaving him standing behind her with a confused expression on his face.

"Mulan?"

"I can't do this," she said, throwing her hands up. "I can't be empress."

Shang slammed the door shut, giving her a reproachful gaze – which she defiantly returned – as he crossed the room to his window. He looked through the latticework from several different angles to see as far to each side as possible. Mulan knew she should feel guilty for worrying him, but she felt more bitterness than guilt. She was tired of appearances. She was tired of keeping it all in.

Shang's rooms were meticulously kept. A sitting room in front had a low table surrounded by straw mats. Through a doorway, Mulan could see a platform bed with blankets folded at its feet. Briefly, she wondered what it would be like to live here, too. To have her shoes next to his by the door, to wake up each morning and see his face. And then she shook away the thought, because it hurt too much.

Shang backed away from the window. "What's going on?"

"I can't do this." Her voice shook. "I never asked to be empress. All I wanted was to live a quiet life in my village. I don't want to give up my family. I don't want to give up…" She trailed off before she said "*you*," but something registered in his eyes. A flash of desire, a flash of pain and just the tiniest glimmer of hope.

"You're serious, aren't you?" he said softly.

"This is my life, Shang. The rest of my life."

Shang shook his head as if to clear it. "You're talking about saying no to the emperor? To the whole thing?"

"Why is that such a crazy idea?" Her words sounded shrill in her ears.

Shang rubbed his temples. He sat down on a chair, only to stand up again and walk in a tight circle around the room, a lion prowling around a cage. "Who would be heir then?" he finally asked.

"There must be someone. One of the ministers. I can't possibly be the only qualified person."

Mulan watched as a myriad of emotions flashed across his face — temptation, doubt, wariness, resolve. "Say something,

Shang," she pleaded.

He sat down, supporting his temple with his hands, brow furrowed. Every moment he didn't reply was agony, but that was Shang. Always deliberate. Always careful.

Finally, he met her eyes. "I can't help you with this decision. My own selfish interests run too strong. But if this causes you such anguish, you need to speak with the emperor."

Mulan swallowed. "I must. I don't know what I will say, but I must."

...

Mulan didn't eat dinner with the court that evening, instead claiming fatigue and asking for Ting to bring a meal to her rooms. Though the handmaiden laid out a seven-course dinner on her table, it sat uneaten as Mulan paced her apartments.

Would Mulan be abandoning her duty if she refused to be empress? Was she just giving up? On her desk lay the letter her mother and father had sent her. What would they think if she simply went home? But along with thoughts of duty came anger. Hadn't she sacrificed enough for her country already? She thought of the life that lay before her if she became empress. Unending years of court intrigue and reports she didn't understand. Living daily under Heaven's watch, with thousands of lives hanging on her every decision.

And she would face this life alone. Or at the very best,

with a political alliance, some foreign prince that she might learn to respect with time, but whom she could not love.

The emperor must have other candidates. Perhaps she could ask him who they were and convince him that one of the others would be better. He would be disappointed, but was it really wise to have a ruler who didn't wish to rule?

The emperor hadn't wanted to rule either. But he accepted his duty and the country prospers because of it.

Mulan pushed those thoughts away. The emperor had been born into this life. She hadn't been. Her selection was arbitrary at best. Mulan had to say something, and she had to do it while the emperor still had time to train a new heir.

The night brought little rest. Shang knocked on her door early the next morning. Mulan, bleary-eyed from fatigue, quietly stepped aside to let him in. His expression was unusually solemn, and shadows under his eyes spoke of a sleepless night for him as well. As he closed the door behind him, Mulan found herself aware of his proximity, the distance between them and the number of steps it would take to close it.

"Will you speak with him?" he asked.

"I have an audience in an hour."

He nodded, and she saw hope flood across his features, dreams that he'd diligently reined in all this time. She took in the lines of his face, allowing herself to look at him more closely than she'd dared to for weeks. His dark, expressive eyes, the curve of his lips. Could they still have the life together they wanted? She reached out and squeezed his arm. "Shang…"

He softened to her touch and, after a brief hesitation, pulled her closer with a gentle hand to her shoulder blade. "I hope…" He stopped, as if afraid to put it to words, though his eyes conveyed what he couldn't say out loud. He radiated heat, and Mulan smelled soap on his skin.

There was a frantic knock on the door. Shang's hand tightened briefly on her back, and then they reluctantly pulled apart. Mulan exchanged a worried look with him as she went to answer the door. An agitated eunuch stood there, one of the emperor's personal attendants.

"Your Highness…" he said. His eyes were so wide that Mulan could see the whites both above and below his irises. A sheen of sweat covered his forehead. Mulan had never seen this servant conduct himself with anything but the utmost composure, but now he shook so hard that the trailing ribbons of his fu tou trembled along with him.

"What's wrong?" Mulan asked.

"It's about the emperor."

Mulan wondered, with a jolt of panic, whether the emperor had somehow received word of her plans. "I have an audience with him in an hour. Does he—"

"He won't be able to speak with you," said the eunuch. He took a shaky breath. "The emperor has collapsed."

CHAPTER SIX

Shang and Mulan stared at each other in shock.

"When?" Mulan finally managed to say.

"He spoke of chest pains after his morning meal." The eunuch's thin voice sounded as if it might break. "And then he fell to the ground."

"Can I see him?"

"That is up to the royal physician. He's currently with the emperor. If you'd like, you can come and wait for him to finish his examination."

The palace appeared remarkably calm as Mulan and Shang hurried to the emperor's quarters. Servants went about their tasks. Gardeners cleared lotus pads off a small lake. Mulan caught a hint of tension in the stance of the emperor's door guards, but she might have imagined it. Strange how everything carried on as normal, even as history was shifting just a few steps away.

Two ministers were already in the emperor's sitting room when Mulan and Shang arrived. Minister Wei, the minister of justice, loomed in the corner, his large frame a menacing shadow to passing servants. Minister Huang of personnel administration paced the room with quick steps, pulling at his sparse moustache. Neither acknowledged Mulan or Shang. After a short while, the remaining three ministers joined them.

The door to the emperor's bedroom was closed, though Mulan could hear someone moving around within. Mulan and the ministers kept vigil, nobody speaking. It felt as if any sudden movement or wayward utterance would somehow cause bad fortune to roll in.

The door opened. The royal physician stepped outside, his brow covered in sweat. "The emperor is awake, but he is not well," he said. "He would like to speak to Mulan."

Never had Mulan felt gazes so vicious as the ones that bored into her back as she followed the physician into the emperor's bedchamber. If only they knew, she thought, the words she'd spent all night preparing. How quickly things could change.

The emperor lay on his bed, propped up by red and gold pillows. Though it had only been a day since she'd last seen him, he looked thinner, more emaciated than before. The skin on his face had a grey cast to it. It was horrifying, seeing the man she'd come to know and respect, transformed into this faded being.

If he dies like this, I'll be trapped as heir. Stepping down would mean civil war. No sooner had the thought crossed her mind than Mulan was overcome with guilt for thinking it.

"Your Majesty."

He shifted to face her, squinting at her features. Mulan got the impression that he was assembling the scattered pieces of her into a picture only he could see.

"I've been expecting something to happen," he said. "But not quite so soon. You might assume the throne earlier than I'd thought." He looked as if he'd slide right off the pillows if he moved too much.

"Don't say that, Your Majesty. You are strong, and the doctor is skilled."

The emperor's eyes twinkled at her blatant lie. "You are scared."

"Yes, Your Majesty." That, at least, was true.

"What do you fear?"

Mulan hesitated, all the words she'd prepared swirling in her mind. She couldn't say them now.

"You fear you are unequal to the task," the emperor prompted.

"Yes." *I know I am unequal to the task.*

He took in a long, slow breath. "Not all rulers believe they are unequal to the task, but all rulers should. If you feel inadequate for the job, it means that you understand the magnitude of the responsibility on your shoulders. This is a good thing."

But what if I can't bear the responsibility? What if I can't pay the price?

The emperor reached for her but faltered. His hand hovered briefly in the space between them before Mulan took it into her own. "I leave this world without worry for China. I know that the country is in good care. You have the Mandate of Heaven. Your reign will be remembered as a blessed time in history."

She was trapped.

The door creaked open. "Your Majesty," said the royal doctor. "You should rest."

The emperor gave Mulan's hand one last frail squeeze before letting go.

Shang caught Mulan's eye when she came out the door. She gave a quick shake of her head. Even if the ministers had not been around, she would not have been able to put to words what had just happened in the emperor's room, what was about to happen, or the cage that had just closed around her. Still Shang seemed to understand. As Mulan sat down beside him, he bowed his head.

The silence stretched. The royal physician came back out. "He sleeps. He may not wake again."

Minutes blended into hours. They continued to hold vigil

in that sitting room. Minister Liu, the minister of rites, lit incense and poured out libations for the emperor's ancestors. The day passed, and night came. The royal doctor moved between the emperor's bedside and the room where everyone waited, though there was never much news for him to bring. Servants brought water and food. Mulan didn't eat and took only enough water to wet her lips.

Before Mulan had returned to the Imperial City, the emperor had seemed to her something like a god – a living, approachable god who'd presented her with military honours, but someone distant and powerful nonetheless. In these past weeks, she'd heard the emperor's stories and his struggles. She'd become familiar with the way he thought, the things he valued, the decisions he regretted. She knew he was a good man.

The night deepened. Candles burned low. Mulan lost track of time in a blur of servants come and gone, incense burned and incense lit.

As the sky began to grey, the royal doctor entered the room again. He didn't speak right away, just stood very still. Mulan knew, from the expression on his face, what he was going to say.

"The emperor has moved on to the next realm."

It was as if someone had hung lead weights from her heart. She looked to Shang, who stared hollowly back. Was it a few hours or a lifetime ago when they'd allowed themselves to hope?

Shang stood, moving with a heaviness that was terrible to see yet impossible to look away from. His expression was stone. Mulan watched, her heart in her throat, as he turned deliberately to face her. Then he fell to his knees and touched his forehead to the ground. "All hail Empress Mulan."

"Shang—" She sprang to her feet, aghast. The truth of the moment descended on her, solidifying, locking her into place.

"All hail Empress Mulan," echoed the royal doctor. He knelt as well.

The servants followed. The head eunuch. A maidservant who had to put down her teapot. Three more eunuchs at the door hailed her in unison.

The ministers were still in their seats. Mulan saw unbridled fury in Minister Wei's face and contempt in the set of Minister Fang's lips. A prickle of danger worked itself through her shock, the sense of a spear point behind her, an archer unseen in the trees.

Minister Liu of rites stood up. He cast a stern look at the other ministers and then turned kind eyes at Mulan, squinting at her from where he stood. Slowly, he lowered himself to the ground.

"Hail Empress Mulan," he said in his thin voice.

Liu's actions seemed to spur a change in the others. One by one, Ministers Fang, Huang and Kin bowed. Only Minister Wei of justice remained now, a hulking presence, terrifying in his fury. Out of the corner of her eye, Mulan saw Shang raise his head. The threat in Shang's eyes was clear, as was the defiance in Wei's.

But then the minister of justice broke his gaze away. He turned to Mulan. "All Hail Empress Mulan."

And then he dropped to his knees and bowed, so that Mulan was the only one left standing.

CHAPTER SEVEN

Mulan woke later that morning with the worst headache of her life. The sun was bright and disturbingly low in the sky. Her pillow was damp. She couldn't be sure whether it was from sweat or from tears.

Was the emperor really gone?

Her maids had left a basin of water in the corner of her room, and she splashed her face. Why had no one woken her? There were things to be done, plans to be made. She would have to address the people and let them know what had happened. And after that... It was too much to think about.

Mulan dressed quickly. Ting was stationed outside her room, and she startled when Mulan opened the door. The handmaid had tearstains on her face.

"You've heard about the emperor," said Mulan.

Ting made a valiant effort to pull up the corners of her

mouth, but that just made her lips tremble even more. She nodded, sniffling.

A large part of Mulan wished to follow Ting's lead and crumple as well, but she didn't have the luxury. "Has anything else happened?"

"I haven't heard, Your Majesty, but I've been here all morning."

Ting had called her "Your Majesty" instead of "Your Highness". It was too much to process. "Can you fetch me some food and paper?"

Ting curtsied, but instead of leaving, she shuffled from foot to foot, moving her lips but not getting any words out. "I'm glad you're succeeding him," she finally said in a rush. And then she ran off.

Mulan stared after her, letting the maid's grief, uncertainty and unexpected devotion wash over her and drain away. Ting's words were a surprising comfort, but they didn't quell the storm of uneasiness in Mulan's head. At first Mulan thought to wait in her room for Ting's return, but she found it too excruciating to be alone. She needed to go out. See for herself that the sun still rose this morning like every other day. And if it hadn't? Well, she should know that too.

She thought over her next steps as she moved down the corridor. First, she needed to find her ministers and discuss their plans. What issues had the highest priority? The funeral for the emperor?

The door to the council chamber was closed, which was strange since it was usually left open unless the council was meeting inside. A familiar voice drifted through the door as she passed. Mulan slowed. When she reached for the door handle, a servant startled her by loudly announcing her name.

The door swung open to reveal all of Mulan's ministers except Shang, crowded around the emperor's small table. They straightened when they saw her.

"Your Highness," said Minister Huang of personnel administration, his round face placid.

Mulan glanced from one minister to the next, an uneasy prickle teasing at the back of her neck. "What are you doing?"

"Just discussing some small matters."

Minister Huang was still calling her "Your Highness". He was technically correct, since she hadn't officially been crowned, but Mulan couldn't help but think there was more behind the choice. She moved to inspect the documents on the table.

"You've been talking about grain taxes," said Mulan. It came out like an accusation. It felt like one, too.

"Just some discussion," said Minister Kin, looking down to pull a handkerchief out of his pocket. "We didn't want to bother you on such a small matter."

"I thought we'd decided not to increase it," said Mulan. "It would overburden the farmers."

"Our circumstances have changed since then," said

Minister Kin. He blew his nose, giving Mulan a moment to ponder what exactly he meant, before he continued. "Crowning a new emperor and ensuring a smooth transition always strains the treasury."

Minister Fang tapped a folded fan in his palm. "We may have to let go of our ideals and bow to reality in times like these. Your Majesty will come to understand this as you grow in experience and wisdom."

Mulan flushed. In the past, these allusions to her inexperience might have made her doubt herself, but these blatant attempts by her ministers to circumvent her authority triggered Mulan's instinct to hold her ground. "If you want to discuss taxes, we can do so at a later time, when I'm present for the entire discussion. I want you to notify me of all council meetings from now on."

Minister Kin bowed. "Of course, Your Majesty. We apologise." He didn't sound apologetic at all.

Mulan took a deep breath, summoning all her strength in an effort to keep her anger from overwhelming her. The emperor was not yet dead a day, and her ministers were already trying to take things into their own hands.

Minister Liu, the minister of rites, stepped forward. He was the oldest of her advisers, grey-haired and hunched over.

"I echo Minister Kin's apologies," he said in a more sincere tone. "It's good that Your Majesty is here, because we need to plan the imperial funeral. The palace astrologer has picked an auspicious day next week to hold it."

"There is the issue of the sacrifice," interrupted Minister Fang.

"The sacrifice on the old emperor's behalf?" Mulan had read about it. She knew that it took place at the tomb, though she couldn't recall any other specifics.

"Yes," said Minister Liu, bobbing his head approvingly.

"What is the difficulty?" she asked warily.

The minister of rites glanced nervously between Mulan and Minister Fang. "The question of who is to offer it."

"Isn't it the next emperor?" asked Mulan.

The ministers exchanged meaningful looks.

"In the past, it has always been an emperor," said Minister Fang. He emphasised the last word.

This time, Mulan didn't bother to hide her anger. "I am the next ruler of China."

"It would be unprecedented, having the offering made by a woman," said Minister Wei, the hulking minister of justice. "It's hard to know how the gods would receive it."

As if belligerent Minister Wei had any true concern for the gods. "When the old emperor named me the ruler of China," said Mulan, "he meant for me to take on all the duties of the ruler."

"The everyday practicalities of ruling, to be sure," Minister Huang of personnel said with a condescending smile. "But surely, for a symbolic sacrifice before the gods…"

But that was exactly it. Symbols were important. It was the first time the people would see her performing an emperor's duties. The act was hugely important, and this was exactly why her ministers didn't want her doing it. With a sinking feeling, Mulan realised she had no allies in this room. It was no coincidence that Shang was not here.

"I will give the offering," Mulan said.

For a long moment, no one responded. Mulan wondered if they would be brazen enough to contradict her to her face.

But then the minister of rites cleared his throat. "The empress is right." His voice sounded all the more delicate after the heated discussion. "We should honour the old emperor's wishes. Surely the gods will be pleased with Empress Mulan's honest wish to perform an emperor's duties to their fullest."

Mulan gaped at him. She had been bracing for a fight, and his words left her momentarily off-balance. "Thank you," she finally said.

Minister Liu bowed. "I'm at your service, Your Majesty."

...

The funeral took place on a fittingly sombre day. Clouds obscured the sun, though no rain disturbed the emperor's procession. Citizens crowded the street, dressed in the white and black of mourning. Wails sounded over the funeral music, at times drowning it out.

The emperor's casket and newly carved spirit tablet were

carried through the streets by Shang's soldiers and guarded by ten pikemen. Mulan followed on horseback, along with the emperor's blood relatives. The emperor's daughters had arrived in the Imperial City two days prior, and Mulan had wept with them over the passing of their father.

Behind the royal family marched servants bearing every conceivable item the emperor would need in his next life: clothes, furniture, books, bronze pots and tureens filled with food and wine. Other servants carried clay figures of horses, attendants and soldiers to serve him in the afterworld. All would be buried with him.

The entire city was cloaked in mourning. Coloured signs had been covered by black cloth. Every bit of gold or red was hidden away. Mulan looked at the grieving faces around her. It was strange to think that all these people were now hers to watch over. Would they grieve her when she died?

The procession exited the city gates, crawling down roads that had been hastily repaired for the occasion, smoothed of imperfections. It seemed to Mulan that even the trees by the wayside bowed to the emperor. Finally, they arrived at a tomb fit for royalty. Stone animals and soldiers watched over a solemn spirit road, while steles carved with dragons and lions proclaimed the emperor's accomplishments. At the end of the spirit road stood a series of palatial buildings – living chambers, a throne room and an underground garden for the emperor to enjoy in the next life.

The largest building was the sacrificial hall, which Mulan entered with servants carrying offerings. Priests brought a newly slaughtered cow and placed it on an altar. Mulan lit a fire under it and watched the smoke billow into the sky. The priest intoned a prayer to Heaven, and Mulan recited ritual words inviting the emperor's spirit to take up residence in these tombs. The sacrifice seemed such a simple and reverent act, incongruous with the arguments leading up to it.

The priest spoke a blessing, and then the procession moved to the underground burial chamber, where the emperor was laid to rest below a massive barrow. Shang and a battalion of imperial soldiers began the long process of filling up the grave. Mulan watched the dirt rain down, the coffin slowly disappear from view, until nothing remained of the old emperor except earth.

...

The mourning period lasted for twenty days in the Imperial City. Music was banned and colours were muted. The palace itself put away its brightest statues and tapestries for the next year. But despite the trappings of mourning, the practical workings of the palace quickly moved on. The coronation was to happen soon, and Mulan spent long hours with the minister of rites, going over everything from rituals to clothing.

With the exception of Shang, Mulan liked the minister

of rites best of her cabinet. His gentle demeanour reminded her of the old emperor, though he didn't have the emperor's authoritative presence. Minister Liu didn't treat Mulan with the same condescension as the other ministers. In fact, the day after the emperor's death, he had pulled her aside to apologise for his colleagues.

"They're not used to advising an empress, but they will come around. I have full confidence in the past emperor's judgment." It had meant a lot, at a time when Mulan feared that the next development, however small, would unravel her.

There was much to be done. The palace astrologer presented Mulan with a list of auspicious days on which to hold the coronation, and she picked the first one that fell after the city's mourning period. With the uncertainty that had surrounded the emperor's succession, it would not be wise to let the country go long without a crowned ruler. The tailor measured her for coronation robes, the finance minister presented her with an extravagant coronation budget, and the minister of public works presented plans for clearing the streets of beggars. When Mulan wanted to spend less and leave the beggars undisturbed, an hour-long fight ensued before the ministers backed down.

On a quiet afternoon, the minister of rites presented Mulan with her coronation gown. The rich gold inner gown was sleeveless and woven of lustrous silk. The outer coat, embroidered in red, blue and black, had bell sleeves that brushed the floor. The ensemble was completed with a thin blue scarf and soft brocade shoes with upturned toes shaped like birds. Mulan hefted the gown in her hands. It was heavy, soft and smooth. After weeks in the palace, she'd become accustomed to luxury, but this gown was truly opulent.

"It's lovely," she said.

Minister Liu bowed.

The pattern caught her eye. "This is phoenix embroidery."

"Yes, Your Majesty. That is the traditional symbol for an empress."

"I thought it would be a dragon." That was what the old emperor had worn on his ceremonial robes. It was also the animal carved on the ceiling of the imperial audience hall and on the throne.

"The dragon symbolises the emperor. The phoenix symbolises the empress. Both are majestic creatures, and both convey great authority."

Mulan smoothed her fingers over the dress. It was true that she was an empress, and that the phoenix was just as noble a creature as the dragon. She didn't want to throw away the trappings of womanhood just to make a point. There was something about it that didn't feel quite right, but she'd fought so many battles already. She needed to compromise, or she'd never be able to work with her ministers effectively.

"Thank you, Minister Liu. It is a work of art."

He bowed. "Your Majesty will be a sight for the heavens."

...

A few days before the coronation, a caravan of travellers arrived from Mulan's home village. When Mulan heard the news, she dropped her soup bowl mid-meal and raced across the entrance courtyard of the palace, trailing a tail of confused servants and handmaidens. She paused, scanning the grounds, her heart filling as she spotted the cluster of riders that had come through the gate. The women stood with their horses, talking among themselves as they stared wide-eyed at the palace around them. Squeals of delight sounded as, one by one, they caught sight of Mulan.

Liwen stood at the edge of the group, regaling a hapless horse groom with detailed instructions. She barely had time to turn before Mulan slammed into her with a hug. As they collided, Liwen shifted her stance and blocked Mulan's shin with her own. Arms guided Mulan's trajectory, and a moment later, the heir apparent of China found herself dumped unceremoniously on the ground. Liwen collapsed next to her, and both of them lay there, laughing so hard they could hardly breathe.

"Maybe I shouldn't have done that?" Liwen asked, gasping for air and surveying the servants standing awkwardly around them.

Mulan picked herself up, dusting off her priceless silk gown. She felt giddy.

"I will pardon you if you're sentenced to death," she said, offering Liwen a hand up. "It's good to see you, friend."

Mulan moved down the line, greeting each woman in turn. Not every member of the militia had come, but a good number had. Ruolan and Wenling, who'd teased Mulan when Shang came to their village, were vocally disappointed that the general was not in sight. Mulan was surprised to see Zhonglin among the group, and she wondered whether the rebellious young woman was here for her sake or simply to see the Imperial City.

"Is that you, Fu Ning?" said Mulan, spotting a figure with a crutch.

The young woman beamed at Mulan, her smile wide enough to match her strong shoulders, and gestured at her heavily bandaged leg. "The physician called it a miracle," she said. "No infections, and it looks to be healing. He said I could make the journey in a cart, and I might even be able to walk without a crutch one day."

"A miracle indeed," said Mulan. The news lightened her more than she'd thought possible. She hadn't realised how much guilt she still carried over Fu Ning's injury.

As Mulan bounced from woman to woman, trying to catch up on everyone's lives at once, a last wagon rolled into the courtyard. The door opened.

"Mama, Baba!"

Mulan ran again, scattering the grooms and footmen

in her way. Her mother came out first, and then her father, who stepped down more slowly, rubbing his bad hip. Mulan slowed, a pang of guilt shooting through her. She wondered who was carrying water every morning for the horses and pigs now that she was gone.

Her parents' expressions, though, showed no hint of disappointment. Mulan's mother pulled her close and held her face between her hands. "My daughter," she said, her voice cracking with pride.

"We've missed you," said Baba, beaming as if he'd unearthed a long-buried treasure.

It took a while to get everyone situated, but eventually the militia women retired to guest quarters and Mulan ushered her parents to her private apartments. She felt shy as they entered the big lacquered doors, conscious of how the apartments, though small by palace standards, were easily twice the size of her home. She felt like a young girl trying on her mother's clothes, not realising how long the sleeves were until she was caught in the act.

"Sit down," she said, motioning to the chairs. "You must be exhausted from your journey."

As Mulan poured tea, her mother admired the delicate blue landscape on the side of the pot. "Imagine being served tea by the empress," said Mama.

"Even empresses honour their father and mother," Mulan said. The tea's warmth spread through her, and she finally relaxed. The room felt fuller than it had ever been. "Are things in order back at home? Will everything be all right while you're gone?"

"The Hongs have promised to watch over the garden and the animals," said Mama. "I worry about our chrysanthemums, but they are in good hands. But come, our garden is hardly the most interesting thing we have to talk about. Tell us how you fare."

Mulan weighed her words. Though she'd dismissed the maids and guards so she could speak freely, she still wasn't sure how much she wanted to burden her parents with her troubles.

"Busy," she said. "A bit overwhelmed, but I'm learning."

Baba nodded. "I'm sure there is much to learn, but you will. You are the pride of China."

"I hope so. Most days I feel as if I have an impossible number of things to pick up. How do I lead a country when I know so little?"

"Well, I have never been royalty, but I have certainly been charged with great responsibility before," said Mama. "When I gave birth to you, I had no idea how to raise a child. I cried when you cried, and I felt overwhelmed every waking moment. But your grandmother told me, 'The important thing is that you love her. If your love is strong enough, you will find a way'. I imagine this holds true for leaders of countries as well. The most important thing is that you love China and care for its people. That, combined with the counsel of your advisers, will see you through."

Mulan thought of her daily battles with fractious ministers and wished she felt the same way.

...

The rest of the day was Mulan's happiest since arriving in the Imperial City. She led tours of the palace for everyone interested. Liwen was especially excited to see the training yards, with their vast stores of practice weapons, and Mulan promised that the militia could train there the next morning. That night, they had a banquet in the grand hall with performances by palace acrobats and opera singers. The chefs outdid themselves with creative uses of wild plants native to Mulan's village. A leafy green Mulan usually stir-fried was instead chopped and mixed into steamed egg, while yellow wildflowers adorned the moulded sticky rice. Everyone ate far more than necessary.

As Mulan swallowed yet another syrupy bite of sticky rice, Liwen came to sit with her. Though it was customary for the empress to eat separately from all the guests, Mulan had insisted on mingling, moving from place to place in the banquet hall throughout the meal.

Mulan's friend fell into the chair next to her with far less grace than befit her ladylike attire. "Is Shang at the palace?"

"He is," said Mulan.

Liwen snatched a clump of sticky rice off Mulan's plate, popped it into her mouth and carefully licked her fingers clean. "I haven't seen him."

"We've both been busy."

Liwen's eyebrows spoke more eloquently than many courtiers, and now they called Mulan a liar.

"It's complicated," Mulan said, fully aware of how defensive she sounded.

Liwen pursed her lips, looking Mulan over as if she were a suit of armour with a missing piece. "You know, you don't have to be empress if you don't want to."

Mulan's first instinct was to glance frantically around to see if anyone had overheard. Her second was to laugh, though it came out harsher than she expected. "The Imperial City isn't a nunnery. You can't just walk away from it all."

"Why not? Leave them to their own devices. Let them run their own lives." Liwen paused, scrutinising Mulan's face. "But you won't do that, will you?"

"The succession was already fraught when the emperor named me as heir. Imagine the chaos if I stepped down. All my ministers want to rule. None would respect my designation of successor. The country could be torn apart." Mulan shook her head. "I gave the emperor my word that I would lead and care for China."

Liwen's smile was a mix of exasperation and resigned fondness. "Did I ever tell you why I travelled across China to seek you out?"

"No, I don't think you ever did." Strange that she hadn't, after all their time spent together.

"I heard the story of how you dressed up as a man to join the army, and I was awestruck at your act of rebellion. I mean, I had long given up on behaving as a virtuous woman should, but what you did was something else altogether." She took a large sip of wine. "It was only after I met you that I realised you were one of the biggest rule followers in existence."

Mulan didn't think "rule follower" was quite the right term, but she understood what Liwen meant. Mulan felt the binds of duty strongly. It was no rebellious streak that had sent her into the army, but her love for her father. Her absolute refusal to let him die a senseless death.

"I'm sorry to be such a disappointment," she said wryly.

Liwen wiped her fingers on the corner of Mulan's napkin. "Ah well, everyone has their faults. Speaking of your ministers, though, I saw a fellow in official robes in the city marketplace. I think he's part of your court. Small man with round cheeks? Rocks on his heels when talking?"

Mulan's gaze snapped up. "That sounds like Minister Huang. He handles personnel administration." She paused. "Huang's not the type who does his own shopping."

"He wasn't buying anything. He was holding court, for lack of a better word. Talking to the people, hearing their woes and so forth."

"I see." Though there was nothing wrong on the surface of it, Liwen's report triggered an uneasy stirring in Mulan's stomach. Ministers were certainly allowed to talk to whomever they wished, but Huang was not one to mix with the masses out of the goodness of his heart.

"Anything particular he talked about?"

Her friend wrinkled her nose. "Anything and everything. He has an oily way to him."

Was he trying to court the people? Ingratiate himself with them? "There's not much I can do if he's simply spending time there."

Liwen sighed. "Impertinent subordinates are a headache, aren't they?"

Mulan followed her gaze to Zhonglin, who was quietly eating dessert across the room. Though there were other women at her table, her chair was pulled slightly away from the others, and she didn't take part in the conversation.

"I was surprised to see Zhonglin here," Mulan said.

"She keeps to herself," Liwen said. "Disappears into the woods sometimes and comes late for training."

Mulan looked at Liwen in surprise. Her second-in-command wasn't the type to tolerate tardiness.

Liwen waved her hand. "Oh, she's been punished plenty. I was hoping the trip here would help her feel a part of the group. The other women would welcome her if she'd simply put in the effort."

Zhonglin turned to look at them, her large eyes bright in the lantern light. Mulan got the impression that she knew they were talking about her.

...

The festivities lasted late into the night. By the time Mulan returned to her apartments, her eyes were falling shut of their own accord. When she saw that a pile of scrolls had fallen off her shelves, Mulan was tempted to leave them. But she'd asked Ting to wake her before sunrise, and she didn't want the maid tripping over them. Mulan scooped up the lot and piled it on her desk. One scroll that had fallen open on the ground was a philosophical treatise on ruling.

The emperor has been given his authority at Heaven's pleasure. It is the duty of the people to serve him as needed. Likewise, the emperor should not overburden his subjects with heavy taxes or requirements of service.

Mulan rolled it back up, darkly amused at the thought of quoting the treatise to her ministers the next time they discussed grain taxes.

She fell asleep the moment she climbed into bed. It seemed just a moment later when Ting woke her and presented her with her old training clothes. Mulan's body protested immensely, but as she dragged herself into the crisp morning, she was surprised at how quickly her spirits recovered. It was quiet in the palace compound. The sun was just coming above the horizon. And the mere prospect of training with her friends instead of layering on ceremonial robes to meet with her ministers brought an undeniable lightness to her step.

The bulk of the local garrison drilled in a field outside the city walls, but the palace had a small training ground for nobility in residence and guards who worked in the palace proper. A good number of Mulan's militia were already there, stretching, talking and rubbing last night's sleep from their eyes.

Liwen crossed the field to greet her. Her hair was in two neat braids down her back, their simplicity speaking volumes about how tired she must have been last night. "Palace life has made you soft, Empress," she said, her eyes sparkling mischievously. "Never did I know Commander Mulan to arrive last to the field."

"Guilty as charged," said Mulan.

Behind her, someone wondered loudly whether the empress was still able to hold a sword. When she turned, she saw only Zhonglin, engrossed in her morning stretches. Mulan's skin prickled in annoyance, but she had a feeling that showing displeasure would be just the reaction Zhonglin hoped for.

"Would you like to lead us in our drills?" asked Liwen.

"Maybe later. I'd like to see where they are first."

Mulan imagined a bit of eagerness in the way Liwen ran back to the others, calling for them to take formation. There was some good-natured groaning, but the women assembled quickly.

Liwen stood in front, calling out and modelling their warm-up form as the women fell in sync. Even after just a few weeks gone, Mulan could see that their movements were crisper, more coordinated. They moved as a unit, and she could sense the energy bouncing between individual soldiers, the awareness they had of each other. Even the snap of their clothing as they punched and kicked sounded in unison. It warmed Mulan's heart to see them doing so well.

The form ended. Liwen called for the women to stand at ease. Every one of their eyes went to Mulan. When she smiled, twenty sets of shoulders straightened.

"Well done, all of you," Mulan said. "Wenling, your kicks have so much more power than before. Ruolan, your control of the staff is much more secure. And all of you move more coherently as a team."

"We've been maintaining regular patrols," said Liwen. "We've had three skirmishes with bandits. One where we brought back prisoners."

"You're a militia. A real one. I couldn't be prouder." The women were too disciplined to move without permission on the training field, but their faces shone. It was a bittersweet moment for Mulan, knowing the progress they'd made, and knowing they'd continue to grow without her.

Liwen clapped her hands. "All right, enough basking in

praise. Regroup for battlefield formations. Go, go, go!"

The women broke and re-formed into groups of ten — some holding shields, others wielding spears. Mulan backed away from the field as different groups took turns attacking each other. Liwen followed Mulan, and they watched side by side in silence.

"I've been training Ruolan," Liwen said suddenly.

"Privately?" It seemed a strange thing to say, since Liwen had obviously been training all the women.

"To replace me." Liwen said it simply and openly, but gently.

And then Mulan understood. Liwen was making good on her promise to leave. Though Mulan had been warned to expect it, the news still hurt.

"Where will you go?" she asked.

"I'm not sure yet. I'll see where the road takes me."

Part of Mulan wanted to ask more of Liwen's reasons, but she resisted. Now didn't seem the time. "You'll let me know before you leave, right?"

"Of course," said Liwen. There was a moment of awkwardness, as Mulan debated whether to say more. And then Liwen jogged off to join the women.

Mulan watched Liwen drill the militia, trying to digest her friend's words. She supposed she had no right to blame Liwen, since Mulan had been the first to leave. And it wasn't as if she'd be seeing much of Liwen even if she stayed with the militia. Still, China was a large place, and without the militia to tether her, Mulan could all too easily see Liwen disappearing into some distant corner of it, never to be heard from again.

"They're good," said a deep, familiar voice at her ear. Mulan jumped, turning to see Shang standing right next to her. His eyes were bright, and his practice armour hung lightly on his frame.

She put thoughts of Liwen aside and inclined her head at his compliment. "It's hard to imagine, but almost none of them had held a sword before they joined. They were farmers mostly. A few from merchant families. But they were so determined."

"Their determination has paid off." His gaze shifted constantly on the field, taking in every aspect of the militia's movements. "I'd be proud to have trained those troops."

Mulan's chest warmed. "Thank you. It means a great deal to hear it from the man who trained me."

His observant eyes moved from the troops to her. "And how are you?"

She could tell by his tone of voice that he was asking about more than her mood this morning. Mulan glanced around, partly to hide her face from his scrutiny, and partly to make sure they were alone. "I'm figuring it out. The ministers have changed since the emperor died."

Shang nodded. "It disappoints me, but it doesn't surprise

me. They have no reason to hide their true leanings now. But whatever they do, you are the empress. Ultimately, you hold the authority."

Mulan felt a twinge of annoyance. She knew she was empress. That didn't make her daily fights with her ministers any less exhausting.

"I've been meaning to say," said Shang. He paused a moment, brow furrowed, gathering his words. "I'm sorry I haven't been around as much these days. It hasn't been completely accidental. I've had trouble with the idea of your coronation and what it might mean... for us. It was juvenile of me, especially at a time when you needed my support. I won't disappear again. And whatever happens, I will always be your loyal subject."

Her chest tightened at the last word. "Subject?" Mulan asked. The air around them was full with everything that hadn't been said.

Shang's gaze softened. "And your friend."

It could have come across as a rejection, but the promise of loyalty was true. Mulan knew this, even as her gut twisted at the loss of what might have been. Perhaps later she would give herself the chance to mourn, to rail at the injustice of the world, but now she was too exhausted to revisit the idea of marriage or fret once more about their future. In some ways, it was a relief to take the offer of friendship at face value.

"Thank you," she said. "I can't ask for a better one."

She saw care and regard in Shang's eyes, even as he worked to mask his regret. "You speak too kindly of me," he said. "But I will do my best to live up to it."

...

Mulan woke to Ting whispering at her bedside.

"Your Majesty."

She groaned, batting the maid's voice away. It was pitch-dark outside. She was exhausted.

"Your Majesty, it's time to begin your preparations." Mulan opened one eye to see Ting's skinny shadow bouncing up and down in excitement.

Preparations? Mulan grasped for understanding, and then the realisation hit her with a zing. The reason she'd tossed and turned late into the previous night. The nerves that had hung over her dreams.

Today was the day of her coronation.

Mulan bolted upright. The sudden movement made her vision cloud over, and she swayed a moment before taking Ting's offered hand and letting the maid lead her to the bath. Mulan usually bathed herself, but Ting had impressed upon her the sheer amount of beautification she'd have to undergo this day. The young maid had shown a surprising amount of pluck, even bringing in her fellow handmaidens to back her up. So Mulan had relented. Still, with one handmaiden scrubbing, oiling and perfuming each limb, Mulan felt more like a chicken being plucked for stew than a royal about to receive her crown. Then she was out of the tub again, wrapped in a luxurious silk dressing gown and taken to her wardrobe.

Mulan found it easier to face the morning by pretending that her clothes were armour. The stiff coronation robe Ting was smoothing down over her shoulders? She imagined it woven with threads of spun gold, the embroidered phoenixes stitched with blazing-red iron. Her sash, hanging loose down her back, was a shoulder guard of blue iron, and the phoenixes on her shoes were spikes and spurs.

"Please keep your head forward, Empress."

A handmaiden gripped a handful of hair, pulling it taut enough to make Mulan's eyes water. The hair, at least, was easy to imagine as a helmet. By the time the maid finished wrapping it around multiple combs and adorning the layered buns with everything from flowers to jade to tiny golden bells, Mulan's coiffure would stop arrows far better than anything the imperial blacksmiths could craft.

The maid inserted one last pin and stepped back. "All done."

She pulled the train of Mulan's robe out as Mulan stepped in front of a full-length mirror. Mulan's reflection was warped and metallic on the coppery finish, but she could see that she was made up as intricately as the finest ladies of court, her face powdered white, her eyes lined with charcoal and her lips painted red as her sash. Her eyebrows had been shaved and drawn back in with blue-black pigment. Tiny silver beads adorned her forehead – tinted with yellow makeup – and three flowers had been painted on her cheek.

"Armour," Mulan said under her breath.

"Your Majesty?"

"Nothing, just talking to myself."

There were many kinds of armour. Mulan would never forget the time she stole her father's that fateful night long ago – lifting it out of the wardrobe in the pitch-dark, stumbling under the unexpected weight of it. She remembered the sweet smell of leather oil as she wrestled it over her head, the sinking feeling as she tugged the belt tighter than it wanted to go, that she was too small and too weak, a failure before she'd even left home. Who was she to think she could live and fight as a man for months on end? Who was she to think she could fulfil a son's duty?

That first night – indeed that first month – failure had followed her around, scratching and biting at her like the fleas that plagued their camp. And yet… here she was, empress of China. During the war, her father's big, unwieldy armour had kept her secrets and kept her alive. Now she needed to trust these ceremonial robes to do the same.

"The minister of rites," announced a eunuch from outside Mulan's apartments.

"Let him in," said Mulan.

Even Minister Liu had cleaned up. His grey hair was combed back and tucked under a crisp black fu tou, and his robe was remarkably unwrinkled. "Your Majesty," he said. "You look exquisite."

"And imperial, I hope," said Mulan.

"That goes without saying."

Servants bowed low as she and the minister left her apartments for the royal courtyard. The midmorning sun shone bright over the procession assembled inside the palace gates. An orchestra of musicians stood at the beginning, tuning their lutes and zithers, polishing their bells. Dancers spun and stretched in colourful robes, waving their long sashes. Lines and lines of soldiers followed, their armour polished so bright Mulan worried it would blind the dancers. She knew without looking that Shang stood at the head of the troops.

In the centre of the processional was a litter lined with gold cloth. It was completely open in the front, and the sidewalls only extended a little past her seat. Yellow tassels hung from the top.

"Your litter, Your Majesty," said the minister.

Mulan stepped in. The bench was wide and padded with a long silk pillow. Someone barked a command, and the four manservants carrying the litter stood. Mulan braced her fingers against the bench as the platform jostled to shoulder height.

Below her, the minister of rites signalled to the bandleader. Drumbeats sounded a low steady heartbeat. Flutes and reed pipes trilled a melody, and then the lutes and erhu joined in. There was another shout, and a team of five men heaved open the palace gates.

If Mulan had thought the music loud before, it was nothing compared to the swell of the crowd. An ocean of faces looked up at her. Young and old, male and female, all craning for a glimpse of her. Heat, sound and energy rolled off that mass of humanity. All those eyes, all the expectations, were overwhelming, and for a moment, Mulan's chest seized in panic. Then she saw a familiar face – Liwen, jumping and waving along with the rest of the militia. And though Mulan couldn't hear them over the noise, she knew they were shouting her name. She waved at them, and then at everyone else around her.

The processional moved on a slow loop through the streets. Once Mulan got over the noise and nerves, she found it a good way to see the Imperial City. The sheer number and variety of faces in the crowd astounded her, and she struggled to comprehend that these people would look to her now for guidance and protection.

The parade had reached its halfway point when Mulan saw another familiar face in the crowd. Mulan's gaze skipped past her at first, but those rosebud lips and perfectly oval face were unmistakable. It was Zhonglin. The young soldier stood far back in the crowd, and she was doing something strange with her hands, putting four fingers in front of her face, and then joining both hands together in two fists. She was out of view before Mulan could get a better look, but now that Mulan noticed the gesture once, she saw others in the crowd doing the same thing. Was it some kind of sign language? A signal?

When the palace gates opened again, the courtyard was lined with the entirety of the imperial staff and army, standing at attention in neat rows like the world's largest chessboard. Soldiers lined the pathway, their backs straight, weapons glinting in the sun. Next to them were eunuchs, draped in blue, green, brown and tan robes as befit their rank. Maids and manservants stood in back, their simple attire pressed and gleaming for the occasion. The minister of rites awaited her at the gates. Mulan exited her litter and proceeded with him towards the great hall.

"Did the parade go smoothly, Your Majesty?" he asked.

"Yes," said Mulan. She marvelled at the stillness inside the compound compared to the riotous celebration outside. "I saw some people in the crowd making a hand signal," she said quietly. "Four fingers across the face, and then double fists on top of each other. Do you know what it means?"

The minister's face clouded for a moment. "Every emperor faces some signs of rebellion. It's sometimes better to ignore, lest you inadvertently fan the flames."

Mulan's eyes snapped to his face. "You think the gesture is

a sign of rebellion?" But Zhonglin had been doing it.

Minister Liu paused to smile and nod at the crowd before replying. "I could be mistaken," he said under his breath. "It's likely nothing. Your Majesty only needs to concern yourself about such things if it becomes widespread."

Mulan dug her fingernails into her palms, concentrating on putting one foot in front of the other. "How would you define 'widespread'?"

"Do not worry about these things now, Your Majesty. It is a day for celebration."

That was like telling someone to enjoy a mountain view as the forest burned down. Did Mulan have a traitor within her own militia?

The great door of the throne room opened before them. Local governors and dignitaries sat in rows beyond. At the front was a dais where priests of the Heavenly Temple awaited along with her ministers. Mulan caught her first glimpse of Shang dressed in ceremonial armour of blue silk. Tigers leapt across his torso after invisible prey. He looked like a warrior from a legend or tapestry, and her chest tightened when their eyes met.

At the very end of the dais sat Mulan's mother and father. It made her heart glad to see her father in his old armour, polished now to shining. Her mother looked like an empress herself in white-and-yellow robes. Neither of them was the type to love pomp and ceremony. Mulan could tell in the way her mother pulled her limbs in from the extravagance around her, the amused tolerance with which Baba observed the busy officials. But when her parents' eyes landed on her, their faces showed nothing but love.

As Mulan took her seat on the throne, a sonorous melody from a stone chime signalled the start of the ceremony. Reading from a scroll, the head priest intoned the long list of an emperor's duties. Mulan was presented with a bronze censer, shaped to look like a mountain in the clouds and inlaid with turquoise and red jewels. Sweet incense smoke drifted out as she presented the censer to the gods and then bowed to her parents.

"All hail Empress Mulan," called the minister of rites. "May she live ten times ten thousand years."

A gong sounded. Everyone fell to their knees before her, and their shouts echoed through the hall. Mulan could feel the reverberations through her feet, like standing knee-deep in rolling thunder. There was power in this room, power in the ritual just performed, and Mulan would either wield it or be blown away.

Finally, the sounds faded to silence. The priest said a last prayer to end the ceremony. The crowd stood, everyone's spirits rising in anticipation of the coming feast. Minister Liu led Mulan to the imperial banquet hall, where she sat at the head table with her ministers on each side. As the coronation guests took their seats, the kitchen staff brought in an array of culinary wonders: roast duck with skin crisped to caramelised perfection; turtle soup and roast bear paw; crab apples in honey; dumplings stuffed with everything from meat, to wild greens, to sweetened lotus paste, and moulded to resemble goldfish, butterflies and flowers.

The food kept coming. The wine kept pouring. Dishes landed in front of Mulan and were whisked away, long after she couldn't eat another bite. She glanced over a few times at Shang, four seats away. He didn't seem to be eating much either.

Along with the food came entertainment. A troupe of acrobats did handstands atop towers of chairs. Sword and fan dancers came next, followed by a one-act opera. Mulan was glad for the spectacle, since it meant she didn't have to talk to her ministers. The entire scene still felt surreal, a raucous celebration that belonged more in a dream than reality.

Finally, the flow of food and wine slowed. The opera singer finished her last aria, and there didn't seem to be any act following. All eyes turned to Mulan.

"Come," said Minister Liu. "We shall now present you to the people."

Together they exited the banquet hall. Mulan was careful not to trip over her robes as they climbed the stairs to a balcony facing the giant palace courtyard. It was dusk now, and a wide band of red stretched across the western sky. The neatly lined soldiers from this morning were gone, replaced by a crowd packed so tightly that Mulan couldn't see the ground. The people – her people – went silent as Mulan came to the railing.

"I present to you Empress Mulan!" said Minister Liu.

If the cheers within the hall had sounded like peals of thunder, the ovation from the courtyard was an earthquake. It went on and on, shaking the palace and everything in it. Mulan feared she'd be knocked down if she didn't brace herself. But the cheers also buoyed her up. She looked at the rapt faces around her, and for the moment, the signs of rebellion she saw earlier seemed like a thing far away. These were the people who had been entrusted to her, and Mulan felt a fierce protectiveness for them.

Finally, after what seemed an eternity, the crowd hushed. Expectation filled the air.

Mulan drew breath, feeling as if she were addressing the universe itself. "The gods have seen fit to put me on the throne. I do not take this responsibility lightly. During the war, I fought alongside China's bravest soldiers to save our nation from the Huns. I swear to continue to guard and guide our country."

There was a shift of energy in the crowd, hard to notice at first, but a feeling of wrongness spread like ripples. Fingers pointed to the sky, and Mulan looked up just in time to see five shooting stars fall below the line of the palace walls.

As their tails faded, a woman screamed.

Voices floated up from below.

"Omen…"

"Sign from the heavens…"

"Gods disapprove…"

Minister Liu paled. "Finish your speech, Your Majesty. Quickly."

Mulan drew a shaky breath. The stars had chilled her, and she couldn't remember what else she was going to say.

"May Heaven look down on our country and bless us," she said.

She looked imploringly at Minister Liu, who signalled for a servant. "Commence the fireworks!"

For a long moment, nothing happened. And then a spark whistled through the air, followed by another, and another, until they blossomed into multicoloured bursts across the sky.

CHAPTER EIGHT

Mulan's dreams that night were of sparks and flames. Fireworks that turned into shooting stars, which transformed into phoenixes, who were swallowed by dragons. Shadowy figures danced among the mythical creatures, occasionally spreading four fingers across their faces. Mulan slept fitfully, vaguely aware that she was in her bed, somehow knowing that she should try harder to rest, because her work was just beginning.

It was still dark outside when she gave up trying. She'd slept only a few hours, despite being up late for the coronation. Even though she'd spent most of the past day sitting down, she felt as if she'd run a hundred li.

She threw off her blankets and walked to the window, remembering the shooting stars and their path across the sky. They'd been a striking sight, falling one after the other.

What did they mean? Were they really a bad omen?

Outside, cicadas chirped and a lone owl hooted. There was no going back to sleep tonight. She had questions, and they wouldn't be answered here in her bedroom.

The wardrobe for her imperial apartment was larger than most guest apartments. Mulan took a lamp inside, brushing past layers of silks and linens. The clothes she wanted wouldn't be hanging up front. Finally, she found her travel bag tucked next to the back wall. Inside were a plain robe and trousers, as well as gloves, a cloak and well-worn boots.

Mulan pulled her hair into a bun, considering her options. Her two bodyguards stood vigil outside her door. They were handpicked by Shang, and she didn't doubt their allegiance or discretion, but she didn't want their company right now.

Thankfully, she'd learned a few tricks in the army. The posts of her bed had long gold sashes to tie back the curtains. She freed one for the night, then quietly lifted the window that opened into the garden. The fragrance of jasmine drifted in.

There was a sliver of a moon – just enough light to show that the courtyard was empty. Mulan slipped outside, wrapped the sash around a large pillar and used it as leverage to climb. Her shoulders burned by the time the roof was in reach. She'd been lax in her training. The tiles were slippery and radiated cold, and she was glad she had her gloves. Once she pulled herself over the edge, she climbed up and over to the other side and dropped back to the ground. Staying up here would be an invitation for an overenthusiastic guard to shoot her down. Not the most auspicious way for a dynasty to end.

Where to from here? She wanted to go out into the city, but she didn't want to do it alone. Thankfully, she knew someone who would jump at the chance to go with her.

Sneaking around the palace, Mulan felt a bit like a misbehaving child. It was fun, actually, running from bush to bush, hiding from maids and the occasional soldier, darting away from the trappings of imperial life in a way she never could during the day. She crossed the palace grounds to the apartments set aside for visitors. The lower-ranked visitors shared large sleeping rooms, while the higher ranked had their own chambers. Mulan looked to make sure the coast was clear, and then rapped lightly on the frame of a wax-paper window.

No answer. Mulan frowned and rapped again. This time, the floorboards creaked. The window opened, and Liwen's groggy face poked through.

"Come with me to the city," Mulan whispered.

Liwen rubbed her eyes and ran her thick night braid through her fingers. "What kind of empress are you?"

"A bad one. Or a good one, who knows? I want to see the city. Come on. You're travelling back tomorrow. Who knows when we'll get the chance to do this again?"

Liwen groaned, but Mulan knew she had her. "Let me get dressed."

A quarter hour later, they were scaling the palace walls in peasant garb and giggling in a decidedly un-imperial manner. They ran a few blocks, turning corners until they were sure no one tailed them. And then they slowed to a more leisurely stroll.

The city was quite messy after the coronation parade. Food scraps, bits of paper and remnants of fireworks littered the dirt streets. At this hour, people were starting to sweep up their doorsteps. Mulan and Liwen walked briskly, quickly enough to avoid talk with bystanders, but not so fast as to attract attention. When they drew near a street corner where some early risers had gathered to talk, Mulan slowed her pace.

"Five of them, brighter than the fireworks after!" one man was saying.

"Gods don't approve…"

"Maybe it was a blessing from the gods."

"Stars falling out of the sky? Those never bode well."

Mulan lowered her head, quickening her steps until the voices faded away. For a moment, she regretted having brought Liwen with her. Though Liwen had seen Mulan humiliated many times on the practice field, Mulan would have preferred to suffer this shame alone.

Well, it was too late for that, and Mulan couldn't exactly pretend that it hadn't happened. "Did you see the falling stars?" she asked.

"I came out to the courtyard right before it happened."

Liwen paused and sucked in her cheeks, making her cheekbones even sharper than usual. "They weren't actually brighter than the fireworks."

"Do you think they mean anything?" *A bad ruler will lose the Mandate of Heaven. His country will be beset by misfortune: war, earthquakes, famine, floods, warnings written in the stars.*

Liwen shrugged and swaggered ahead. "I think Heaven's signs are impossible for man to decipher."

"You don't believe in omens?"

"I wouldn't say they're all false, but I've seen enough of them fail to be sceptical. Even if those stars were from the gods, how do you know they were meant for you? Maybe the gods wanted to send a message to someone in a neighbouring realm."

Mulan walked in silence. After a while, Liwen glanced over at her. "You disagree?"

"My grandmother believed in omens," Mulan said quietly.

Liwen cocked her head. "I never met your grandmother."

"You would have loved her. She was always cooking and having people over. If she was in the mood, she'd read their palms while they were there, or sometimes even burn an oracle bone for them, if they were at a crossroads. It seemed silly sometimes. We'd tease her about her lucky crickets, but she also seemed to know things. She had an intuition."

"What do you think your grandmother would say about the stars?"

That was a good question. Mulan couldn't imagine her grandmother sitting her down and telling her that the gods were against her, and that she should just give up now. But she didn't think Nai Nai would dismiss the omen out of hand either.

A light-footed figure ran across the street ahead of them. Someone familiar. "Was that—" Mulan stopped.

"Was that Zhonglin?" said Liwen.

The two of them exchanged a look. It seemed impossible, but...

Mulan sped up, and Liwen followed, hurrying to the crossroads where she'd seen the person. She skidded to a stop in the middle of the intersection and looked around. Dusty streets, covered market stalls. One old man sat on his doorstep, knees akimbo, looking at them. No one else.

"Maybe it was a look-alike," said Liwen at her shoulder. "Someone who lives around here."

Perhaps, but this was the second time in two days that Mulan had glimpsed Zhonglin in a place where she wasn't supposed to be. "Was Zhonglin with you during the coronation parade?"

"Yes," said Liwen. Mulan sighed in relief, but then Liwen frowned. "Actually, I don't remember seeing her with us. I'd assumed, but I didn't think to look for her. Why do you ask?"

"I thought I saw her in another part of town. By herself."

Liwen gave a pragmatic shrug. "Perhaps she was cross

with us. It wouldn't be the first time."

"I'd like you to keep an eye on her."

"You suspect something?"

"She was making a hand signal," Mulan said, modelling it for Liwen. "One that might be associated with rebellion."

Liwen's eyes widened, and her forehead creased. She took a moment to digest Mulan's words. "Shall I confront her?"

Mulan thought for a moment. How exactly should one handle a possible traitor? "No, but watch her. If she really is hiding something, we might learn more by observing her first."

Liwen nodded, frowning, and then she skipped forward without warning.

"Where are you going?"

A large two-storey building stood at the street corner. Posted on its walls, halfway in the shadow of its overhanging eaves, was a piece of paper. Liwen stopped in front of it.

"What's this?" Mulan asked.

Liwen moved aside for Mulan. Her frown deepened.

The paper looked to be a tract written in well-formed calligraphy.

Hens should not announce the dawn. A woman in the palace will only bring Heaven's judgment on us. The gods have made their displeasure known through the stars.

Cold sweat broke out over Mulan's forehead. This was far more brazen than hand signals in a crowd. The words taunted and condemned her. Reading them felt like peeling off her skin, but she couldn't stop.

Liwen ripped it off the wall. "You need to tell your ministers."

"For all I know, my ministers wrote these," said Mulan. She felt as if she were on the wrong side of a leaky dam. How many holes could she plug before she should simply give up and run?

Liwen raced ahead. She stopped three streets down to tear down another tract, and then four streets after that to remove yet another. Mulan ran after her. "Liwen," she hissed. "You're attracting attention."

Indeed, people were turning to look at them. Liwen turned a cold glare back at the closest few. "There's nothing to see here," she said, grabbing Mulan's arm and pulling her away. "You can't let rebellion sit in the open like this," she hissed under her breath. "That'll just encourage it to grow. Even I know that."

Curious stares followed them. Mulan felt eyes clinging to her back, sliding along her skin. "What kind of power do I really wield if I have to silence all my detractors to keep it?"

•••

The next morning, all the travellers from Mulan's village gathered to begin their journey home. Mulan tried to appear upbeat as she saw them off.

"Are you sure you don't want us to stay longer?" asked Mama.

"You miss home," said Mulan. "And I wouldn't want to bore you with all my duties here. I'll be fine."

It was hard to say that with a straight face when Mulan had three seditious posters confiscated from across the city hidden under her bed. She hadn't shown them to anyone. Her instincts warned her against showing weakness to her ministers, and she didn't have it in her to tell her parents. She'd already caused them far too much worry throughout the course of her life. She didn't want to pile on any more. Although Mama and Baba had enjoyed the novelty of palace life, Mulan could tell that they were tired and eager to go home.

After saying farewell to her parents, Mulan moved on to the women of her militia, who were lined up with their horses and bags. She said her goodbyes one by one, stopping momentarily when she got to Zhonglin. The young woman had packed her bags and now sat cross-legged on the ground, finishing up a bowl of oxtail soup. She took her time lowering the soup from her mouth when Mulan came to stand in front of her — long enough to hint at a snub but not long enough to confirm it. The bowl she held was from the palace kitchen. Mulan wondered if she intended to keep it.

"Did you enjoy your time at the capital?" Mulan asked.

"Very much so," Zhonglin said, wiping the grease off her

mouth with the back of her hand. Was that self-satisfaction that Mulan sensed, or was she just imagining it? Either way, she was relieved that Zhonglin would be leaving and Liwen would be keeping an eye on her.

Thinking of Liwen made Mulan realise she hadn't seen her among the travellers. Mulan scanned the grounds for excessively intricate braids.

"Looking for someone?" said Liwen's voice at her ear.

Mulan jumped back and looked her up and down. Liwen was wearing a long blue gown with wooden sandals – hardly travel-worthy.

"I'm not leaving," she said airily.

Her words brought Mulan up short. "You're what?"

"I'm staying here. You need a friend."

Something inside Mulan rejoiced at the idea, but she tamped it down. "You can't stay. They need you back home."

"I've put Ruolan in charge of training, and she can keep an eye on" – Liwen glanced over Mulan's shoulder at Zhonglin – "any troublemakers in the ranks. I'm not going to leave you here with the wolves."

That one statement, said with so little fanfare that Liwen might as well be discussing the morning's exercises, lifted a mountain of weight off Mulan's shoulders. She blinked back a sudden prickling behind her eyes. "Thank you."

The travellers mounted their horses and gathered by the gate. Mulan bit down on her cheeks and waved as her parents' carriage rolled away. Liwen squeezed her hand, and Mulan squeezed back.

"Festivities are over," Mulan murmured. "Time to run the country." A country full of uncooperative ministers and peasants who didn't want her rule.

"It's too bad your grandmother never taught you to commune with the spirits," said Liwen. "We could use their advice right now."

"I thought you didn't believe in all that."

"I don't really, but you need all the help you can get."

•••

Liwen had spoken in jest, but her words still made Mulan wonder. It was true that Nai Nai had never explicitly taught her about fortune-telling, but Mulan had spent a great deal of time with her over the years. She'd watched her crack many an oracle bone, and she remembered the steps she took. Grandmother had always said that it was Mulan's ancestors who spoke through the bones. Mulan wondered if her ancestors were sticklers for details. Surely they'd cut her a little slack if she got something wrong, wouldn't they?

By the time Mulan retired to her apartments that night, she had made a decision. Ancestors were supposed to offer guidance, and she was in desperate need of guidance. No one could argue with that.

Mulan opened her bedroom door. Ting stood outside,

fiddling with one of her hair ribbons.

"Ting, can you go to the kitchen and ask them for ox shoulder bones?"

The maid dropped the ribbon. "Bones, Your Majesty?"

"Yes. I'd like them whole. It's better if they're quite dry."

"Would you prefer that I send up some soup instead?"

"No, just bones. And if they don't have any that are dry, have them set aside some fresh ones for me."

As Ting went off with a wrinkled brow, Mulan built up the fire in her hearth. It felt like a fitting act of faith, preparing the fire before she knew if she had any bones. And besides, she was restless. Thinking of Grandmother had brought back memories, along with a deep yearning to see her again. Burning bones would not bring Nai Nai back, but perhaps it would make her feel closer, for just a moment. When the flames were as high as the fireplace would allow, Mulan laid a poker at its heart and settled down to wait.

The maid came back a half hour later, still clearly perplexed by the errand. "The kitchen gave me these," she said, holding out two roughly triangular bones.

Mulan took them. They were smooth to the touch. "Thank you. This will do."

In a jar on Mulan's desk was an impressive array of calligraphy brushes: a goat-hair brush thicker than two of Mulan's fingers, a weasel-hair brush with a needle-fine point, plus rabbit-, raccoon-, and rooster-hair brushes. Mulan considered for a moment and took the weasel-hair brush. She poured water on the inkstone and ground her stick to make a smooth black liquid. Carefully, she set one shoulder bone on the table and wet her brush. She loved the smell of freshly ground ink.

A sudden set of nerves struck her as her brush neared the bone. Was she really about to speak to her grandmother? What did she want to say? Practically speaking, she needed a question that would yield a specific and useful answer.

Does China face imminent danger? Below the question, she wrote *yes* and *no*.

The ink glistened, taking longer to dry than it would on paper. Mulan blew on it until the sheen gradually dulled. From her soldier's bag, she took out an awl and painstakingly drilled a hole in the centre of the bone. Then she laid it in front of the fireplace and carefully drew out the poker she'd left in the flames. The tip glowed a dull red. Mulan didn't stop to think. Every moment of hesitation meant the poker would lose more of its heat. Deliberately, Mulan pushed the tip of the poker into the hole she'd drilled.

A crack echoed through the room. Sparks flew up from the poker. Mulan blinked, stunned. Bones didn't give off sparks, did they? And she could have sworn that for a moment, the sparks had formed the shape of a dragon. Blinking again to clear the afterimage, Mulan knelt down to inspect the bone. A long fissure ran through it now, right across the word *yes*.

Though she was sweating from the fire, a shiver travelled through her entire body. Even the jagged shape of the fissure radiated a sense of threat. Was this really a message from her ancestors?

She had one bone left. Trembling, Mulan wrote a second message.

Is the danger in the north, south, east or west?

She moved through the steps more quickly this time, both out of familiarity and urgency. This bone cracked loudly too, but there were no sparks. When Mulan bent down to inspect it, she saw that another fissure had formed. This time, it crossed through the word *north*.

•••

Shang didn't hide his surprise at finding Mulan at his door. It was very late. Indeed, Mulan had been surprised to see a lamp still lit in his window.

He'd clearly been preparing to sleep, as he wasn't wearing a shirt, only a pair of trousers. Mulan averted her eyes, but not before she caught a glimpse of his well-muscled chest.

"Mu— Empress," he said.

"I'm sorry to come this late," she said. She clutched the oracle bones, wrapped in cloth, to her chest. "I had some questions you might be able to answer. Can I come in?"

Unspoken was the uncomfortable truth that she didn't really need to ask. She was his empress and could do whatever she wished. But Shang moved aside and waved her in.

Shang retreated into the back room, where she heard him rustling through his clothes. Mulan waited up front, wondering vaguely about the impropriety of this – the two bodyguards she'd left outside, the guards and servants who had seen her leave the palace grounds, and what they all might say about her late-night movements. But then, stars had fallen at her coronation, and people were openly rebelling in the streets. What difference would one more scandal make?

Shang came back in, dressed in the long robe he'd worn earlier in the day. For a moment, they hesitated.

"Would you like to sit down?" he said.

"Yes, thank you."

She bypassed the couch and perched on the edge of an hourglass-shaped wicker stool. Shang sat facing her and rested one elbow on his knee, waiting for her to speak.

"The spy commanders report to you, is that right?" she asked.

He straightened. Mulan could tell that her question surprised him. "That's right. Ever since I became minister of war."

"What do you know of threats coming from the north? What is the situation with the Huns?"

"They've never been friendly to us. We dealt them a blow when we defeated Shan Yu, but the Hun people are made up of many tribes, with many leaders able to unite them.

One tribal leader has been consolidating power. His name is Ruga."

"Do you see any movements from them? Any preparations for war?"

Shang frowned. "No overt movement towards war. There's been a few skirmishes along the border, but they've been careful never to let anything escalate into war. Why do you ask?"

Mulan realised she was still clutching her oracle bones to her chest. Shang had never seen her grandmother do anything like this. She wasn't sure what he'd think.

She laid the bones down on the table.

"My grandmother used to crack oracle bones," she said, unwrapping the cloths. Little specks of ash dotted the bones' undersides. "I was worried tonight, so I cracked two in order to ask about threats to the country. The bones say there is a danger from the north. I'm not sure it's a military danger. I'm not even sure if the oracle bones can be trusted, but it's hard to think of the north without thinking of the Huns." She wondered if she should tell Shang what else she'd seen, the sparks and the image of the dragon, but that seemed too private.

Shang bent over the table to inspect the bones. Mulan forced herself not to fidget as he picked them up, frowning, and read the inscriptions, then tilted them to look at the fissures. She couldn't quite read his expression.

He met her eyes. "Do you trust what your grandmother taught you?"

"I do."

"I'll send more spies up north. See if they can find anything."

Mulan hadn't realised how much tension she'd been holding until it melted out of her shoulders.

"Thank you," she said. She thought she should say something else, about how much she appreciated his friendship, or what a relief it was that he believed her on this, but none of those words actually came out. The room started to feel uncomfortably silent. She became deeply aware that it was only the two of them in this room, at this late hour.

"I should go," said Mulan.

"Of course," said Shang before she finished speaking.

Mulan resisted the urge to look furtively around as she walked out. She was the empress, after all. She could come and go as she pleased. Her bodyguards fell in step behind her, stone-faced as ever. The streets were mostly empty, though the few people about did double takes and fell into hasty bows as she passed.

She was not far from the palace gates when she heard a gate sentry announce a visitor. Mulan paused, causing her bodyguards to stop suddenly behind her. The gate sentries screened everyone seeking entry into the palace, but they only announced guests of import. It was far too late for any normal guest. Mulan had been too far away to catch the name.

She walked closer, her bodyguards trailing behind her. A mass of servants had gathered there. As they noticed her, individual staff members turned and hurriedly bowed, nudging others, until a wave of obeisance rippled through the crowd.

Mulan looked to one of the gate guards, who quickly ran to kneel in front of her.

"Who just arrived?" she asked.

"It's an official envoy from the north," said the soldier. "He says he represents the Huns."

CHAPTER NINE

W hy are they here?" Minister Fang of public works blinked his wide eyes slowly as he spoke, making him look even more like an owl than usual. "They were not invited."

"The Huns don't exactly have a history of doing as they are asked," said Minister Huang of personnel administration. He didn't stand near the other ministers but instead rocked back and forth on his heels next to the wall.

Mulan took a deep breath, trying not to groan. It had been twelve hours since the Hun envoy arrived, and the palace was in a panic. This was impressive given that the envoy had merely been a messenger announcing the coming arrival of the ambassador this evening. The full retinue hadn't set foot in the palace and her ministers were already expecting a crisis.

"What could they want? Trade?" asked Minister Kin. "An alliance?"

"Tread carefully with them, Your Majesty," said Minister Wei in his booming voice. "They're not trustworthy, and they have powerful armies."

"The empress is aware of that," Shang said wryly.

"Ah, but the empress must be careful not to offend them with talk that is too direct. They may not be used to a woman speaking thus."

"Unlike you, Wei?" said Shang, an edge to his voice. "The picture of diplomacy and good manners?"

Mulan pushed back from the table, bristling at being discussed in this manner when she was right there in the room. Her chair scraped loudly across the wood floor. She was exhausted from a night of poor sleep, and her tight layered bun was making her head ache. "I will be as polite as circumstances dictate," she said. "And I see no point to further speculation. We'll find out what they want when they arrive."

As the ministers turned to go, Mulan caught the eye of the minister of rites. "Minister Liu, if I may speak to you privately."

Minister Liu's eyes widened briefly before going back to their usual squint. "Of course, Empress."

Mulan waited until the rest of the ministers had left. "You didn't say much during the meeting, Minister. Do you have any opinion?"

"I'll reserve my opinion until after we hear from the ambassador," he said. Minister Liu had such a quiet voice, he probably wouldn't be heard in the council room even if he'd wanted to speak up.

"There's something I want to ask you about," she said.

"I'm at your service, of course."

Mulan hesitated a moment before pushing past her self-consciousness. "My grandmother taught me the art of reading oracle bones."

"You never fail to surprise me, Your Majesty." His tone was one of good-natured amusement rather than disdain.

"I only know the basics, but I cracked two bones last night. It predicted a danger from the north, right before the envoy arrived."

He nodded. "And you think there's a connection?"

"It seems like a great coincidence, don't you think?"

Liu straightened out of his usual stoop. "Do you still have the bones, Your Majesty? I can consult the palace astrologer to see if he has any insights."

"Yes, I'll have them brought to you," said Mulan, encouraged that he seemed to be taking her seriously. "Thank you."

He bowed. "I'll let you know as soon as I learn anything."

• • •

The ambassador from the Huns arrived that evening, right on

schedule. Mulan didn't watch the retinue enter the Imperial City, but Shang's soldiers informed her that the ambassador had arrived with three wagons and a staff of five. She granted them an audience the next afternoon.

It would be the first time she gave an audience in the great hall as empress. The palace staff was kept busy all morning preparing it for use. Dust had gathered in the weeks since the last emperor's passing. Furniture had to be oiled, decorative tureens had to be polished, the floor had to be mopped, and curtains and rugs had to be beaten out. Even the carved dragons on the ceiling of the hall had to be dusted off. Mulan wondered if part of the reason for the ambassador's quick arrival was so he could watch them scramble.

Mulan's throne stood at the end of the hall, ensconced in a miniature gold pavilion with arched roofs that tipped up at the corners. Carved dragons danced across the entire wooden structure, green on red columns. The back wall of the throne pavilion was not a real wall, but rather a series of heavy gold screens.

As the time for the audience drew near, Mulan waited behind the screens with her advisers, hearing the murmur of the crowd gathering on the other side. Shang stood beside her, his bulk a reassuring presence in the high-ceilinged hall.

"He'll be looking for weakness from you," he said. "Anything that his warlord can exploit."

"Then I won't show him any," said Mulan.

Out of the corner of her eye, she saw his lips curve into the slightest of smiles. She looked around at her other ministers. Kin scribbled notes on a piece of parchment, and Huang paced back and forth, each dispelling nervous energy in his own way.

"It's time," said Mulan.

The crowd quieted as Mulan's cabinet stepped out. She peeked through a crack in the screen as she waited to be announced, feeling a bit like a child at a window. Her tall throne rested on the raised floor of the pavilion, and her officials fanned out in a half-moon around it. Lower officials and courtiers filled the floor below, a colourful mishmash of bright silks. There was an air of anticipation – many of them had long waited to see Mulan perform her official duties as empress. Some of the faces were already familiar from her coronation. Mulan recognised the son of a powerful family who wanted lower taxes on their silk factory, and a monk whose curiosity had lured him to court. She also caught sight of Liwen, and that calmed her nerves somewhat.

A gong sounded, sending vibrations along the floor. A herald called out with exaggerated intonation, "Her Imperial Majesty, Empress Mulan."

As Mulan stepped through the curtain, every man and woman bowed to the ground. It was like watching a field of millet bend to the wind. "Hail Empress Mulan. May she live ten times ten thousand years!"

Mulan stood firm as the crowd's chant crashed over her. *Look like you claim this as your due. Look like an empress.*

The herald drew breath again and called out in a clarion tone. "His Excellency, Balambar, ambassador from the Huns."

Five men approached down the red carpet in the middle of the room. Their clothes, though foreign, were very fine. Each man wore a hat trimmed with furs, and leather boots with upturned toes. Their tunics and slacks were constructed of colourful wool and silk panels. These envoys were a far cry from Shan Yu and his ragged troops.

The man at their head had the richest furs and brightest silks. Mulan could barely see his fingers under the numerous gold rings he sported. He stepped forward and bowed on one knee, very pointedly not kowtowing like Mulan's own subjects. "His Majesty, Warlord Ruga, conveys his congratulations to Her Imperial Majesty on her recent coronation." He had a smooth, rich voice. "One imagines it must be overwhelming to go through so many changes in such a short time." He stopped to scan Mulan's face for a reaction. When she didn't give him one, he continued. "Our unworthy retinue brings gifts of gold, silver and wool to adorn Her Majesty's palace and person."

Two of the men brought forward a chest. A murmur ran through the crowd as the men opened it to display bolts of dyed cloth surrounded by gold and silver ingots.

Mulan flicked her hand, and two imperial servants rushed forward to receive the chest. "We thank King Ruga for his well-wishes."

The ambassador inclined his head. "He does what any monarch would do. China is indeed favoured by the gods to have such a lovely blossom grace its throne."

Out of the corner of her eye, Mulan saw Shang's expression darken. She too heard the insult in those words. Flowers were beautiful and delicate. Ornamental.

She bared her teeth in a thin smile. "I'm quite fond of flowers myself. After you're settled in the state guesthouses, you must tour the imperial gardens. There's a particular variety called snow lace, a white blossom with rose-tinged petals. I collected it myself from the Tung-Shao Pass. Are you familiar with that region?"

The ambassador's smirk froze on his face. The Tung-Shao Pass was where Mulan's regiment had defeated Shan Yu's men. There were already multiple ballads commemorating how Mulan used a rocket to trigger the avalanche that buried his entire army. "Yes, I am familiar with that pass."

"I'm glad," said Mulan. "It's the mark of a good ambassador to know his host nation's land and history, and I'm sure you are one of the very best."

Shang turned his head slightly and caught her eye. There was just the barest hint of an upturn at the corner of his mouth. Mulan bit the inside of her cheek to keep an imperial expression on her face.

The ambassador bowed deep. When he straightened, he'd regained a portion of his smug veneer. "King Ruga wishes also to convey his desire to visit in the spring."

That was unexpected. Mulan didn't know the last time a leader of the Huns had come into Chinese territory. "We would, of course, be honoured to have His Majesty as an esteemed guest," she said carefully. "Provided that he comes in peace."

Balambar inclined his head. "I am glad you also desire peace, Your Majesty. Warlord Ruga's son will accompany him. Prince Erban, as you may have heard, is a great warrior and scholar. The prince is of an age to find a bride. His Majesty would like to take that opportunity to open up discussions of an alliance."

Mulan felt the blood drain from her face, even as she struggled to keep a calm facade. There was a choking sound from Mulan's left, and she made a pointed effort not to look in Shang's direction. She shouldn't have been so surprised to get a marriage proposal. It was what the emperor said would happen and what Shang had predicted. She just hadn't expected it to happen so soon.

"We will entertain any proposals," she said. "But His Majesty should know that my first duty is to my people, and my priority is to ensure a smooth transition into my reign. Some affairs of state may have to wait a few years."

"We do hope His Majesty and Prince Erban's proposal will not be one of them," said the ambassador. "Despite his reputation as a fierce commander of armies, King Ruga much prefers diplomacy to war. He finds the latter to be excessive expense and trouble, though sadly unavoidable at times."

Breaths hissed out across the room. Mulan felt her face flush. For the first time, she felt glad for her heavy white makeup. "China is a country of strength and will, Ambassador. We do not regard circumstances as unavoidable, but rather we work to control our own fates, whether by plough or sword." She stood up. "I've enjoyed our conversation, Balambar, and look forward to having you around the court. Do not hesitate to ask for anything you need during your time here."

...

Her ministers swarmed her after the audience.

"Well done, Your Majesty," said Minister Fang, cheerfully tapping his fan against his palm. "You handled that audience very well."

Mulan was so surprised at the praise she didn't know what to say. She motioned all of them to the council room.

"The man was impudent." Minister Wei had waited until Shang closed the door to speak, though he spoke so loudly that anyone outside would have heard him anyway. "It was right and proper to put him in his place."

"I couldn't let him insult us." Mulan took her seat at the head of the table, disoriented at the vocal support. Her ministers were in better spirits than she'd ever seen.

"I'm quite optimistic," said Minister Wei. "The peace they offer could be quite good for China."

There was some deeper implication to the minister's words, but Mulan was having trouble grasping it. "What do you mean?"

"The alliance, of course. It's a good turn of fortune."

"Alliance?" said Mulan. And slowly, it dawned on her why her ministers were so happy. "You mean the prospect of a marriage to Prince Erban."

Minister Wei looked at her as if she'd just forgotten the name of her own country. "Of course, Your Majesty," he said.

Perhaps it was good that her heavy imperial robes kept Mulan from jumping to her feet. "Minister Wei, we're talking about an alliance with an entity that is not trustworthy in the least. I would have thought you'd treat an offer like theirs with more caution."

"But certainly, Your Majesty knows how powerful their armies are," Minister Fang said with a condescending smile. "A friendly overture from them is far better than another war."

"War is by no means a certainty at this point," said Shang. "I have my spies watching the border."

"But you can't deny that the Huns are the greatest threat to us at the moment," said Minister Kin, tapping his notebook.

"And they are willing to discuss an alliance! It is hard to see a better match. The royal family of the Nanzhao empire was lukewarm to the idea of an imperial marriage at best, and the Balhae king to the north is without sons as of yet."

"Wait," said Mulan. "How do you know that the Nanzhao royal family was not interested in an imperial marriage?"

Minister Kin's finger froze mid-tap.

"Have you been communicating with them behind my back?" said Mulan.

Minister Huang cut in smoothly. "We are your ministers. It is our duty to see to the nation's well-being, and that involves foreign communications."

"Hogwash," said Shang. "Making marital overtures without the empress's knowledge is far beyond your authority."

"Forgive my bluntness, General," said Minister Wei, "but you may not be completely unbiased where the empress's marital plans are concerned."

Mulan drew a sharp breath. Her closeness to Shang was no secret, but no one had ever spoken of it this plainly before. The manner in which Wei spoke galled her too, as if they were two men discussing a prize sheep.

Shang's eyes flashed. For a moment, it seemed as if he was going to leap across the room. Minister Wei, the only man in the room who could match Shang for size, levelled a gaze back in challenge. Mulan looked between them frantically, wondering if she should say something before things got out of hand. Wondering if she could get away with punching Wei herself.

The minister of rites cleared his throat. "If I may interrupt," he said, his thin voice floating above the tension. "Your Majesty has seen the threat from the north yourself. I have queried the palace astrologer about your bone reading as you requested. Perhaps hearing his perspective might shed some light on this subject."

Mulan took a deep breath and let it out, doing her best to dissipate the heat in her belly. "Send for him."

Shang relaxed out of his forward coil, slowly and deliberately lowering his arms to his sides. Wei crossed his arms over his chest with a sneer. No one spoke as they waited. Every once in a while, Minister Kin sniffed or Minister Huang scratched his nose. Mulan sat motionless, grappling with the realisation that she was losing control of her cabinet.

The door opened again. "The royal astrologer," announced a eunuch.

The astrologer was an older man with grey hair at his temples. He entered the room like a mouse entering a lion's den, glancing nervously around and shrinking back at Shang's glare.

He bowed low to Mulan. "Your Majesty," he said. "May you live ten times ten thousand years."

Mulan motioned for him to stand, more aware now than ever of the need to act like an empress. "I hear you looked at my prediction."

"Yes, I inspected your oracle bones. Your Majesty is a very gifted fortune-teller." He stopped, folding his fingers nervously. "The bones do indeed speak of a threat from the north, but I found a mitigating factor within the stars. Right now, the constellation known as the Azure Dragon is in the northern palace of the sky. The azure dragon is a symbol of friendship, which means that danger to the north can be mitigated with friendly overtures."

A prickle of ice travelled from Mulan's heart to her gut. "And the stars at my coronation. Is there any meaning to those?"

The astrologer paled visibly. "Forgive me, Empress. I do not wish to overstep…"

"Tell me your reading. You will not be punished for its content."

The astrologer sucked in a breath. "Five falling stars…" His voice trailed off, and he drew breath to try again, shaking visibly. "Five falling stars fell in the middle palace, Your Majesty. That is the section of the sky that symbolises earthly kingdoms. And falling stars are generally a sign of…"

"A sign of what, Astrologer?" What patience Mulan had was rapidly dissipating.

The astrologer fell prostrate on the ground, a quivering lump of fear. "Heaven's displeasure."

Mulan stared at the astrologer, summoning all her

willpower to keep herself from disintegrating in the same way. She wasn't sure what was worse, the pronouncements of judgment or the humiliation of getting them in front of her entire council.

She drew a slow breath. "Thank you for your insight. You are dismissed."

The man needed no further encouragement to leave. Mulan waited until the door closed behind him. She was keenly aware of everyone's eyes on her, and equally aware of the need to show no emotion.

She turned to Minister Liu. "You knew he was going to say this?"

"Yes, Your Majesty. I spoke to him earlier."

"When did he first give you his reading?"

"Last night. Before the Huns presented their marriage proposal," he said.

That did little to unravel the knot in Mulan's stomach. She turned her gaze to her ministers. "And you all feel that the best course of action is to agree to the marriage alliance."

"The Huns are too powerful," came Minister Huang's smooth voice. "The last war nearly destroyed China."

"We *won* the last war," snarled Shang. "Thanks to the woman at the head of the room."

"But at what cost?" said Minister Wei. "The deaths on the battlefield, the crops and houses burned. We came close to losing the entire country."

"And there is one other thing to consider," added Minister Liu softly. "Wars are much more successful if the common people are behind them. The last emperor was greatly loved. And… while I'm sure Your Majesty will soon be just as beloved, there will be an adjustment period."

That was a gut punch. Mulan thought of the hand signals at her coronation, the posters of rebellion. "The Huns are untrustworthy. They've always wanted to conquer us. This is just another way for them to wrest control. What's to stop them from assassinating me after the marriage?"

"Marriage alliances are carried out all the time between enemy countries," said Minister Fang. "I understand that you are new at politics, but affairs of state must be decided with rational logic, not the whims of the heart."

Mulan itched to smack the arrogant expression off his face. "Do you feel I am making decisions irrationally, Minister?"

There was a long silence in which Mulan refused to drop his gaze. Finally, Minister Fang bowed. "No, Your Majesty. I just wish to emphasise that all rulers have a duty to marry for the good of China. An alliance with a foreign power would be far more advantageous than an internal one."

Waves of fury radiated from Shang on the other side of the room. Mulan felt as if she were getting herded into a snare.

"Thank you for your advice, Minister. I assure you that everyone here takes their duty to country with utmost gravity. I will take your words under consideration. This meeting is adjourned."

• • •

The cloud of the meeting hung over Mulan long after she left the council room. Was a marriage alliance with the Huns truly her only choice? Every one of her instincts told her to run from it, but was she only against the marriage because she was still in love with Shang?

The thought occupied Mulan for the rest of the day. She retreated to her apartments. When they became too stifling, she went out into the gardens.

They were peaceful in the afternoon hour. Well-groomed trees bent over mirror-like ponds. Vases of colourful flowers adorned stone steps. A network of exquisitely carved covered walkways and pavilions offered shade while still allowing a visitor to feel the breeze. The garden looked like paradise, but it was deceptive. Mulan knew how much work it took every day to coax the plants to do the workers' bidding, the constant effort required to beat back chaos.

Could I have escaped this life? What would have happened if the emperor had not collapsed when he did? Would Mulan have gathered the courage to ask him to choose someone else? Would he have agreed? She wondered again if he'd had any other candidates. With the country turning against her so soon, it was hard to believe that she was the best choice. And yet, what alternative was there? Her ministers had more experience, though their recent dealings had eroded her trust in them. But was that just her pride talking? Minister Liu was the most reasonable of them all, quiet, even-tempered and soft-spoken, but Mulan could see him being trampled by his stronger-willed colleagues.

Of course, Mulan wasn't doing a very good job of holding her ground either.

A rustle sounded in the bushes. Mulan looked up just in time to see an enormous hawk with red-tipped wings fly out from a bush. There was a person too, who ducked behind a rock garden. Someone who looked familiar...

"Zhonglin? Is that you?"

No response. Mulan wondered if her paranoia had finally got the best of her. But she was certain she'd seen someone. And she was certain the gardens were supposed to be closed to everyone except the empress.

Mulan knelt and unstrapped the knife she kept on her ankle. "I know there's someone there. Show yourself."

She glanced towards the archway at the garden's entrance, where her bodyguards waited. Before she could call for them, Zhonglin stepped out.

It was indeed her. The last time Mulan had seen her, she'd been gathered with the rest of the militia in the courtyard, preparing to leave for their home village. She shouldn't be here.

Mulan smiled brightly, banishing any suspicion from her

expression, pouring every bit of relief she could muster into her voice. "Zhonglin," she said. "You gave me a scare. I didn't realise it was you."

Zhonglin bowed. "Good evening, Empress." She spoke carefully, picking her way between flowered shrubs towards the walkway.

"I didn't expect to see you here," said Mulan. "I thought you'd returned home."

Zhonglin came to a stop and stood at attention, her hands clasped behind her back as she did when awaiting orders on the training field. "Commander Liwen asked me to stay here to assist her."

That was a lie, and Mulan didn't like having Zhonglin's hands out of sight. "It is good of you to help. And what were you doing out in the garden tonight?"

"The commander wanted me to examine it for vulnerabilities."

"By yourself?"

"Yes, Your Majesty."

Mulan nodded, keeping her expression neutral as she ran through her options. "Walk with me, Zhonglin, I'd like to hear more about what you've found."

Hesitation flashed for a brief moment across Zhonglin's pretty face. And then she bowed. "Of course."

Mulan stayed back from Zhonglin until she saw for sure that both the girl's hands were empty. Even then, she kept a casual grip on her knife as they walked. A quick glance towards the garden entrance showed that Mulan's guards had spotted Zhonglin. She could see their confusion and panic as they hurried towards her.

"Tell me," she said to Zhonglin. "How does the Imperial City strike you, now that you've had time to experience it?"

"It's very big," said Zhonglin. With her large eyes, she looked so innocent. "And busy."

"Do you like the busyness?" Mulan asked. Her guards were halfway there, and Mulan did her best to exude calm. She'd gone hunting enough times to know that a trapped animal was the most dangerous.

"I prefer somewhere less crowded." Zhonglin watched the guards now, too. The girl held no weapon – at least, not that Mulan could see. It was hard to get a good look without being obvious about it.

Mulan gave her bodyguards a friendly wave and addressed Zhonglin again. "To be honest, I prefer quieter places myself. I'd much rather go for a ride outside the city than take a stroll in the marketplace."

The guards arrived in a clatter of armour, glancing confusedly back and forth between Mulan and Zhonglin as they tried to discern the extent to which they'd failed at their duty.

"Ah, good, you're here," said Mulan cheerfully. "Take this woman under custody."

The guards gaped, thrown by the mismatch between Mulan's tone and her instructions. Zhonglin turned to run.

"Get her!" ordered Mulan.

The first guard tackled Zhonglin in a bear hug. A knife flashed in the girl's hand, only to be wrestled away by the second guard. Zhonglin kicked and screamed, but it wasn't long before they had her subdued and bound.

"Thank you," said Mulan. "Bring her this way."

CHAPTER TEN

L iwen broke into a grin when she opened the door.

"Glorious, blessed Empress, to what do I owe the pleasure of..." She trailed off as she caught sight of Zhonglin standing behind Mulan, her hands bound and escorted by two guards. For a moment, she simply stared, her eyebrows creased together.

Liwen's surprise was a relief to Mulan. If Liwen had shown fear upon seeing Zhonglin, or had simply taken her appearance in stride, it would have made Mulan wonder. But Liwen simply looked perplexed. It was one less thing to worry about. Mulan loved Liwen like a sister and didn't think she could handle any more betrayal from within her own ranks.

"Zhonglin," Liwen finally said. "Why are you here?"

"I found her in my garden," said Mulan. "She said you'd asked her to stay in the Imperial City."

Comprehension lit Liwen's face. She met Mulan's eyes, and a quick understanding passed between them.

Mulan turned to her bodyguards. "Take the prisoner in and wait outside. We'd like to talk to her alone."

The two soldiers glanced nervously at each other.

"Did you hear me?" said Mulan.

They hurriedly took hold of Zhonglin's arms. The girl didn't resist as they escorted her in, but the heat in her glare made no secret of her thoughts.

Liwen's elegant guest quarters, with its simple yet delicate furnishings, made an unlikely interrogation room. Liwen moved an hourglass-shaped wicker stool to the middle of the room. "Sit her here."

The guards manoeuvred her into position, and then the more senior soldier cleared his throat, his gaze darting between Mulan, Zhonglin and Liwen. "Will Your Majesty be safe, with us outside? Her legs are not bound." He'd failed once in his duty by letting Zhonglin into the garden. Clearly, he knew that another failure would seal his fate.

"We'll be fine," said Mulan, in no mood to offer any further reassurance. The guards exited, looking more like schoolchildren fearing a whipping than royal soldiers. The door closed behind them, and suddenly the room was silent, with no clinking armour or heavy boots to drown out the wrongness of the moment. The air felt thin, as if a stray move could tear a hole in the space around them. Months ago,

Mulan had taken this girl under her wing. She'd committed to mentor her. How had things come to this?

"You lied," Mulan said. "You were supposed to go home with the others. Liwen never asked you to stay. Why are you here?"

Zhonglin turned defiant eyes on Mulan. "When I offered my sword up for the militia, I didn't hand you control over my entire life. Where I go and what I do is my affair."

Liwen's hand snapped out. There was a smack and a muffled grunt. Before Mulan realised what had happened, Zhonglin was doubled over and gasping for breath.

"You'll address the empress with the proper respect," said Liwen. "People have been sentenced to death by a thousand cuts for a fraction of the impertinence you just displayed."

Zhonglin stared at the ground, her jaw set, blinking back tears.

Mulan put a restraining hand on Liwen and addressed Zhonglin again. "I saw you in the crowd at my coronation ceremony. You were making a hand signal like this." Zhonglin rolled her eyes upwards to watch Mulan replicate it. "What does it mean?"

"It's a symbol for your reign," the girl said under her breath.

"Is it a symbol of rebellion?" asked Mulan.

Zhonglin stared stonily at the floor.

"Answer the empress," said Liwen.

A wave of fury washed over Zhonglin's face, and she spat

on the ground. "Fine empress you are, interrogating your most inconsequential subjects for treason. You pretend to rule, but you can't even control your own ministers."

Mulan was too stunned to reply.

"Most women don't have the option to say no to men or refuse their orders. You are the empress. You have the strength of the spirits, of women who came before you and who will come after you. Why let your decisions be made for you?"

Liwen struck Zhonglin again, hard enough to knock the breath out of her. Mulan's former second-in-command looked just as shocked as Mulan felt.

Zhonglin coughed and spat blood out of her mouth. The blow hadn't extinguished the fire in her eyes. "Everything I've said is true. What are you going to do, execute everyone in the kingdom who doesn't kowtow to your liking?"

When Liwen lunged again, Mulan put up her arm to block her, though she wasn't exactly sure why.

"Who are you really?" Mulan asked.

"I'm your loyal subject, Your Majesty." Her voice was flat, thick with mockery. Rage flooded through Mulan, and for a moment, she thought she might strike Zhonglin herself. Instead, she pivoted and threw open the door to the room.

"Guards."

Her soldiers rushed in, relief washing across their faces when they saw Mulan in one piece. If they were surprised to find Zhonglin more ragged than before, they didn't show it.

"Keep her under guard. I'll want to speak more with her later."

Zhonglin didn't utter a word as they led her away. For a long moment, neither Mulan nor Liwen said anything. It was not a good feeling, watching a member of her beloved militia, even a rebellious one, dragged away like a criminal. A soldier she'd trained was working towards her ruin. That betrayal hurt far more than the constant undermining from her ministers.

"Was she a spy?" Mulan asked, more to herself than Liwen. Did someone hire Zhonglin to undermine her reign? To sow discontent?

"She didn't give us many answers," said Liwen. "That makes me think she's protecting someone."

"We need to find out what she was doing in the Imperial City."

Zhonglin's arrest raised so many other questions. Had she been working against Mulan from the beginning, or had she only turned against Mulan after she was named heir to the throne?

"There's the question of when she was recruited," said Liwen, as if reading her mind. "And who recruited her."

"The Huns are a logical place to start," said Mulan. "Can you investigate the ambassador for me? Ask around and get a feel for his movements. I don't trust him."

Liwen gave a grim nod. "I'll see what I can find."

• • •

Mulan knew she wouldn't be able to sleep that night, but she supposed she should try. She had Ting draw her a bath and then dismissed her for the evening. Now that every other aspect of her life stood under the kingdom's scrutiny, her nightly bath was one of the few times she still owned.

The water was delightfully hot, turning her skin bright red. Mulan soaked until the water grew tepid, then towelled off and slipped on a heavy silk nightgown. She'd kept most of the old emperor's furniture when she moved into his apartments, but she hadn't felt right sleeping in his old bed. She'd had them bring in a new one, and it was one of her favourite things about her apartments. Once she let down the gold curtains on every side, it became her own private tent, a place of safety within a palace that felt less secure by the day. She climbed in there now and curled under the silk covers, pulling her knees up to her chin. From outside came the pad of cloth-shoed servants traversing the outdoor walkways, interspersed with the occasional jingle of armour.

Most women don't have the option to say no to men or refuse their orders. You are the empress. You have the strength of the spirits, of women who came before you and who will come after you. Why let your decisions be made for you?

Why should she be so haunted by a traitor's voice? Yet

Zhonglin's words weighed on her now, prodded her and mocked her. She was empress, yet she felt so powerless. If only she did have the strength of women who came before her.

As the footsteps outside faded to quiet, Mulan gave up on sleeping. She climbed out of bed and pulled on the wool pants and tunic she'd been issued as a soldier. Her hair was still in its nightly plait, so she rolled it up on her head and pinned it. Then she slipped out the window, climbing a pillar to the roof as she'd done before.

Though summer was around the corner, the night air still had a nip to it. By the time Mulan crossed the rooftop of her apartments and dropped to the other side, her cheeks and fingers were thoroughly chilled. Once back on the ground, she kept her head down and hurried along like a servant with a late-night errand.

The training ground was quiet as Mulan approached. One lone guard stood in front of the small equipment house. "Announce yourself!" he barked.

"Fa Mulan."

The soldier squinted in her direction, scanning her well-worn clothes, before he jumped and fell to his knees.

"Empress! Forgive me." Was he knocking his head on the ground?

"Stand," she said. "I need a few practice weapons."

He missed the keyhole several times in his rush, but the door finally swung open. A few spare racks of weapons shone grey in the moonlight. Mulan waved him aside and scanned the pickings. There was nothing of particularly good quality here, since the expensive weapons were in storage with the commanders, but she wasn't looking for quality. She was looking for a distraction.

A battered quiver hung in the corner alongside a well-worn bow. She grabbed those, as well as a few javelins.

"You can lock it back up," she told the still-mortified guard. "I'm going to the archery range."

"Will you require assistance, Empress?"

"No. Just stand watch."

The guard dropped out of sight as she rounded the corner to the archery range. The wind picked up noticeably as she stepped out into the open field. She shivered. At the far end of the field were circular targets and a few man-shaped ones. She wrestled one of the latter forward. It smelled of straw and mould, and its surface was pockmarked by old arrow wounds.

"Poor man, always used for target practice. Would you like my job instead?"

The target didn't answer.

There was something deeply meditative about archery. Raise the bow, breathe in. Draw the bow, breathe out. Aim, breathe in, hold... and release. A dull thud sounded as her arrow found its victim. Mulan couldn't see very well in the darkness, but there had been a burst of movement around the target's shoulder. Passable, but it wasn't where she'd been aiming. Truth was, she'd let herself get out of practice. It was a humbling thought.

Shang's voice echoed in her head. *Stray thoughts cause stray arrows. Leave the rest of your life off the battlefield. Here it's just you and your enemy.*

All well and good, but who were her enemies? Zhonglin? The people who hired her? The Hun ambassador? Or someone else altogether?

She drew another arrow, and this one went into the target's thigh.

The Hun ambassador was just a messenger. Any threat from him was secondary. He was the tool of a larger enemy.

Her next arrow went into the target's stomach. She supposed the Huns were a natural enemy, but they could also be allies. Wasn't that the point of diplomacy, to make allies of your enemies? Did making someone your ally require making him your husband, too?

Something whizzed by her ear. Mulan dove to the side as a chunk of straw exploded off the target. Her quiver clattered as she landed, spilling its contents on the ground. She grabbed an arrow and nocked it as she rolled into a crouch, blood racing as she scanned the darkness. Where had that arrow come from?

Gradually she made out a familiar form at the edge of the field, tall and broad of shoulder. She recognised the alertness of his stance, the confidence in how he gripped his bow.

Relief washed over her, and something harder to categorise.

Aiming her bow at the ground, Mulan walked towards him. "Don't surprise me like that. I might have shot you."

Shang was dressed simply. There was no sign of the embroidered silks that adorned him during the day. He looked like the man who'd trained her, the untried young captain who'd taken a mess of new recruits and turned them into soldiers.

The stern look he shot her also hearkened back to those times. "That's the least of your worries. I could have been an assassin. My arrow could have hit you instead of that chunk of mouldy straw."

"So you risked your life to teach me a lesson? That doesn't seem like proper strategy. Besides, if your guards are doing their jobs, then I don't have to worry about assassins in the palace."

His features were hard to see in the darkness, though she got the impression he was trying to hide a smile. "You really should be more careful about wandering these grounds alone, Empress."

For some reason, it hurt more to hear him use her title when it was just the two of them, bantering in the dark.

Mulan squared her shoulders. "I'm sorry. I needed to be alone, for my own sanity."

Shang shifted the angle of his face, and the moon illuminated his eyes. They were the same colour as the surrounding night, but somehow they felt brighter. "What's on your mind?" he asked.

"I had some problems with a member of my militia. She's been acting suspiciously for weeks, and I was relieved to send her home. But today I found her sneaking around my private garden. She wouldn't give me a straight answer about what she was doing."

"You believe she was a spy?"

"I can't think of a better explanation."

"What did you do?"

Mulan had forgotten how fierce Shang could look sometimes. He used to terrify her as a recruit. Shang had a way of looking at people as if he were trying to spear them with his pupils. Mulan didn't fear him now, though she could feel the energy radiating off him. It made her glad he wasn't her enemy.

"So far, I've had her placed under guard. I know I need to go back and question her. I just…"

They both fell quiet. Mulan noticed, as she often did now, how he was standing a little further away than felt natural, how his eyebrows knit together when he looked at her. Still, there was something about the anonymity of darkness that made things feel closer to what they'd been before. Perhaps it was the clothing they wore tonight, or simply because it was so cold and uncomfortable outside. But it felt like they weren't empress and general, but Mulan and Shang.

She kicked at a clod of dirt under her foot. "And then there's the Hun warlord, pushing his son on me."

"I don't like the Huns, but as empress, you must consider their proposal."

It was a statement that any of her advisers might have made, but her rage came on so quick and strong. "Don't tell me how to be empress."

The air between them stilled. She could sense her words floating where she'd spat them, but she couldn't bring herself to take them back.

Though Shang didn't take a single step, he seemed to retreat nonetheless. "My apologies, Empress." His voice was as stiff and formal as Mulan had ever heard him.

Her anger drained away, leaving only heaviness. "I'm sorry. I don't mean to be so short." The wind picked up, sending straw swirling around their legs. "I suppose my plan for coming outside and clearing my mind didn't work out too well."

He chuckled at that. "I think you had the right idea," he said. "Nothing like some hard training to get your mind off your troubles." Mulan jumped when he snatched her bow out of her hand. "But archery isn't going to work. You need to sweat."

"What exactly do you mean?"

He walked to the edge of the field. When he came back, he held two dull practice swords and bulky padded armour.

"Come on," he said, handing a set to her. "This is how you clear your mind. You've been spending too much time sitting on a throne and not enough time doing real work."

If he meant to get her blood racing with that challenge, he succeeded. She pulled the armour over her head and hefted the sword.

Shang raised his weapon. "Ready?"

And just like that, she was back on the battlefield, her world narrowed down to the edge of his blade.

Mulan attacked first. With her first lunge, she knew that Shang was right. She *had* been spending too much time on the throne, and her body was eager to move and fight. Shang brought his sword up to parry, and Mulan countered with another blow before he could recover. *Keep driving. Keep him guessing.* She sensed him recovering after his initial surprise and felt his energy rise to match hers. His parries became faster and faster, until finally a counterstrike knocked her off-balance. The force of the impact rang down her arms, and she ducked out of the way. They circled each other, gulping down the frigid air.

"Why don't we do this more often?" Mulan asked. Her arms and lungs stung, but she was awash in exhilaration.

Shang's voice had a bitter twist to it. "You know why."

Mulan wished he hadn't said that. Not now, when she was feeling better than she had in weeks. So she charged him again. This time he was ready, spinning out of the way and slicing his sword down at her head. She dropped and swung her leg out, trying to sweep his feet from under him, but he jumped. Mulan whirled out of range, though not before the tip of his sword caught her sleeve. If it had been a real sword instead of a dull practice one, it would have sliced the cloth off and perhaps her hand with it. Her sword clattered to the ground.

"You're slow, Empress," he said.

She backed up, keeping an eye on his weapon. "I'm out of practice. And I'm living with the weight of the empire on my shoulders."

"Nonsense," he roared, and Mulan was transported back to their training days. "That's the type of thinking that'll get you killed. You're the empress. You have the strength of a million men behind you."

She threw a handful of straw at his face. "A million men and women, you mean."

The straw didn't even reach him, but still, it drew his eye long enough for her to break away. Mulan sprinted for the edge of the field, where she'd stashed her javelins. A quick check to make sure their tips were still wrapped, and then she threw one at Shang. It went wide. She grabbed the remaining javelin and charged.

Now she was really improvising. The javelin wasn't meant to be used in hand-to-hand combat. It was lighter than the spears she'd trained with, and the balance was off. But it gave her the advantage of reach, and she was determined not to give Shang an easy win. Mulan pressed her attack, trying to snake the spear past his guard as he parried and dodged. Every time he tried to move in past her spear point, she whirled the shaft around to drive him off. At one point, she caught him so hard in the ribs that his breath whooshed out, but he didn't even slow. Heavens, she'd forgotten how near indestructible he was.

Mulan overreached with one attack and fell forward, her spear embedding itself diagonally into the ground. Shang raised his sword and brought it down hard on the spear handle. The wood splintered with a crack. As he lifted his sword for another blow, Mulan grabbed what was left of her spear with both hands and threw it over her head in a desperate block. A second crack rang through the darkness, the vibrations numbing her palms. She tried to spin away, but her spear wouldn't budge. The edge of his blade had cut into the wood.

They stared at each other across their weapons, both struggling to catch their breath. Mulan's blood ran hot from battle, even as the wind sent chills across her skin. The two of them were standing so close that the warmth of Shang's breath brushed her face. If they lowered their weapons and took a half step forward, they would touch. Mulan's gaze flickered to Shang's lips, and she looked away, mortified. But she could tell by the shift in his expression that he'd noticed.

Perhaps she was imagining it, but he had the look of a man tempted, a man struggling to gather his will, yet not quite succeeding.

Would it be bad if she wished for him to succumb? Mulan's heart beat wildly, throwing itself at her rib cage with staccato bursts. She couldn't afford to be weak – she was empress. But if Shang were the one to fail, perhaps she might be just a breath slow to stop him. Just one kiss, here in the dark, where nobody could see…

Shang set his jaw and wrenched his weapon loose. As he backed away, Mulan's entire being deflated. She'd known, in her gut, what would happen. Both of them were far too disciplined to do anything out of line. She'd known, but her chest still burned as if she'd swallowed a brand.

"Well fought, Empress," Shang said. There was a huskiness to his normally steady voice, and the hot iron in her chest twisted deeper. "Be sure to stay in practice. The kingdom needs your leadership."

The kingdom needed her leadership. That was the awful truth of it. Here they were, the two most powerful people in the Middle Kingdom, and yet they had no control over how their lives should proceed.

•••

Liwen knocked on Mulan's door early the next morning. Locks of hair had escaped her braids and fell in kinked strands around her face. Dark circles lined her eyes. Still, she was animated.

"I found something," she said, pushing her way through the door. "The Hun ambassador went into the city last night with his retinue. I followed him to a restaurant, and then I decided to go back to his quarters and see what I could find."

She handed Mulan a piece of paper. "This was under a false bottom in his personal chest."

It was written in the script of the Huns. "Can you read it?" asked Mulan. She knew that Liwen had learned different scripts from the nuns who raised her, but her friend had never been incredibly studious.

"I was up late trying to read it, and I've deciphered enough to know it's a list. This here is 'a herd of twenty fine horses'. This says 'riding rights in the eastern territory'. Here it says 'governorship of Yangzhou region'. And this says 'fifty gold ingots'."

Mulan ran her finger over the paper. "Why keep a list like this? Why keep it hidden?"

"Bribes, perhaps?" said Liwen. "Promises to those who would switch their allegiance?"

That had crossed Mulan's mind, too. "We need to talk to Zhonglin."

Mulan flung open the door to her room. The maid outside curtsied. "Bring a message to the guards currently in charge of the prisoner Zhonglin. I intend to question her. Have them make sure she is awake and alert, and summon me when she's ready."

As the maid left, Mulan closed the door and paced her room, tapping out her misgivings on the hardwood floor. There was a knot in her stomach that wouldn't loosen.

"She may not talk," said Liwen.

"She may not," Mulan agreed.

Neither of them spoke after that, because what followed was too horrible to say. Mulan needed to know what Zhonglin knew. If Zhonglin didn't volunteer the information, there was a long tradition of methods employed by rulers to wrest it out of her. But the idea of Mulan actually using such methods herself, much less on someone who had been under her command…

"I can handle the questioning if you'd like," said Liwen quietly.

Mulan shook her head. Was she falling victim to delicate female sensibilities? Did that make her weak? "I don't want to get used to having people do my dirty work for me."

"All emperors do."

"And empresses?"

Liwen pressed her lips together. "My offer stands, if you change your mind."

A knock sounded at her door. Mulan locked eyes with Liwen.

"Ready?" asked Liwen.

Mulan closed her eyes and nodded. Had the old emperor had to make such choices? Had he ever been betrayed? She steeled herself and opened the door.

A soldier stood there. When he saw Mulan, he fell to the ground, pressing his face to the floor.

"Your Majesty…" He kept speaking, but his words were too garbled to understand.

"Soldier, what are you doing?" asked Mulan. She stared down at him, unable to comprehend his actions. He continued to babble incoherently.

Liwen came to the door. "What's happening?"

The guard cowered, knocking his head on the floor, rocking back and forth in full armour like a hysterical turtle. Mulan could make no sense of his rambling, and he seemed oblivious to anything she said. Finally, she grabbed him by the shoulders and pulled him to standing. Not an easy feat with a fully suited-up guard.

"Soldier," she said, shaking him. "Soldier!"

The guard stopped abruptly, eyes wide.

"Soldier, you're making no sense."

"Your Majesty, please forgive us," he rasped. "We don't know what happened. Our lives are forfeit, but please, spare my family."

"What are you talking about?" asked Mulan.

He drew a quivering breath. "We don't know where the prisoner is. She's disappeared."

CHAPTER ELEVEN

The guards had placed Zhonglin in a holding cell for wrongdoers caught within palace walls, a small brick building with thin slits for windows and a thick wooden door. There had been two guards on duty – one stationed by the door, and the other on the opposite corner. Both collapsed at Mulan's feet in the same way the first guard had.

"Calm down," Mulan said. How was she supposed to sort anything out amid all this carrying on? "I have no fondness for executions. Just tell me what happened."

From what Mulan pieced together from their reports, nothing out of the ordinary had occurred. Just after sunrise, a guard had peered through the window and seen Zhonglin asleep in the cell. An hour later, she was gone. None of the brick walls showed any sign of tampering. The stone floor was untouched, and the windows had no loose bricks.

"Close the palace and city gates," said Mulan. "Send out soldiers to search. She may not have gone far."

"And what of the prison guards?" asked Liwen.

Mulan paused. The soldiers were all watching her, terrified in a way that no human being should be when looking at another. How did one live with this kind of power day after day and not let it change her? *I am not a god.*

"Hold them for questioning," she said, averting her eyes. And then she left.

Liwen hurried after Mulan as she cut across the palace grounds. "Where are you going?"

"To the state guesthouses."

The doors to the Hun ambassador's apartments were closed. The ambassador was known to keep late hours, but the servant at the door opened it for Mulan.

"Her Imperial Majesty!" he announced.

Mulan didn't slow as she entered. Ambassador Balambar had been sitting with two of his scribes, and he stood hurriedly as Mulan swept in. This power, at least, she would let herself enjoy. Despite all that was going on, Balambar was still a guest in her city, and she would enter as she pleased.

"Your Majesty," Balambar said, his thick black eyebrows arching in exaggerated surprise. "To what do I owe this pleasure?"

"I had a prisoner escape today from the holding cells in the palace," she said.

Mulan watched him for a reaction, but he remained unperturbed. "That is distressing news, Your Majesty. May I or my staff be of service in tracking down this prisoner?"

"Have you seen anything suspicious around here recently?"

"Nothing that I've noticed, Your Majesty."

Mulan looked around. It was a very clean apartment. Nothing seemed out of place. There was nowhere for a fugitive to hide, and besides, the ambassador wouldn't be so stupid as to hide Zhonglin in his apartments.

"Deal honestly with me, Balambar," she said. "Deal honestly with me, and I will deal honestly with you."

•••

Mulan was back at her ancestral temple. It was dawn, and fog still covered the ground. Through the mist, she saw hints of red and pink blossoms on a background of muted green. The smell of rich earth filled her nostrils. A hawk's cry rent the air, and a brown-and-red streak flew over her head.

Mulan walked up the steps of the temple, batting at the fog with her hands. She could see someone on the bench in front of the altar, just a shadow in the haze, but somehow Mulan knew who it was.

"Grandmother!"

Mulan ran to her, wrapping her in a tight hug. Her grandmother's frame was small, but Nai Nai felt strong, full of energy like she'd been years ago. Nai Nai squeezed her and rubbed her back. She smelled of jasmine and anise.

Tears flowed down Mulan's cheeks. "Nai Nai, you're here."

"Are you surprised to see me here?" Grandmother sounded faintly amused. "Where else would ancestors be?"

"Yes, but..." Mulan gestured helplessly at the spirit tablets lining the walls.

Grandmother held Mulan out at arm's length. She looked just the same as in Mulan's memories. The melon-seed-shaped face, eyes that danced, and cheeks wrinkled from smiling. "My soldier granddaughter has grown up. Empress of China. You make us all proud."

Mulan shrank back at her words. "Not now, Grandmother. There's nothing to be proud of now."

Two white eyebrows arched. "Whyever not?"

"It's all a mess. I've barely been crowned and everything's falling apart. I'm not sure I can do this."

Grandmother tapped her cane on the floor. "My granddaughter? Admitting defeat? That's not the girl I remember. My granddaughter went off to war. She showed all the boys what she could do and saved all of China."

That victory felt so distant now. "But this is different. I used to command troops, but now I can't even control my own council. The old emperor told me I would have wise people helping me rule, but instead my ministers undermine me at every turn."

"Maybe you need a new council. Give this one the boot."

Mulan got a mental image of her tiny grandmother marching

into the council room and running her ministers out with wild swings of her cane. It was an oddly satisfying thought, if only for a little while. "It's not just the council that's the problem. I need to win the hearts of the people."

"You already have those, my dear."

"Maybe I did before, but there were symbols of rebellion at my coronation."

Nai Nai pursed her lips. "Symbols of rebellion?"

"There was a hand signal."

Now Grandmother's eyes sparkled. "What was the symbol, now? Something like this?" She fanned her fingers and then placed both fists together in an exact imitation of what Mulan had seen.

"Yes, that's it!"

Grandmother fanned out her fingers. "A fan, covering the face. A coy maiden, if you will, with secrets. And this" – she put her fists together – "is the maiden holding a sword. A symbol for the warrior queen. Hidden strength." Grandmother caught her eye. "Looks like a sign of devotion to me."

"Devotion?" Mulan stepped back. "But Minister Liu said..." She drifted off. The minister of rites had implied straight away that the signal was a sign of rebellion. He'd reminded her time after time that she didn't have the love of the people. And Mulan had believed him, because Minister Liu had been the kindest of her advisers, the only one who'd never talked down to her or gone *blatantly against her orders.*

"Could he be lying?" Mulan asked.

*"There's only one way to know for sure," said Grandmother.
The fog grew thicker, chilling Mulan's skin. Grandmother's voice
grew softer. "Oh, and maybe talk to the palace astrologer too. See
if there's anything he'd like to tell you."*

...

The scents of jasmine and anise lingered around Mulan's bed
even after she awoke. Mulan wiped her eyes with the back
of her hand, and it came away damp. Her body mourned
the memory of being held and comforted. How long had
it been since she'd been able to lean on someone like that,
with no worries of what it might mean, or how it might
hurt her? Could the dream really have been a visit from her
grandmother's spirit? Or was it simply a dream? And the
things Grandmother had said – were they true?

There was one way to find out.

Mulan opened her bedroom door and was glad to find
Ting stationed there. "Ting, can you come in for a moment?"

"Of course, Your Majesty." Ting watched with interest as
Mulan closed the door behind them and looked through the
windows for bystanders.

"I need to entrust you with something sensitive and
important," Mulan said finally.

The maid perked up, her upturned nose lifting the

slightest bit. "Anything, Your Majesty."

"First, I need you to summon Liwen. Then I need you to find the palace astrologer and send him here as well, but I need you to do it discreetly. I don't want anyone to know that I'm looking for him."

Ting's eyes widened so much that her entire forehead lifted. "Is there danger, Your Majesty?"

"I'm not sure," Mulan answered honestly.

Mulan watched the maid struggle to compose her excitement into a more serious expression.

"I'll do it, Your Majesty," Ting said fervently. "I won't fail you." The maid curtsied, bouncing the slightest bit. Despite all on her mind, Mulan suppressed a smile. Ting might be starstruck and idealistic, but Mulan trusted her to do her task.

It didn't take long after Ting left for Liwen to arrive. Mulan wondered if her friend had been waiting to be summoned. Liwen walked heavily, her head uncharacteristically lowered, though she looked up to greet Mulan.

"Any news?" Mulan asked.

"No sign of her so far. We're still searching," said Liwen. Her face clouded. "I should have kept a better watch on her."

"You did what you deemed was best at the time," said Mulan. "We can't expect ourselves to be clairvoyant. Keep up the search, but there's something else I'd like you to look into."

Liwen waited.

"This hand signal." Mulan replicated it herself. "Minister Liu told me it was a sign of rebellion, but I've never heard its meaning firsthand from someone who used it. I want you to go into the city and ask around. Talk to people. See if they recognise the symbol and know what it means."

Liwen gave a focused nod. "I'll see what I can find."

Two hours later, a satisfied Ting escorted the royal astrologer to Mulan's quarters. He came in with his head down, shuffling like a kicked dog. It almost looked as if the maid was dragging him, although she was actually quite gentle in her herding.

"He saw me coming for him at his workshop, and he tried to leave out the back door," said Ting. She spoke sternly, though her narrow face was triumphant. "I was too quick for him, though."

That didn't sound like the behaviour of a man with a clear conscience. "Thank you," said Mulan. "You've done a fantastic job. Please keep watch outside while I speak with him."

Ting beamed. "Shall I send a bodyguard in?"

"No. I'll be fine."

Mulan remembered how nervous the astrologer had been during his last royal audience. She wouldn't have thought it possible for him to be even more frightened, but somehow he managed. He fell on his face the moment Ting let him go, his entire body trembling.

"Your Majesty."

"Sounds like you're a hard man to track down," said Mulan. It was strange speaking to the top of someone's head. She seemed to be doing that a lot recently.

"Forgive me, Your Majesty. I had some tasks to do in the city."

"And it was important that you leave out the back door?"

He cowered.

Mulan thought it better not to press him further about his escape attempt, lest he disintegrate completely. "I had some questions about your predictions. I was hoping you could explain them to me. You said that the stars corroborated the prediction from my oracle bones, is that right?"

"Yes, Your Majesty," he said to the floorboards. "The constellations tell of a threat from the north."

Mulan suppressed a new flicker of unease at the reminder. "But the stars also said that the threat could be mitigated with an offer of goodwill. Can you tell me more about the offer of friendship? Do the stars offer any other clues?"

"Astrology is an inexact art, Your Majesty." The man's fu tou had fallen askew with all his prostrating. "The way the stars aligned, it suggested an alliance. An offer of friendship..."

"Are we going to have this whole conversation with your head to the floor, Master Astrologer? Please stand up."

His knees wobbled as he got to his feet.

Mulan cocked her head. "Why are you so nervous?"

"I… Your Majesty…" His mouth clamped shut. His eyes bugged, out, and then he threw himself on the ground. "I have to care for my ailing mother, Your Majesty. The medicine is expensive. I meant no harm…" His words tumbled out in an undecipherable jumble.

"Slow down. What are you talking about?"

The man kept blubbering. "Do what you must with me, Your Majesty, but please, I beg you. Spare my family."

Why was everyone convinced she was going to wipe out their bloodlines? Mulan stepped closer. "I can't understand what you're saying."

The man pressed himself flat on the ground. "I lied about the prediction, Your Majesty. There was never anything about an offer of friendship."

The words filtered slowly into her understanding. Even after she deciphered their meaning, it was a long, drawn-out stretch before Mulan fully grasped their implication. "There was nothing? What do you mean?"

"He offered me money to add that in," said the astrologer. "He said it wouldn't make much of a difference, and it was best that we make peace with the Huns anyway."

Mulan stared at him. The prediction had been a lie. Not a miscommunication, not even a biased interpretation, but blatant sabotage.

"Someone told you to do this. Who?" Though the suspicion was already uncurling in her gut.

The astrologer abruptly quieted. He lifted his head and looked around wildly.

Mulan gritted her teeth. "Answer me, Astrologer. May I remind you that anyone you could possibly fear is under my authority."

His voice dropped to a whisper, so soft that it was just shy of impossible to make out his words. "The minister of rites, Your Majesty."

"Minister Liu paid you to lie to me?" Part of Mulan wanted to believe that she'd misheard the astrologer.

"Yes, Your Majesty." Still almost inaudible.

"But why?"

He whimpered. "I don't know."

Someone knocked on the door. Both Mulan and the astrologer jumped. Mulan stepped away to retrieve her sword from the closet, ignoring the astrologer's yelp of fear when she unsheathed it.

"Who is it?" she called through the door.

"It's Ting, Your Majesty." The handmaiden's voice came tentatively. "Lady Liwen is here to see you."

Mulan's knees softened with relief. "Let her in."

When Liwen swept in, her gaze went first to Mulan's sword, and then to the astrologer. "I take it a lot has happened."

"You could say that," said Mulan. She turned to Ting. "Take the astrologer to my back room and have one of my bodyguards watch him."

She waited until the maid and astrologer were gone. "Did you find anything?" she asked Liwen.

Her friend pulled something white and spherical out of the folds of her skirt and offered it to Mulan. It was a meat bun, slightly compressed and soggy. "I had the kitchens make me four dozen of these to sell in the streets. Whenever someone bought from me, I asked them about the hand signal. Not everyone knew of it, but those who did said it was a sign of celebration. Nobody knows where it came from, but it seems to have popped up a few days before the coronation."

"Celebration?" asked Mulan. Despite the bun's ragged appearance, it smelled temptingly of meat juices and ginger. Mulan wondered how long it had been since she'd eaten.

"Celebration and devotion to the warrior empress."

"I see." Devotion, not rebellion, just like her grandmother had said. She put the bun on the table. "My ministers have been lying to me. And they bribed my astrologer to steer me towards an alliance with the Huns."

Liwen took this newest revelation in stride. "Why would they ally themselves with the Huns?"

"I don't know. And I don't know where Zhonglin fits in. If she knew that the symbol wasn't one of rebellion, then why didn't she just tell me? She's a proud girl, but refusing to defend herself to the point of arrest..."

"She didn't stay under arrest very long," said Liwen. "Maybe she knew she had a way out."

But how did she get out? Who helped her escape? Why go to these lengths? There were so many pieces to the puzzle. "Maybe Shang will know something."

"You're in danger," said Liwen abruptly.

Finally, Liwen put into words the growing sense of unease that had plagued Mulan the entire morning. Things had moved beyond simple political games. As soon as her ministers knew that their treachery was discovered, they would act to save themselves.

"I need to move quickly," she told Liwen. "The minister of rites must not know that he's been betrayed."

Mulan swept out the door and into the back room of her apartments, where the astrologer sat cross-legged on a straw mat, watched by a bodyguard and Ting. The handmaiden had picked up a paperweight of white jade and now tapped it threateningly against her palm. The astrologer's head snapped up as Mulan entered.

Mulan cleared the room of all but Liwen, the astrologer and herself.

"After you leave this room," said Mulan, "I want you to head home as you normally would. Do not stop and speak to anyone. Once you're home, stay there. Do not leave for any reason until I summon you. By confessing to me, you've earned yourself the possibility of clemency. But if I suspect that you've said anything of our conversation to a single person, you will be punished as fully befits your crime. Do you understand?"

"Yes, Your Majesty." He kowtowed repeatedly. "Thank you, Your Majesty."

Mulan looked to Liwen. "Trail him. Make sure he stays silent."

...

An empress was never truly alone. Never had Mulan been more acutely aware of this. Though she stood on her own in her bedroom, one maid always waited just outside the door. Her bodyguards constantly circled her apartments. And the palace compound outside bustled with officials and sharp-eyed servants.

In some ways, the lengths Mulan had gone in order to ensure the astrologer's silence was just theatre, holding an umbrella to stay dry as she stood knee-deep in water. Did it matter whether the astrologer told anyone of their conversation when countless people saw Ting search the palace for him? When dozens of servants witnessed the handmaiden escorting him back?

But what else could Mulan have done? After several weeks with Ting, she trusted the handmaiden's loyalty and judgment. Her bodyguards were handpicked by Shang, and Mulan didn't think they would betray her. As for the possible witnesses, bystanders and passers-by, Mulan could only hope for the best.

There was a state dinner that night to send off several of

the emperor's distant cousins who'd come for the coronation. Mulan smiled at Minister Huang's oily compliments over shark fin soup and ignored Minister Fang's veiled insults of her intelligence. Shang never showed up.

After dinner, Mulan stopped by Shang's quarters. No one answered the door. A passing servant told her that the general was out on a long training exercise.

"When will he return?" Mulan asked.

The servant bowed. "Late tonight, Empress."

She couldn't afford to wait until tomorrow to speak with Shang. Sending him a message didn't feel safe, and waiting around for him was too conspicuous.

"Let me into his rooms, please."

There was an inkpot and parchment on his desk. Mulan worded her note carefully.

I'm feeling out of practice after our last training bout. Can we meet again, same time and place?

She tucked it under his ink stand so that only one corner was visible.

There was no sleeping that night. The moon rose. The palace grew quiet. Mulan paced her room. Her ministers were traitors, but they were powerful, with allies both within the palace and without. If she acted to remove them, could she prevail?

The water clock in the corner of her bedroom dripped lower. Lines on the porcelain ticked off the passing hours.

Mulan changed into her soldiering clothes, pinned up her hair and slipped out the window. This time, she did make an effort to stay hidden as she made her way to the training grounds, skimming along rooftops, ducking out of the way whenever she heard guards or servants.

The practice field was empty, and the guard was at his usual post by the weapons shed. Mulan took a wide circle around him onto the archery field. She settled down next to a musty straw warrior.

She was early, according to her calculations. Mulan probably had a quarter hour to wait. The wind bit at her as she crouched by the target. She had no way of knowing if Shang would be here, but he was an observant man. If he'd returned to his quarters tonight, he would have found her note. And if he read her note, he would come.

A rustle in the darkness jolted her out of her thoughts. Mulan stood. Her legs were slightly cramped, and she shook them out. It was hard to see anything.

A shadow detached itself from the surrounding night, but the silhouette did not belong to Shang. It was too narrow, too delicate. Mulan stayed completely still, imagining herself a part of the straw soldier, willing the newcomer to go. But the other person on the field didn't leave. Instead, he walked closer, heading for Mulan's position without wavering.

"Who's there?" she called out.

The shape moved closer, and a familiar thin voice spoke.

"Your loyal servant, Your Majesty," said the minister of rites.

CHAPTER TWELVE

True fear coursed through Mulan's body – the realisation that something was very, very wrong.

It was the minister who broke the silence first. "Your Majesty shouldn't be wandering the grounds this time of night without a bodyguard."

The shadows moved. More shapes resolved themselves out of the darkness – the hulking frame of the minister of justice, the quick-stepping minister of personnel. One after another, they came out, her entire cabinet save Shang.

"What are you doing here?" asked Mulan.

"We might ask the same question of you, Your Majesty," said Minister Liu.

"I'm empress. Can I not go where I please?"

"You're certainly allowed to go anywhere you like, but there are risks." He looked so small, stooped there with the giant field behind him. So harmless.

"You've been having me followed," said Mulan. Not just during the day, she realised, but even during those times she thought she'd been sneaking out alone.

"We've been keeping track of Your Majesty's movements, for your protection."

"Don't lie, Minister." It was a relief to finally speak plainly. "You've betrayed me, all of you."

Minister Liu drew a sharp breath, as if he'd been asked to consider a distasteful recipe. "We prefer to think of it as loyalty to China. The country must have stable leadership from someone with experience in these matters. A strong ruler who can handle the challenges of leading such a great country."

A ruler who is not a woman. "I was chosen by the emperor as his heir. You dishonour his memory."

"The emperor was a wise man, but his judgment waned with old age."

There were more movements now. More shapes stepped out, outlined in the bulky edges of armour.

Mulan took a step back, bending to retrieve her knife from her shin. Her heartbeat sped up in a way she only knew in the moments before a battle. "Regicide? Heaven will judge you."

"We would never commit such a crime." Minister Liu spoke as if explaining an obscure bit of history. "We simply suggest that Your Majesty take a brief trip to the countryside to rest. Ruling has been hard on your health, and some time away would do everyone much good."

The soldiers formed a semicircle around her. Mulan unsheathed her knife. How hard had her ministers had to look in order to find soldiers willing to raise hands against her? One soldier moved in ahead of the others, and Mulan kicked out his knee. He went down with a grunt. When Mulan raised her head, she faced a wall of swords.

The minister's voice carried over the blades. "We've ordered our soldiers not to kill you, but Heaven will forgive us if you trip and fall on one of their blades. I advise you to drop your knife."

Mulan looked around. The moon was down. All around, she saw nothing but shadows. But did the palace ever truly sleep?

"Treason!" she yelled. "Treason against the empress!"

This time, the soldiers moved as one. The points of their swords formed a curved wall, just a hand's width from her skin.

"I'd hope you wouldn't think us so incompetent as to allow anyone within hearing distance," said Minister Liu. "Please drop your weapon, Empress. I'll remind you that gold tends to dull mortal fear of the gods, and we have given these soldiers plenty of gold."

She dropped the knife.

"Bring her to the wagon."

The soldiers shifted formation, allowing Mulan to march, surrounded, off the field. Now that she was closer to them, she could see that they had covered their faces with handkerchiefs. *Cowards.* Did she know any of these soldiers? Did Shang?

On a cobblestone path next to the practice field was a large wagon. Not an imperial carriage, but a closed, boxy cart that might be used to transport a prisoner.

One of the soldiers opened the door. It was empty except for a wooden bench. "Get inside, Your Majesty."

Was there a hint of hesitation in his voice? She looked at his eyes, but they were just as cold as all the others. Mulan stepped in. The wood of the bench was rough, the kind that would easily leave splinters.

"Where are you taking me?" she asked.

Minister Liu moved to the door. After all this, he still looked like a pleasant, doddering scholar. "Your Majesty will find out soon enough," he said, squinting at her as if she were another scroll in his collection.

And then he smiled and closed the door.

•••

The wagon jerked and began to roll. Mulan had the overwhelming urge to bang on the door and shout to be let out, but she didn't want to give them the satisfaction. Instead, she gripped the rough wood of her bench, digging her nails into the underside as they rolled away. Her head spun. The world tilted. She gripped harder.

Six days. It had only been six days since her coronation. Six days for her to lose her country, to be ejected from her own palace in chains.

The wagon had no windows, only a narrow slot at the front that allowed the drivers to look in on her. Mulan launched herself from the bench, clinging to the slot as if the wagon had no floor to hold her up. She narrowed her eyes at the two soldiers sitting in front.

As they reached the palace gates, Mulan caught a glimpse of four guards on duty. Was there any chance they were loyal?

She banged on the wall. "Help! Let me out!"

The closest gate guard flicked an uninterested eye towards the wagon and waved them through with his halberd. As soon as the wagon cleared the gates, one of the drivers reached back. Mulan barely got her fingers out of the window before the soldier slammed the panel shut.

Mulan's self-control dissolved. "Damn you!" She pounded the wall. Splinters lodged in her fist. When her hands hurt too much to continue, she kicked at the wagon until the vehicle jostled over a rut and she lost her balance. Pain bloomed in her elbow and hip as she landed on the floorboards. She lay on the floor, her cheek pressed against the wood. What would her ministers do now that she was gone? What were they planning?

The wagon rolled on. The bumps on the road imprinted themselves into Mulan's joints. She marked time by the gradual warming of her cabin and the brightening rays of light through the cracks around the door. After a few hours, the wagon stopped and the back door opened.

Light streamed in. Mulan threw a hand up to save her eyes. As her vision finally adjusted, she saw that the guard had placed a plate of steamed vegetable buns on the floor next to her. After she ate, the guard placed a chain around her ankle and allowed her into the woods to relieve herself.

This became the routine. Travel in the back of the wagon until mealtime, when she was given food and water and let out. At night they gave her a thick silk blanket – far too luxurious for a prison cart. Morning brought another meal and more travel. The landscape went back and forth between grassland, farmland and the occasional hilly forest. From what Mulan glimpsed during the times her captors let her out of the wagon, she could tell they were headed north and east. Were they bringing her across the border? To one of the summer palaces up north? She supposed it didn't matter. Wherever it was, it would be far away. She would be irrelevant, tossed aside. She'd failed to keep her vow to the old emperor.

Mulan made notches on her bench to keep track of the days. Four, five, six, seven… At first she tried her best to maintain her dignity. In the mornings, she wrestled with her increasingly tangled hair and tried to pin it up. She attempted to keep her face clean, even if the rest of her picked up more grime by the day. But as the days passed, her hair became more knotted, the dust on her face more thickly layered and harder to wipe off. Empresses kept up appearances. Prisoners had no reason to. Mulan's guards never spoke to her and always avoided her eyes. They simply fed her, locked her up and continued on their way.

•••

Empress.

Mulan pulled her covers closer around her. The silks were soft against her cheeks, though the pillow hurt her head.

Empress. Wake up.

Mulan's eyes snapped open. There was no pillow, only floorboards. The wagon was cold and dark. Though she could see nothing, she had the distinct impression that there was someone, or something, in the wagon with her. "Who's speaking?"

You're stronger than this.

The voice was female, not quite human. It gave Mulan the impression of a crowd, multiple voices speaking at once.

Your people need you.

"My people rejected me," whispered Mulan.

You know better. Your people love you. It is only your enemies who seek to hide you away.

The wagon's floorboards pressed against Mulan's ribs.

"They're doing a pretty good job of it."

Only because you let them. Take stock of your advantages. Use them to free yourself.

"Can I walk through walls?" she asked, an edge to her voice now. "Conjure a sword out of thin air?"

You are the empress. You have the strength of the spirits, of women past, present and future. Your jailers cannot keep you if you do not wish to be kept.

Recognition zinged through her. "Who are you?" Mulan asked.

That's not the right question. Who are you?

Abruptly, she was alone. That presence, that feeling of something other, was gone. What had it been? A spirit? A host of spirits? She didn't like the idea of ghosts haunting her sleep. Still, the presence had not felt malevolent.

Take stock of your advantages. Your jailers cannot keep you if you do not wish to be kept.

Were the spirits right? Could she get out?

What were her advantages? Her guards were armed. She had no weapons.

No, that wasn't quite true. She had no sword or knife, but weapons did not have to be forged as such. Her hair was still in a messy braid that had fallen out of its bun days ago. Tucked in her robe was the hairpin that she'd used to fasten it, which the guards hadn't thought to confiscate. The pin was as long as the span of her fingers and had a rounded

211

point that could be sharpened. And there was the chain that the guards used to shackle her when they let her out. It was heavy, with a decent amount of length.

Also, advantages didn't have to be physical. They could also be psychological. Prisoner or not, she was still empress of China. The guards knew that. Mulan had seen the flashes of hesitation in their eyes. Though they'd been bribed or otherwise convinced to turn against her, they feared her, and they feared Heaven's retribution if they harmed her. This was why they didn't search her thoroughly before they threw her in the wagon. It was why they gave her decent meals and a blanket fit for royalty at night, and why they hadn't tied her hands. If they needed to, they would raise arms against her, but they would be slow. They would be prone to mistakes.

And because she was a woman, they would underestimate her.

The next time Mulan's guard let her out into the forest, she found a small stone and tucked it into her robe. She got to work when the wagon went on its way, hoofbeats and clattering wheels masking the scrape of her hairpin against stone. After a day, it had been sharpened to a serviceable point. She tied it to her forearm with several strands of her hair.

That night, she huddled under her blanket, going over her plan. She would have one chance to surprise and overpower her guards. Mulan ran over scenarios, trying to imagine every possible way this could pan out, every point at which her plan might go wrong. She fell asleep a few hours before dawn. The spirits whispered in her dreams.

When she woke, sunlight streamed through the cracks in the wagon. Voices drifted in from outside – her guards awake and preparing their morning meal. Mulan sat up, feeling for the sharpened hairpin, her heartbeat quickening until she found the pin tied securely where she'd left it.

Footsteps drew closer. A key rattled inside the wagon's lock. As always, Mulan blinked against the light until the guard at the door came into focus.

He was the older of the two, thick-skinned and wind burned, the one she'd come to think of as more hardened. It had been the other guard who had hesitated when ordering her into the wagon the night of the coup. She'd hoped for that one.

The soldier didn't make eye contact as he laid a bowl of rice porridge on the floor of the wagon, though he watched her eat it. Mulan finished it off quickly, strangely conscious of any porridge that got on her face as she tipped the bowl to her lips. She placed the empty bowl on the floor and pushed it towards the guard. The wagon stood high enough that the bowl was at the level of his thigh. As always, he put the bowl to the side and then held out the shackle for Mulan. She scooted to the edge of the wagon, presenting her ankle. As he moved closer, she flexed her forearm, letting the hairpin drop into her hand. The soldier's armour covered his chest and the tops of his shoulders. Though he wore guards on his forearms, his upper arms were covered only by cloth. Mulan tightened her grip on the hairpin.

As the guard bent over her ankle, she thrust the hairpin into his armpit. He roared in surprise and dropped the chain, which Mulan grabbed and threw over his neck. She flung herself backwards as hard as she could, pulling him into the wagon with her. As he fell, she guided him to her left and wrapped her legs around his torso like a monkey on his back, tightening the chain around his neck. He gasped and choked, grabbing and pulling at the metal rings as Mulan pulled, her entire body bowed with effort.

It didn't take long. The soldier's movements weakened, and then he went limp. Mulan held on a few more moments to make sure he was out, and then she untangled herself and dragged him away from the wagon door. His sword belt she hastily unbuckled and put on herself. There was a dagger too, in a sheath at his waist, and his keys. She grabbed them both.

"Laoxie!" The call came from outside.

Mulan froze.

"Laoxie, you still back there?" There was caution in the other guard's voice, but he wasn't scared yet. Mulan picked up the chain and crept to the back of the wagon. She pressed against the sidewall, weighing out a good length into her hands.

"Are you there?"

The other soldier came around the corner, freezing when he caught a glimpse of his fallen comrade. In that moment, Mulan flung out the length of her chain, swinging from the hip and putting all her weight behind it. The chain links smashed into his handkerchief-covered face. When he stumbled back, she launched herself out the door and planted a foot in his chest. He fell. She followed up with a kick to his head.

Silence. The whole fight had taken less time than she'd spent eating her breakfast, but Mulan's throat burned with exertion. She shook with the leftover energy of battle.

Mulan looked back at the first soldier, lying in the wagon. He was still unconscious, but she didn't know for how much longer. Quickly, she crouched and lifted the second soldier's arm over her neck. She tried to stand, stumbled, adjusted her feet, and straightened again. Why were men so heavy? The soldier's feet dug trails in the dirt. She threw his torso into the wagon, and then, grunting, heaved his legs up one by one. A moan sounded as she shoved him the last of the way in. Mulan didn't check to see who it came from before shutting the door.

The keys wouldn't fit in the lock. Mulan fumbled with them. Her hands shook as another moan sounded. Finally, the key slid in. The bolt snapped into place. Mulan pulled the handle to make sure the door was locked, and then she ran.

CHAPTER THIRTEEN

The terrain was hilly. Mulan ducked under tree limbs and brushed leaves away from her face as gnarled branches left gouges across her skin. Her breath rasped loud in her ears. Shouts sounded in the distance, and was that a banging sound? Maybe she should have killed the soldiers, but killing someone in battle was different from killing someone she'd already rendered defenceless. And there was something about striking down her own subjects that felt wrong, even if they'd betrayed her.

She kept running, skirting around rust-coloured boulders and doing her best not to kick up red dust. The uneven ground took a toll on her ankles – it was a wonder that she hadn't tripped and fallen yet.

The noises gradually faded. When she could run no more, Mulan doubled over, hands on her knees, and vomited her breakfast onto the ground. Her head felt too light for comfort. There was a stitch in her side, and her left calf cramped painfully. All those days in the wagon had weakened her.

"What do I do now?" she asked the trees.

But the spirit voices remained silent. A rodent darted across her path. A falcon dived into the brush after it.

It was only a matter of time before her ministers would start looking for her. Whom would they send? Mulan had no way of knowing how many people her ministers had managed to turn.

She saw now how blind she'd been about them. She'd been so awed by their education and experience that she didn't see the malice and cunning behind their every move. Mulan had soaked in their poisonous words, carefully calculated to chip away at her confidence. And because of that, she'd let them catch her unawares. It killed her to think about them in the Imperial City, carrying out their agenda unhindered, telling whatever lie they pleased about her fate.

She needed to stop them, and that meant getting back to the Imperial City. The road Mulan had just fled was a major thoroughfare. If she could find a way to follow it safely, she could backtrack the way she came.

Mulan picked her way through the forest, at a slower pace this time. After a while, she found a small footpath and followed it until the trees opened up to a wheat field. A single farmer ploughed the rows with an ox. Mulan took a step towards him, a call for help forming on her lips, and then stopped. If the man was disloyal to her, then he could turn her in. If he was loyal and helped her, his actions could put him in danger. Either way, it was better if he didn't know of her presence.

But she couldn't go much further without supplies. Already, Mulan was hungry after throwing up her breakfast. Could she take food and provisions from this man's house without letting him know? Even from this distance, she could see the threadbare condition of his clothes. Somehow, she didn't think he had much to spare.

Mulan looked around. There were many fields here, one next to the other. If there were peasants working these fields, then they would have a landlord. Landlords meant large houses, food and supplies.

Mulan retreated to the cover of the trees and ran her hand over her hair. She undid the bottom of her braid and did her best to tie any loose strands back in. She wiped her face with her sleeves, though she had no idea if that made her skin cleaner or dirtier. Her sword was the most conspicuous thing on her. After some thought, she gathered a bunch of branches, tied them together with her sword belt and tucked the sword in the centre of the bundle. Mulan continued along the edge of the fields with the bundle slung over her back. The farmer didn't look in her direction as she passed him. As she walked, she came across other workers, but they paid her little mind.

At regular intervals, she passed mud-brick cottages with thatched roofs, modest dwellings that made her glad she hadn't raised the grain tax. Finally, Mulan came upon a large rectangular villa made of clean-cut bricks and roofed with green tile. Two rows of white-paper windows stretched across the low front wall, while fine latticework on the windows and carved lintel beams signalled money and power. This, she could work with.

Mulan skirted around to the back. There were windows here as well, most likely looking into bedrooms. One lay open a crack, and Mulan eased the shutters wider. Inside, she glimpsed a bed, a heavy wooden desk and a wardrobe. Gingerly, she looked around and climbed in.

The room was quiet. Round windows looked out into a small central garden. Mulan could hear someone talking in the distance. Perhaps some pots banging in the kitchen? She pulled open the wardrobe door, wincing when it creaked. Long robes in varied colours hung next to each other alongside trousers and hats. It looked like the closet of a young man. The silk clothes were too nice for travel, but a linen robe might do. The trousers seemed long, but perhaps she could roll them up.

Bundling the clothes under her arm, she turned her attention to food. Should she risk a trip to the kitchen? No, kitchens were filled with servants, and she didn't want to press her luck. But there was a bowl of fruit on the table. Mulan grabbed three pears, hoping they wouldn't be missed, and then went on her way.

It was too risky to take the same path back, now that her arms were full of contraband. Mulan cut directly into the trees instead, tramping through the underbrush to get out of view. She went only a short distance before she could no longer resist biting into a pear. Sweet, heavenly juices flowed over her tongue. Mulan demolished that pear and a second, and though she wanted to continue to the third, she saved it for later. Mulan rubbed the juice from the corners of her mouth with the relatively clean skin on the top of her wrists. Then she did her best to wipe her sticky hands on some leaves. She continued walking, holding her new clothes gingerly until a trickling sound led her to a small spring.

The water, sparkling as it burbled over rocks and twigs, was the most beautiful thing Mulan had seen in days. It was all she could do not to drop everything and plunge her head below the surface, but caution won out. Carefully, Mulan laid her new clothes on a stone and submerged her hands. The water was icy, numbing her fingers immediately, but Mulan didn't care. She scrubbed her hands and nails vigorously, and then moved on to her face and neck. She cleaned the rest of herself as thoroughly as she dared without leaving herself too vulnerable, sighing with euphoria as the dirt melted off. Then she tore off the cleanest strip she could find from her old clothes and bound her chest. Her new clothes went on next, and then her sword belt. She finger-brushed her hair, tucked it under her new fu tou, and examined her reflection in the rippling stream.

Voices drifted through the trees. Mulan froze, and when it became clear that the voices were coming closer, she snatched up her belongings and ran behind a stand of trees.

"It's a good caravan," said a man in a low voice. "Four wagons. Looks like they have silks and spices."

"Any soldiers?" Another man, with a rougher voice.

"A few hired mercenaries. But they don't look like they're expecting an attack. We can take out four or five of them before they even know we're here."

Bandits. Mulan put a hand to her sword, though a moment later they passed the spot where she hid, their voices growing softer in the direction of the Imperial City. They were probably setting up an ambush further down the road. If she stayed in the forest a little longer before rejoining the thoroughfare, she could avoid them. They were more interested in plundering merchants than bothering a lone traveller.

But what about the caravan she'd heard them discussing? The bandits had been going towards the Imperial City. That meant their intended victims were coming toward them, about to head into a trap.

She made a quick decision and doubled back, away from

the ambush. After a while, Mulan ventured out of the foliage. This section of road was really just wagon ruts in the dirt, curving quite a bit around trees and boulders. The road was remote and isolated, the perfect place to surprise victims.

A quarter hour later, a wagon train came into view. There were four wagons carrying silks and spices, just as the bandit had said. The caravan was attended by men who were armed to varying degrees. Seasoned travellers, judging by the wear on both their clothing and their wagons. They didn't look to be expecting an attack.

Mulan did a quick check of her disguise. Robe buttoned up and crisp. Pants discreetly rolled at the ankles. Hair tucked tolerably neatly under her cap.

She bowed as she approached. "Good day to you."

A man with a sun-aged face and wide nose greeted her from the front of the caravan. "Hello, traveller. Is the wind at your back today?"

"Your caravan is in danger." Abrupt, perhaps, but Mulan couldn't think of a better way to lead into it. "There are bandits half a league down the road, planning an ambush."

The man's friendly expression morphed into a mixture of wariness and suspicion. "Bandits? How do you know?"

"I overheard them discussing their plans."

He scrutinised her, taking in her fine clothes and her sword. Mulan shifted, uncomfortably aware of how flimsy the piece of cloth was that bound her chest.

"You just happened to overhear them?" asked the man.

"You're free to believe me or not. It's not my skin that's at stake. But at the very least, be on your guard."

The leader exchanged a glance with two men behind him. After a moment, he turned back to Mulan. "Thank you," he said, in a voice that didn't sound grateful at all. "We'll be on our guard."

Mulan watched the wagons as they rolled past her, frustration warring with disbelief as they disappeared around a bend. The men did seem to be more alert now than before, but still, were they really going to enter headlong into an ambush? And what should she do now? Follow them on the road, or try to wait out the impending fight?

Morbid curiosity won out. She followed the merchants, sticking just close enough to catch an occasional glimpse of their wagons without appearing threatening. Ahead of the caravan, the road passed through a gap between two hills and disappeared into a sharp turn. Mulan's spine prickled. This was the perfect spot for an ambush.

She sped up, her stomach tightening. The caravan still moved forward, though they slowed and shifted their formation, drawing closer together and putting their packhorses between the wagons. The foremost riders reached the shadow of the first hill. All was quiet. Mulan slowed, her stomach knotted. Perhaps the bandits wouldn't attack.

Arrows rained down from the hills. The merchants

shouted, putting up shields and ducking behind wagons. Thuds sounded as sharp points embedded themselves in the wooden planks of the carts. Horses whinnied and danced. One arrow bounced off a horse's flank, and Mulan realised that its blanket was thicker than she'd thought.

There was a great cry. Bandits rushed in from between and around the hills as the caravanners raised their weapons to meet them. Mulan crept closer, her hand on her scabbard. She was within a stone's throw of the battle now, yet no one paid attention to her. Now that she was closer, she could see that the merchants were quite skilled with their weapons. They held their own, and the leader's horse was trained to kick at enemies. A few bandits lay dead, while others had fled. The caravan might well make it out of this, but the fight was far from over.

Mulan's muscles tensed, ready to carry her towards or away from the battle, though she didn't know which way. She needed to get back to the Imperial City. If she died out here, no one would ever know what happened to her. Her ministers would have free run of the palace.

She rushed into the fray.

The first bandit she came across didn't even see her. Mulan cut him down from behind. She locked eyes briefly with the surprised merchant who'd been battling him, and then she ran off to find another fight.

Now that Mulan was in the thick of battle, she no longer

had the element of surprise. She set her sights on another brigand, a grizzled man who swung his sword like a mace. As she neared, one of the caravanners stepped in her path, sword raised to attack, and she realised he had no way of knowing that she wasn't an outlaw.

"Stop! I'm a friend!" she cried, parrying desperately.

It was enough to get the merchant to hesitate, and Mulan took that moment to charge someone else who'd cornered a caravanner against a wagon. The masked man turned to meet her attack. He was fierce, but no match in skill to Mulan's usual sparring partners. She cut him down, then realised it was quiet.

All the attackers lay on the ground, dead. Horses pawed at the ground, restless and jumpy. The merchants leaned against their wagons or slumped over their knees, breathing heavily.

"Who's hurt?" asked the man with the weather-worn face.

"Over here, Guozhi," called a man. He was bent over another merchant, bandaging his side.

Guozhi strode over for a closer look. "Deep?" he asked.

"He'll need to ride in the wagon."

These merchants seemed far calmer after combat than Mulan would have expected.

The leader turned to her. "Your help is appreciated, stranger."

The contrast between the man's suspicion earlier and his

gratitude now snapped Mulan's patience. "You wouldn't have needed my help if you'd heeded my warning."

Guozhi didn't reflect Mulan's anger back at her. "I see we've offended you, young master. You were under no obligation to come to our aid."

"Heaven knows why I did it," said Mulan. Part of her suspected that her anger was simply the aftermath of battle, the residual heat after fending off a mortal threat, but knowing this did not make Mulan feel it any less. There was something too about her disguise, being anonymous after weeks of court scrutiny, that loosened her tongue. "It's pure folly to walk right into an ambush. I should have left you all to your fate."

Once again, her barbs didn't faze the caravan leader. "You're insulted because you think we didn't listen to you. But you're mistaken there. We took precautions. We're not as helpless as you might think."

Mulan took a closer look at the men around him. Their skin was sun darkened and bore scars, their sword arms and wrists well muscled. As Mulan watched, one of the men took out a cloth and casually wiped off his bloodstained blade.

"You're soldiers, not merchants," she said. But she could have sworn those wagons were trade wagons.

"Nowadays we trade. I grew tired of the soldier's life, but we don't fear the dangerous roads. This isn't our first ambush, and it won't be our last. If we turned around at every warning of attack, we'd be much poorer men." Guozhi scrutinised her. "Now, stranger, you know our story. What is yours? Why does a young man such as yourself travel these roads with no companions?"

Mulan wished she could check if her overly long pant legs had rolled loose. "My name is Ping," she said carefully. "I've run across some troubles of my own."

"Troubles you'd rather not talk about."

Mulan didn't respond.

He looked around. "You have no luggage?"

"No," she said. His questions were making her nervous. "I'll be on my way now." She turned to leave.

"Wait," said Guozhi.

Mulan stopped, though she didn't relax.

Guozhi walked around to face her again, giving her a long, measuring look. "I don't know your story, but you waded into a fight that wasn't your own, at risk to yourself. I'm not one to take debts lightly. Our caravan is headed towards the Imperial City. If you wish, you're welcome to travel with us for as long as our paths converge. The roads are safer in these parts with company."

It was a tempting offer. After this skirmish, Mulan had no doubts that the roads were dangerous. Plus, her ministers would have a much harder time tracking her down if she travelled with a group. But could she manage this disguise all the way to the Imperial City? "I don't want to bring my trouble upon you," she said.

"Have you broken the emperor's law?"

"No," she said emphatically.

"If you're loyal to the emperor – or empress, I should say – then we don't fear any trouble that might come for you. It's up to you, Ping, what you choose, but our caravan is open to you. Will you join us?"

•••

The merchants were pleasant travel companions. They didn't have an extra horse to ride, but one of their party found a mare that had been abandoned by the bandits. The horse took to Mulan quickly, following her movements with curious brown eyes and accepting her offered treats with dignity. Guozhi was a strong and efficient leader, running the caravan much like a military unit. When he rode alongside Mulan, he told her stories about his time in the army. She learned that he'd fought in some of the same battles as her father.

After living openly as a woman for so long, Mulan needed some time to remember how to travel as a man, to speak with a lower voice and be mindful of when and where she undressed. Once again, she learned to spread herself when she sat and to belch without hesitation. She spoke loudly and shouted above others when she needed to. It was freeing, after her long stay at court. At night, the caravan camped outside rather than spend money on inns. Mulan was self-conscious every night getting into her bedroll, but no one seemed to suspect she was anyone but whom she claimed to be.

On the third day, they passed by their first walled city, and Guozhi asked for volunteers to go in for supplies.

"I'll go," said Mulan. She hadn't heard any news from the Imperial City since the coup, and she was eager to learn more. Two others also volunteered: a skinny man called Little Fan and a man Mulan only knew as Chef. They took one horse to carry their goods.

This town was not as large as the Imperial City but still sported walls and a bustling marketplace. Walking into a crowd put Mulan on edge, but after a while, she realised that no one gave her a second glance. She was one face among hundreds, and she began to relax.

Chef took charge, leading them through the stalls, charging past piles of fruits and vegetables, cages of chickens, and tubs of swimming fish. Little Fan needled Chef to buy dried mutton as Chef weighed his coin purse in his hands, accusing Fan of wanting to bankrupt them all. Mulan didn't voice an opinion, though she looked longingly at the greens.

Chef caught her looking. "Those will wilt on the road," he said. But he passed some coins to a farmer for a bag of persimmons.

In addition to the persimmons, Chef picked a bag of mung beans, several sacks of rice and some flour. Sensible fare for the road. After they loaded their horse, they turned back towards the city gate, but the streets had become much more crowded since they came in, especially near the city square. People crowded shoulder to shoulder in the dirt courtyard, and Mulan could hear someone speaking over the crowd.

"Is someone calling out news?" she asked.

They made their way closer and squeezed into the back of the crowd. Mulan wrinkled her nose at the smell of concentrated humanity and stood on her toes to see. A man in imperial uniform stood on a podium – really just a sawed-off log – in the middle of the square.

"… taken time to retire to the countryside, to rest from the strain of leading the country," he was saying. "The ministers will attend to the business of government while she is gone…"

Mulan's jaw went slack. She nudged a man next to her. "Who's he talking about?" Her voice came out higher than it should have, and she coughed to disguise it.

The man barely glanced at her. "Empress has taken ill."

Taken ill. Mulan balled her hands into fists. The empress was perfectly fine. The only threat to her health came from her own cabinet.

"When will she return?" shouted a man from the crowd.

"She will return when the royal doctor has deemed her adequately recovered," answered the herald. He must have said all he meant to say, because he stepped down and the crowd began to dissipate. Around her, Mulan overheard snippets of conversation.

"Offer up prayers for her health…"

"Strange for the empress to leave with no warning…"

"… women have weaker constitutions…"

Mulan realised she was trembling. There were probably heralds like this crisscrossing the entire country. Soon all of China would think she'd abandoned her office because of a weak constitution.

"Ping!"

Mulan wasn't sure how long Chef had been calling her name. "Sorry, what?"

"You planning to return to our caravan, or were you just thinking you'd stand there forever?"

"Sorry," she mumbled.

The square cleared out after the announcement. Mulan, Chef and Little Fan followed a stream of people through the gate.

"So much for trying to catch a glimpse of the empress at the Imperial City," said Little Fan, tossing the bag of persimmons over his shoulder.

Chef grunted. "Royals. Unpredictable lot."

"I thought she was all right. My two nieces loved her, but that was before she retreated to the far countryside. I don't know, maybe she wasn't suited to the stresses of running a country. It does seem pretty different from fighting a war." Fan turned to Mulan, who shrank back in anticipation of his question. "What do you think of the new empress?"

She attempted a nonchalant shrug. "I don't pay attention to these things."

"Oh, come on. The first female empress in history is hardly everyday politics. You must have some thoughts about her qualifications."

"There's more to ruling than ability," said Mulan, unable to fully disguise the bitterness in her voice. "The most competent man in the world will drive a country to ruin if he wields his power for his own gain. A ruler needs to be honest and honourable, to rule with the good of the country in mind."

Chef patted Mulan's shoulder with a meaty palm. "Look at that, our Ping is a philosopher. So do you think our empress has these elusive qualities?"

"Yes," said Mulan after a pause. "Yes, I do."

A cloud hung over Mulan for the rest of the evening, as anger and guilt warred in her head. Her entire country thought she'd abandoned her people and run off to the countryside. She urgently needed to make things right, yet here she was wearing men's clothing in the middle of nowhere.

Her companions noticed her mood. At one point, Guozhi remarked good-naturedly, "If this is how cities affect you, then I'll be keeping you by the caravan for the rest of the trip."

Mulan grumbled an apology and retreated to be by herself. At least she could take solace in the fact that they were making good time towards the Imperial City. She guessed they'd be there in a week if nothing delayed them. Mulan wasn't sure what she would do once she got there, but she hoped she could find Shang or Liwen. She sent up a prayer to her ancestors that they were safe.

The next morning, Mulan was packing up her bedroll when someone shouted that an armed rider was approaching. The ambush was still fresh on everybody's mind, and there was much shuffling as people scrambled for weapons. Mulan grabbed her sword from where it lay on the ground and hurried towards the road to get a better look.

"Good day, travellers," a male voice called out.

Mulan's bones went soft. Though she couldn't see the speaker, she would recognise that voice from the bottom of the ocean.

"Good day yourself," came Guozhi's voice. "Does fortune smile on your travels?"

Mulan regained her footing and moved quicker, nearly tripping in her haste to see the visitor. Could it really be? She circled around a wagon to get an unimpeded view. And then she stopped again, unable to move, because she'd been right. Sitting astride a horse, talking to Guozhi, was Li Shang.

CHAPTER FOURTEEN

The sight of him hit her with almost physical force. It was definitely Shang – the wide shoulders, the stubborn jaw, the strength and confidence in the way he sat astride his horse. He wasn't wearing imperial livery, though. Instead, he was wearing the plain, functional armour of a private guard, the kind hired by rich families to protect their homes.

"Have you seen a young woman travelling alone in these parts?" asked Shang.

Mulan felt strangely bodiless, as if she were floating in the space above her head. The initial shock was wearing off, but her relief was tempered by a nagging sense that something was wrong. Why was Shang in disguise? He didn't seem to have spotted her yet. Every last bit of her wanted to call out to him, but it felt dangerous to give him away.

"No," said Guozhi. "The road has been quite empty."

Shang nodded in a way that suggested he'd been getting

the same answer over and over.

"My name is Li. I'm a private guard for House Fong. We've had a maid run off with my mistress's jewellery. She's a young woman, unmarried. Quite pretty…"

His gaze landed on Mulan, sending a jolt through her, and his eyes widened a brief moment before moving on. "My mistress is eager to get the jewellery back before it's sold," he said, continuing with only a slight hitch. "It's valuable to the family."

Guozhi shook his head. "We haven't seen anyone fitting that description."

Shang looked up at the sun. "Yes, unfortunately I'm thinking this might be a lost cause. Are you travelling west?"

Mulan realised her mouth was open and snapped it shut. So he'd been looking for her. And he was probably doing so without her ministers' knowledge. She wished she knew what was happening at the Imperial City.

"Yes, we're travelling towards the Imperial City," said Guozhi.

Shang nodded. "Tonight I'm staying at the Inn of Three Fountains at Wen village, thirty li up the road." He made eye contact with Mulan again as he named the inn, and she gazed back with a hundred questions that went unanswered. "If you hear of anything at all, please leave a message for me there. My master is a generous man and will reward any help you provide."

"We will keep an eye open," said Guozhi.

Shang bowed. "Thank you. May the wind be at your backs."

And then he rode off.

...

Mulan tore her gaze away from Shang's disappearing form. Then she rushed back to her bedroll, avoiding everyone's eyes and hoping no one had noticed her reaction to seeing him. Her hands shook so much that it took her two tries to tie her bedroll tight enough to load onto her horse. Shang was alive. That in itself sent waves of relief through her limbs. Was he still in danger? What had transpired since the coup? The important thing was that he was here, and that he'd seen her.

And he'd told her where he would be tonight.

Mulan's horse pranced when she mounted, sensing her nerves. She shushed the creature, knowing that she couldn't risk giving herself away just yet. If Shang was hiding his identity, he must have a reason to do so.

It turned out that Shang's calculations were good. By the end of the day, the caravan had travelled just beyond Wen village. Mulan did her best not to fidget or pace as the group set up camp for the night. Chef served up a delicious meal of yams and rice that stuck in Mulan's throat.

After dinner, Mulan rolled out her blankets at the edge of camp. She lay down as usual and closed her eyes, pinching her forearm to the rhythm of her favourite marching song so she wouldn't drift off to sleep. Gradually, the breathing of the men around her evened out.

Mulan opened her eyes. Though the fire had gone out, the sliver of moon in the sky was bright enough for her to see clearly. All around her, the only movement was the steady rise and fall of blankets on all sides. She sat up carefully, stopping at every shift or sleepy snort that punctuated the night. Through the trees, she could make out Little Fan standing guard. His attention was directed away from the camp, towards the mysteries of the forest. Mulan made her way quickly in the other direction, weaving around sleeping bodies and ducking behind a tree when she finally made it past the edge of camp. Sneaking back in would be harder, but she'd worry about that later. She continued until she was sure she was outside of Fan's guard route, and then she stopped to get her bearings.

The moon cast confusing shadows. The road was a stone's throw away through the trees, but it didn't seem wise to travel openly. It would take longer to pick her way through the forest, but if Mulan hurried, she might be able to get there and back before the night was half-over.

A twig snapped behind her. Mulan jumped, her hand going for her sword. She caught sight of Shang at the exact moment he said, "It's me."

Mulan ran at him, not bothering to slow as she neared.

They collided hard enough for her to knock him back a half step. The impact jarred through her, the wooden scales of his armour leaving imprints in her skin. He probably couldn't even feel her through the layers of gear, but still, she clung to him desperately.

Shang wrapped his arms around her and squeezed her tight. Mulan tucked her head under his chin and blinked back tears. He smelled of spice and armour oil. She breathed in deep.

"I knew the ministers were lying." Shang's words vibrated through his chest and against her cheek. "You wouldn't have left like that."

Mulan backed away to look at him, wondering at how the moonlight illuminated angles of his face she'd never noticed before. "How did you find me? What happened?"

She sensed a sudden tension from him and waited as he took a breath to dispel it. "The morning after you left, the ministers told me you'd gone off. They fed me the same story about needing to rest in some far-off palace. It was ridiculous. They knew it, and I knew it, but they stuck to the story. I went looking for Liwen, but I couldn't find her either."

Mulan's heart dropped. "Liwen…"

"She's safe," he assured her. His voice was deep and resonant against the forest's night-time thrum. "At least, she was when I last saw her. They had her locked up in a holding cell."

Mulan clenched her fists. "They must have seen her following the astrologer home."

"I was lucky to find her there when there were no officials about. I pulled rank to get her released, and she told me everything." Shang gave a mirthless laugh. "When we tracked down the minister of rites again, we were greeted by assassins. Liwen is good with a sword. I'm glad I had her with me."

"She's deadly," said Mulan, wishing she could have seen that fight. And then she realised the full meaning of Shang's words. "Assassins?"

"Four of them. Dropped right down from the ceiling. Liwen and I fought them off and fled the palace; then we split up to find you. Some people around the city said they'd seen a prisoner's wagon being sent in this direction. I followed, and a few days later, there were rumours of imperial soldiers needing to be rescued from a locked carriage." Even in the darkness, she could sense him raise an eyebrow in amused admiration. "Your work?"

His comment awoke a bit of pride. "They were scared to lay hands on me, which made them slow. Gave me room to attack."

"It's always dangerous to underestimate you," Shang said.

She smiled genuinely for the first time in weeks. That plan, at least, had gone well. But she was still a fugitive, and now she knew that her strongest allies at the palace had been forced out.

"Have my ministers taken control of the army?" she asked.

Shang was silent for a moment. "I don't think so. I made contact with Commanders Fan and Hong of the palace garrisons before I left. They are loyal to you. Some of the other commanders might have been turned—"

"Some soldiers, too," said Mulan, thinking of the ones who had captured her.

Shang nodded. "Some soldiers, too, but I have to believe that I still command the majority of my troops. That's probably why the other ministers wanted to kill me."

Mulan believed him. No one who'd served under Shang would doubt his ability to command loyalty. He had a presence about him, projecting confidence while conveying that he truly valued the soldiers under him. Still, all that loyalty would do little good if he couldn't even get close to his troops.

"What now?" she asked, half to herself.

"We take your country back."

Mulan stifled a bitter laugh. "What shall I do? Assemble a new army and march in at the head of it? What kind of empress am I, if I can't even control my ministers?"

"Do you think they could run the country better than you?"

Shang's tone stopped her. He wasn't delivering a pep talk. He was serious.

Mulan thought of her ministers, of the bribes they'd accepted for power, of the tricks they'd pulled behind their back. If there was one thing that she learned these past weeks, it was the crucial truth that there was more to leadership than knowledge.

"No. I'm a better ruler." And for the first time, she truly believed it. "They want power to suit themselves. They'll sell out the country if need be. Indeed, they already have. I may not have their lifetime of experience, but I have the people's best interests at heart. I'm willing to listen, and learn, and admit what I don't know."

Shang nodded. "You are the appointed heir and the rightful empress. And you're more capable than you think. They tried to get you out of the way, but they failed. Remember that."

She wanted to believe him. She had to believe him.

"We need a plan," she said, racking her brain. What could the two of them do out here against five ministers entrenched in the capital? "No matter what we do next, I'll need the support of the military. Are there other commanders you can contact? Troops within riding distance?"

Shang nodded. "There are several within three days' ride."

"Go find them," Mulan said. "Determine where they stand. Make sure they're still loyal to you and to me." She paused, the image of Shang captured by his own soldiers flashing through her mind. "Be careful."

"I will," said Shang. "Will you come with me?"

It was tempting, the thought of riding with Shang again.

"No," she said. "If they turn on you, it's better that we're not both there to be captured. You said there were commanders in the Imperial City who are loyal to me, is that right?"

"Yes, I trust Fan and Hong with my life."

She took that in, continuing to think out loud. "I'll travel with the caravan back to the Imperial City and find those two. I need to get a better idea of what's happening inside the palace. Once I do, we can decide our next step."

It wasn't a watertight plan, but it was the best she could do right now.

"Once you get back into the capital, contact Master Tsai at the Three Bamboos Teahouse," said Shang. "He's a longtime friend, and he can lead you to Fan and Hong."

They fell silent then. The plan was set. The next step was to carry it out. They had no more reason to stay together, though Mulan found herself searching for one.

After a long moment, Shang exhaled. As the space between them threatened to expand, Mulan fought the urge to reach out and grab hold of him.

"Shang, thank you. For everything."

He took her hand. Though she couldn't see him in the darkness, she sensed the intensity of his gaze, felt his energy through his fingers.

"Take care of yourself, Empress." The emotion in his voice

belied the formality of the title. "I don't know what I would do, if..." He paused, and his grip tightened.

Something knocked loose in Mulan's chest. And at that moment, she was finally sure of one thing.

Reaching up, she pulled Shang to her. It wasn't a gentle coaxing. She pulled from her core, as he'd taught her to do in their fighting lessons, leaving him no question as to what she wanted. She caught him off guard, and he fell forward, taking a half step to catch himself. She felt him exhale as his mouth fell open in surprise. Before he could speak, she met his lips with hers.

His response was instantaneous, scooping her to him with one arm and pulling her towards him. She moulded herself to his chest, sighing as she felt his hands go to her shoulders, then to her back. When he found the curve of her hip beneath her boyish clothes, Mulan discovered that she was the one who couldn't keep her balance. She clung to him, lost in the touch of his lips on hers. Slowly, he bore her backwards. Mulan was vaguely aware that there was a tree behind her and she was leaning against it, but it was a fleeting awareness that disappeared as he trailed kisses down the side of her face and her neck. She wished she could remember how to breathe.

Shang stilled. Mulan drew in a deep breath, feeling as if she were breaking through the surface of a lake. He leaned a hand against the tree and pulled back, ever so slowly, to look at her. The moonlight caught one side of his face. He had the look of a man beholding an oasis in the desert, overcome by its beauty, yet terrified it would disappear.

"I've thought about doing this for so long," he whispered, his voice catching. And he leaned down to kiss her again. This time it was a gentle brush against her lips, one that sent shivers across her skin even as a new ache uncurled in her core.

Footsteps shuffled to their left. "Who's there?" called a man.

At first, the voice didn't register, but when it did, it snapped Mulan back to reality. Shang jumped away, reaching for his sword as he scanned the darkness around them.

Guozhi. Mulan was almost certain it was the caravan leader who'd called from the trees. After a frantic look at Shang, Mulan took stock of her own appearance. She was flushed and out of breath. How much of that was obvious in the darkness? She smoothed down her clothes, hoping everything was in place. Her lips felt warm and pleasantly numb.

Shang stood coiled, ready to flee or fight.

She reached for his shoulder. *From my caravan,* Mulan mouthed.

Their eyes met, and a silent communication passed between them. Shang backed away, first one step then another. Mulan fought the pull of his leaving, willed her feet to stay still. He caught her eye one last time, and then he disappeared into the trees.

It felt as if a piece of herself had peeled away. Mulan yearned after him, her feet ready to carry her into the trees. Maybe she was wrong to send him off alone. Maybe she would never see him again.

"Anyone there?" Guozhi called again.

Mulan clamped ruthlessly down on her rapidly multiplying doubts. Now was not the time to fall apart. How much had Guozhi seen?

"It's Ping," she called as Guozhi stepped out. She should have deepened her voice more.

The caravan leader wore none of his daytime armour. It looked like he had simply thrown his cloak on over the tunic he slept in, though he held his sword unsheathed. He approached cautiously, scanning the shadows.

"Ping, is it just you? I thought I heard someone else."

"I was talking to myself," Mulan said.

Guozhi stepped into a patch of moonlight. He scrutinised Mulan's face, and she wondered how much he could see.

"I've been a caravanner for a long time, Ping," he said. "I deal with a good number of people, both in my caravan and in my business dealings. I've learned to trust my own eyes and ears. There was someone else here, and that had been more than a conversation."

Mulan scrambled for words as her mind whirled. Did he know she was a woman? Did he know she was empress? Would he be loyal, knowing her deception, or would he turn against her?

"I've been a caravanner for a long time," Guozhi said again. "And I get a sense now of what I need to know, and what I can let go. A history, a secret, a cut sleeve… none of that matters to me except as it affects my men. I know you recognised that private guard the moment you saw him. And I know he was just here. Our caravan owes you a blood debt. We've offered you our protection, and we've allowed you to keep your secrets. That hasn't changed, but I need to know if your friend places us in any greater danger."

He'd given a subtle emphasis to "friend," in a way as to suggest he hadn't really meant that word at all. Slowly, his phrases reassembled themselves in her mind. *A secret, a cut sleeve…* the latter was a reference to an old story, an emperor who'd been so loath to disturb his sleeping companion that he'd cut the sleeve off his robe rather than wake the young man. Guozhi had seen what happened with Shang, but he thought Mulan was a man who loved other men. Or at least, he was giving her permission to claim to be one.

Tentatively, Mulan tested out her voice. "You're right. The guard and I have a long history together, but he is no danger to us. If anything, he would help us in times of trouble. But… I don't expect him to come back for a while."

Guozhi scrutinised her still, until Mulan worried her disguise would simply disintegrate under his gaze. Finally, he spoke again. "You'd better get some sleep. We have an early morning tomorrow."

...

The next day, Guozhi treated Mulan as if nothing had happened. The caravan packed up without much ado and set off on the road again. Mulan rode in silence, light-headed from sleep deprivation and doing her best not to attract attention to herself. About halfway through the morning, they came across another walled city. Mulan once again volunteered to go into town with Chef, and she ignored Guozhi's knowing glance when he gave her permission.

The road leading in from the gate was backed up, so crowded that Mulan couldn't lift her arm without hitting someone. She was too short to get a good view of the city square, but Chef craned his neck and peered above the crowd.

"A crier from the Imperial City," said Chef. And now Mulan could hear the exaggerated intonations of his announcement. "It's no use trying to get past the crowd to the market. We might as well stay and hear the latest news."

As they moved closer, the energy of the crowd rubbed off on Mulan, and not in a good way. Voices around them had the sharp pitch of worry. Mulan caught glimpses of eyes opened wider, brows creased, mothers clutching their children. She smelled sweat and fear.

"Something's happened," she said.

They pushed forward now. Mulan spotted a crier installed

on a block in the middle of the square. People crowded around him, shouting questions that Mulan could not yet separate from the roar of everything else.

Mulan leaned close to an old woman next to her. "What is happening?"

The woman looked at her, annoyed. "There's been fighting. Hush, I'm trying to listen."

"Fighting? What do you mean?" But the woman had managed to thread her way deeper into the crowd. Mulan moved to follow, but she felt a hand on her shoulder.

"Ping, stop," said Chef. "I heard the news. A northern outpost has fallen to the Huns."

CHAPTER FIFTEEN

Ice crystallised on Mulan's skin, packed around her heart.

"I want to get closer," she said.

They jostled their way towards the increasingly nervous crier, who was now shrinking away from the people around him. Indeed, it looked as if the crowd might crush him before the Huns got a chance. He answered questions in clipped, loud phrases, his eyes scanning for an escape route.

Mulan picked up the rest in bits and pieces. The attack happened a day ago, a surprise invasion that had taken the Chinese troops unawares and driven them from the region. The Huns now controlled the steppes just south of the border and were likely to continue towards the Imperial City. Able-bodied men should prepare to enlist.

"Prepare? Where do we go?" asked one man.

"More word will be sent," said the herald.

Chef gave a disgusted grunt. "Come, we'll learn no more here."

Though it killed Mulan to walk away after hearing so little, she knew Chef was right. There was too much chaos here to learn much more.

Mulan's thoughts swirled as she and Chef fought their way towards the markets. The herald was giving the official version of events, but there was far more going on. Mulan was familiar with the northern outpost that had been overtaken. It was at a strong strategic location, built on high ground with heavy fortifications. If the Huns had taken it over so easily, that meant the army failed to mobilise as it should have. The crier's command to wait for instructions about enlisting also hinted at disorganisation within the ranks. Things were falling apart in the Imperial City.

But why were the Huns attacking at all? Just a short while ago, they'd been pushing for a marriage alliance. Mulan was fairly certain that one reason her ministers hadn't killed her was so they had the marriage to dangle in front of the Huns. But perhaps the alliance was slipping out of the ministers' control, too. Perhaps the Huns sensed the growing chaos in the capital and decided they could take the country without the trouble of diplomacy.

The crowd finally thinned enough so Mulan and Chef could move freely. Chef took the lead, and Mulan followed, lost in her dark thoughts. She watched passively as he haggled with the vendors. Chef grew gruffer with every purchase, and though Mulan was distracted, she noticed more coin leaving his purse than last time.

"No persimmons today," grumbled Chef. "Everyone's raising their prices in case of war."

War. But they'd just come out of the last one, and they'd lost so much. The thought caught like a bramble in Mulan's chest. How many soldiers had been killed on the border? And what were her ministers doing to defend the country? All signs suggested that they were failing in their duties, and China was about to pay the price. Her country was hurtling towards war. Mulan needed to do something, yet she was deposed, anonymous. Powerless.

"How many days are we from the Imperial City?" she asked Chef.

"Five days," he said. "Maybe more if talk of war clogs up the roads."

Five days to get back. Once there, she'd have to find Shang's loyal commanders. That could take half a day if not more. And then, if they were still loyal, they'd have to find a way to muster the troops...

It could be weeks before she could march troops to the border. And she hadn't even considered what her ministers might do to thwart her. An invading army could do a lot of damage in that time.

"Something on your mind, Ping?" asked Chef, strapping a

bag of rice to their horse with more vigour than was strictly necessary. The animal snorted in disapproval.

"Just the fate of the country," she said.

"We fought off the Huns once." Chef sounded as if he spoke out of routine, rather than true confidence.

"Things feel different this time."

Part of her wanted Chef to argue, but he merely grunted. "This'll test the empress," he said.

●●●

Mulan was back at her ancestral temple. She knew she was dreaming, and she resented the knowing. Here she was, at the place she always retreated to for comfort, and she couldn't even escape the knowledge that it wasn't real.

The air had a grey cast to it. The spirit tablets dedicated to her ancestors stood undisturbed, with the lightest sprinkling of dust on top. A single stick of incense burned on the altar, its orange tip the brightest point in the room. A thin thread of fragrance tickled her nose.

Just as Mulan had decided she was alone, a movement outside the door caught her eye. A wisp of grey hair, the fluttering of robes. Mulan hurried out into the garden. There was Grandmother, bending down to smell a chrysanthemum.

Though Mulan's feet made no noise in this dreamworld, Grandmother looked up.

"My granddaughter!" she said cheerfully. "I thought your

cross-dressing days were behind you."

Mulan looked down and realised she was still in Ping's clothes.

"Come," said Grandmother. "Give me a hug."

Nai Nai's embrace was surprisingly strong. Her hair smelled of flowers.

Finally, Grandmother pulled away. "You look down," she said.

"China's falling apart." Mulan felt like she was constantly repeating this refrain. "I've left the country in bad hands, and I fear what might happen next."

Grandmother took out a knife and trimmed off a wilted flower. "Well then, get up and fix it. My granddaughter is more than capable."

"I wish I had as much confidence."

Nai Nai tossed the flower into a nearby pond, clapping delightedly at the multicoloured koi that scattered beneath the surface. "You're capable. I know this, your father and mother know this, and I daresay many others do as well. But you're right that this is a daunting task. Perhaps you might feel better with some guidance."

Mulan waited for Grandmother to deliver advice, but instead Grandmother moved past her towards something she couldn't see. Mulan turned, and a chill ran across the back of her neck. It was a strange landscape she was in. A quick check over her shoulder showed that she still stood in front of her ancestral temple, next to flowers, groomed paths and a pond. But just a stone's throw away, the garden met a curtain of mist. Behind it, Mulan recognised the woods where Guozhi's caravan currently camped. She wondered if she would find her own sleeping body if she looked hard enough.

"Don't look for yourself," said Grandmother. "That's too disorienting. Look at what's right at the border."

Feeling like she'd been caught in an act of narcissism, Mulan directed her gaze towards the mist. The air shimmered at the interface, especially where it touched a thick tangle of branches. Something large and round lay on the ground directly below it.

"What's that?" Mulan asked.

"Whatever it is," said Grandmother, "it looks interesting."

• • •

Mulan opened her eyes. Tree branches scratched the sky overhead, layered like the overlapping snores of her caravan mates. The transition from sleep to wakefulness had been quick and disorienting, as if she'd blinked and been suddenly transported from one place to another. There was no grogginess, no residue of sleep in her mind. She felt preternaturally calm, and though everything around her was crisp and clear, Mulan somehow knew that the world was vivid only for her. If she got out of her bedroll and left the camp, no one would stir.

She let her bedroll fall away. Guozhi slept on his side a few paces to her left, his sword within arm's reach. Chef snored loudly next to him. Mulan turned in a slow circle, scanning the branches around her and comparing them with the image from her dream. She saw where the branches crisscrossed in patterns like crooked fingers, and she lowered her gaze to the ground below. There, something round and pale shone in the moonlight.

The camp sentry walked a circle around the sleepers, passing right by the object on the ground. Mulan couldn't tell what the thing was. It wasn't quite white, but it was lighter than the ground around it, and smooth. A very large rock perhaps? Mulan waited until the sentry passed, and then she headed towards it, taking care not to kick any sleeping bodies. Her feet made no sound.

Now that she was closer, Mulan could see that the object was as wide as a small saddle. She bent down. It was smooth to the touch, like bone. Mulan brushed some dirt off the top and felt ridges. A tortoise shell, left by a very large tortoise indeed. But the creature who had used it was long gone. This shell was desiccated and light.

It was perfect.

She picked it up, surprised at how little weight it had, and walked with it deeper into the forest. The choice of place seemed an important one, though she couldn't put into words what she was looking for. She needed a patch of dirt without much underbrush. She wanted it to be private yet not too far. Special but not frightening. She was looking for a feeling, the same one she'd felt when she embraced her grandmother.

Finally, she stopped at a small clearing. Three trees

stretched out overhead, bending their branches together like old women over a batch of dumplings. Here.

Mulan laid the shell down as she cleared the ground for a fire. There were plenty of fallen branches and twigs for fuel. She piled some up, stepped back to look at it and then piled it twice as high. Some dried grass served as kindling. The first spark from her flint caught and flared. Flames grew and licked at the fuel she'd gathered.

As the fire burned, she turned her attention to the tortoise shell. The rounded carapace had a breathtaking pattern like a marbled chessboard, but it was the flat plastron, the part that covered the turtle's belly, that she needed. Mulan pulled at it, unsure of how to separate the two halves. The shell came apart in her hands.

She had no brush. She had no ink, for that matter, but she did have her dagger.

A quick intake of breath. A light slash across her palm. The blood welled up quickly, almost eagerly. Mulan touched her finger to one droplet, watched it change shape and cling to her fingertip. She wrote in shaky, clumsy script: *How do I save China?*

The first words were almost dry by the time she wrote her last. Mulan blew on the shell until her words darkened to dull rust. The fire was crackling now, tall white flames reaching towards the sky. It was far more robust, far hotter, than it should have been, the breath of a dragon, the surface of the sun. Heat from the flames pressed at Mulan's face as she brought the shell towards it. She edged closer until she thought her skin might blister and peel, and yet she continued, gritting her teeth against the searing heat. She was far beyond the laws of nature now, too far gone to fret over the limitations of flesh and blood. Only when she knew beyond doubt that her next step would turn her to soot did she stop and throw the shell in.

It exploded into a cloud of smoke and ash.

CHAPTER SIXTEEN

Mulan gagged and choked. She clutched at her mouth, but hot air and dust passed through her fingers as if they hadn't been there at all. How could one shell possibly create so much ash? It swirled around her, burning her skin, working itself under her eyelids, pushing and pawing at her until she fell to the ground.

And then there was sudden, absolute silence.

Nothing moved, and neither did Mulan. She lay there, dreading how her raw skin would hurt when she moved, wondering if the absence of pain was real or just a moment of peace before it all set in again.

Gradually, she became aware of cool air rushing into her lungs. A gentle breeze brushed her skin. Her eyes opened of their own accord, and she found that they were moist and whole. Mulan blinked and staggered to her feet. Her skin shone smooth and untouched in the moonlight. Her legs, though they remembered the pain of moments before, held her weight.

A cricket chirped, and a chorus of cicadas joined in. Mulan looked again at the forest around her. There, standing below the largest tree in sight, was her grandmother.

"Nai Nai!"

She'd just seen her grandmother in her dream, but this was different. Mulan knew, with a certainty as sure as the forest roots, that she wasn't dreaming this time. She was awake, and her grandmother had returned to the world.

Nai Nai was solid when Mulan threw her arms around her, though perhaps a little *less* solid in a way that Mulan couldn't explain. Was she a trifle lighter? Softer at the edges? But it was unmistakably her.

Grandmother rubbed Mulan's back. She was so short that her hand landed at the bottom of Mulan's shoulder blades. "My girl. My strong, brilliant girl."

Were they going to have this conversation again? Mulan opened her mouth to reply, but then she saw other women fanned out behind Grandmother. There were more than a dozen of them – some young, some old, and though they looked as solid as Nai Nai, there was something distinctly otherworldly about them, the slightest strangeness in how their bodies caught the light, a sense of unfathomable depth to their eyes. They were all looking at her.

A chill went down Mulan's spine, and yet... as they smiled at her, aspects of the women began to look familiar. The firm set of one's mouth. How another stood with one hand on her hip, so much like Mama. The way one woman's hairline curved into an exceptionally pronounced widow's peak, just like Baba's.

These were her ancestors.

As Mulan's knees went soft, an elderly lady smiled, her dimples eclipsing her heavy wrinkles. "You've done well, daughter."

"That's my grandmother Fa Lin," said Grandmother, leaning in towards Mulan. "Your great-great-grandmother. She came to our village from the south."

"A long journey," said Fa Lin. "We walked for a month to escape famine."

Mulan clutched at Grandmother's not-quite-solid shoulder as the crowd of women gathered around her, fussing and clucking among themselves.

"She has your nose, Fa Lin," said the one who'd stood with her hand on her hip. "And such strong hands. The hands of a warrior."

"And what would you know about being a warrior, Meixiang?" teased the woman with a widow's peak.

"I know plenty about being a warrior and a leader," said Meixiang. "I raised nineteen children, and I once hit a robber over the head with a cooking pot."

Another woman reached out and fingered Mulan's robe with slender hands like Baba's. "This needs washing, doesn't it?"

"You're not at your silk farm any more, Xing," piped up another voice. "She has no time to wash up. She's trying to save China."

Sashes and gowns swished around her, creating less of a breeze than they should have. Giggles and murmurs. Touches on her arms, shoulders and back, as if her ancestors wanted to convince themselves that she was real. It was starting to overwhelm her.

"I don't understand," Mulan said, craning her neck to see who'd just straightened the back hem of her robe. "Why are you all here?"

"We're here because you need help," said Nai Nai. "Your enemies work against you. You're in need of counsel."

Mulan thought of the oracle bones and the dreams, the voices in the wagon. "You've all been helping me."

"As any good ancestors should. But we shouldn't hog all the credit. We – your loving family – were summoned to help you, but there have been others, too."

"Others?"

"You've met one of them already," said Grandmother.

Plants rustled behind Mulan. Footfalls sounded, carrying a solidity that the other feet in the clearing didn't share. That bit of reality amid this otherworldly crowd triggered Mulan's sense of danger more than any of the spirits thus far.

Mulan grabbed for her sword, only to realise she'd left it by her bedroll. As her hand closed around empty air, she turned and found herself face-to-face with Zhonglin.

The girl looked much as she had the last time Mulan saw her – rosebud lips, oval face, large eyes. Skin that – now that Mulan thought about it – was paler than it should have been given the time she spent under the sun. She wore armour of well-polished mail, far finer than anything she'd owned as a militia member. Zhonglin showed no ill effects of her recent imprisonment. She looked healthy, strong. There was something more to her now, too. A glow? A shimmer? But only when Mulan looked out of the corner of her eye.

Grandmother laid a hand on Mulan's shoulder, whether to comfort or restrain her, she wasn't sure. Mulan's gaze darted back and forth from Zhonglin, standing there calmly, to her smiling ancestors, and back.

"You?" was all Mulan could say.

The young woman knelt and bowed. "At your service," she said, with no trace of mockery.

"But…" Mulan's mind spun. The things Zhonglin had said. The blatant challenges to her power. The hand signals of rebellion – except they hadn't been rebellion. They'd been the exact opposite.

"You made me think you were a traitor."

Zhonglin shrugged, and Mulan caught a hint of that

independence, that defiant spirit that had so nettled her on the training field. "I never actually pretended. I simply didn't correct you when you leapt to conclusions. And perhaps I was a little less polite than you were used to." She held herself now with an authority that she didn't have before, and there was an echo in her voice that spoke of centuries, if not millennia.

Mulan thought back to Zhonglin's comments. How the girl had challenged her on everything from failing to deploy her militia to failing to control her ministers. Her gibes about Mulan getting out of practice with her weapons. Zhonglin had made Mulan angry, dangerously so. But had she also spurred her to action?

"You goaded me on purpose."

Zhonglin snapped a loose string off her sleeve. "There were things you needed to hear."

With the girl in front of her now, more pieces fell into place. That first battle against Dafan's bandits, Mulan had come so close to calling off the raid, and it was Zhonglin's mistake that had forced her hand. And then there were Zhonglin's actions in the Imperial City. The hand signals of support at the coronation. The way she'd led Mulan and Liwen to seditious posters around the city the next morning, posters that had convinced Liwen to stay in the Imperial City with Mulan instead of travelling back home. Even the oxtail soup Zhonglin had been eating the day she pretended to leave with the militia – a subtle reminder at a time when

Mulan needed oracle bones.

"Did you leave that treatise on my floor?" said Mulan. "The one warning emperors against imposing too heavy a tax burden?"

Zhonglin's lips twitched. "You're clever. I can see why the emperor chose you."

"Why didn't you just tell me who you were?"

"A leader needs wisdom, selflessness, intelligence and compassion. All of that, you have. But a leader must also believe she's worthy to rule. If I'd stood by your side and told you how to act, it would not have made you an empress."

"What are you?" Mulan asked.

"I am..." Zhonglin pursed her lips, looking over Mulan's shoulder as she searched for the right words. "... the embodiment of an ancient magic that aids the sisterhood of rulers. Think of me as a messenger with particular talents that may be useful to you."

"And what might those be?"

Zhonglin smiled. "I call spirits."

"You summoned my ancestors."

"You needed support, and you needed comfort. The women of your family were most suited to that task, but it's just the first step."

Grandmother scratched her chin. "We're not really military people, you see. Though some of us would have been quite good at it, if we'd thought to try."

"A queen needs trustworthy advisers," said Zhonglin. "Your own ministers have been self-serving and deceitful, but I can remedy that for you, if you'd like."

"If I'd like?" Why was this woman/ghost/ancient asking permission now, after all this time?

"We can only do so much without your participation. You've had challenges, and they will only increase. We can offer you help, but you must accept it."

Mulan shook away a sudden bout of dizziness. It was too much. The sudden appearance of her ancestors. Zhonglin's return not as a traitor, but her secret protector.

Grandmother laid a hand on Mulan's arm. "I've spent much time with this one these past weeks," she said. "She wishes for you to succeed, as do the ones who sent her."

Mulan wondered briefly what was real and what was not. Was it really her grandmother who stood here, assuring her that Zhonglin was to be trusted? But it was only a fleeting thought. She knew in her gut that this really was Nai Nai by her side, and she would trust her to the edge of the earth.

"Show me more," she said to Zhonglin.

The spirit waved her hand in an arc. Silver sparks trailed her fingers, leaving the outline of a doorway in midair. Through it, Mulan saw a forest quite different from the one in which she currently stood, with giant silver-trunked trees and gnarled branches. Much of it was obscured by mist.

Zhonglin beckoned for Mulan to follow her through.

Mulan stepped up to the threshold, then stopped. None of her ancestors were following her.

"Go on," said Grandmother. "Talk of war and armies is beyond us. We'll speak again later."

What lay beyond? A spirit land? Would she be able to come back? Mulan stepped through, suppressing a shot of panic as the portal closed behind her. With the closing came the muffling of all the forest sounds from before. The silence was disorienting. She turned in a slow circle, taking in her new surroundings. The forest was ancient, judging from the size of the trees and the heaviness of the air. Mulan saw now that she stood in something more than a simple grove. The trees' branches and roots had been shaped into chairs of living wood. They were arranged in a circle, and Mulan had the suspicion that if she touched these chairs, they would feel warm. In the centre was a table carved from a single enormous stone.

Mulan looked at Zhonglin. The girl/spirit/creature was watching her reaction.

"What now?" Mulan asked.

"We wait for the others."

That was when Mulan noticed another portal opening on the other side of the grove.

"There they are," said Zhonglin with a satisfied tone.

A woman walked through. She was tall and dressed in full armour, though it was of a different style than Mulan's, made of stitched leather instead of metal or wooden scales, and painted with sword-wielding figures.

The woman looked around, assessing the room like a general surveying a battlefield. Her eyes landed on Mulan. "This is her?" she asked Zhonglin.

Zhonglin made an expansive gesture. "May I present Fa Mulan, empress of China."

The spirit bowed low, clasping her hands in front of her. "It is a great thing, that a woman has come to rule," she said. "I am called Fu Hao, and I offer my unworthy advice."

"Fu Hao..." Mulan stuttered. "General Fu Hao?" Mulan knew her history. Fu Hao had been a celebrated military leader, commanding troops of thousands. "Please, stand up. Do not bow for me. It is I who am unworthy to take your advice."

The general had barely straightened when a second spirit walked through the door. This one was young. She looked like she hadn't even reached her full height, and her chest was still flat. "Empress," she said. Two buns on either side of her head bobbed with her bow. "I am Xun Guan."

"I know you, too," said Mulan, with a growing sense of disbelief. "You led a charge through enemy ranks when your city was under siege. And you were but a girl."

Xun Guan smiled impishly. "Sometimes it's easier for a small group to break through enemy defences, if it's done right."

After Xun Guan came two more women. One was stunningly beautiful, with long lashes and straight teeth. The other woman was short and solid, with the most muscular shoulders Mulan had ever seen on a woman.

"We hear you lead an all-female militia," said the beauty. "I am Lin Siniang, and this is Liang Hongyu. We both led female contingents in our day."

"The recruitment process was slightly different," said the strong one.

Siniang smiled elegantly. "True. My contingent started out as sister wives and concubines," she said. "My husband didn't want helpless consorts, so we became sisters-in-arms. Hongyu recruited her soldiers the more traditional way."

After Siniang and Hongyu came commanders and pirates, Han Chinese and fierce tribeswomen, women in riding gear and women in full armour. One by one, they took their places around the table.

"Your war council, Empress," said Zhonglin. "At your service."

Mulan counted around the table. Twenty strong, fierce women in all, waiting on her to speak. "I'd never dreamed..."

Though Mulan had spent the last years embroidering the names of woman warriors on her tunics, they'd felt more like legends than real flesh and blood. Knowing their names hadn't kept her from feeling like an anomaly, both in the army and later in the imperial palace. But now these legends of the past were seated around her table, women just like her. And they looked as if they expected great things.

"The Queen's Council wishes for you to succeed," said Zhonglin. "The women around the table, your sisters in spirit from the past and the future, want to see you to victory. Command us."

Mulan surveyed the circle of waiting faces. "I don't know how to lead a council full of spirits."

"The same way you would lead any other council," said Zhonglin. "We've lived our lives as mortals. We earned our stripes on the battlefield, and we've learned from our mistakes."

Zhonglin had said "we".

"You were also a warrior, then? Was Zhonglin your real name?"

Zhonglin's lips parted in a coy smile. "I had some skill with a sword in my day."

"Enough chatter," said Fu Hao. "The empress has a campaign to wage."

Fu Hao's voice reminded Mulan of Shang's, the way her words rang out and demanded attention. Mulan's spirit rallied to the challenge. The Huns were at her doorstep. She needed to stop them.

"What is your first move, Empress?" asked Fu Hao.

Mulan thought for only a short moment before answering. "I need to seek information. I need to know where the enemy is, and what they're doing."

A high-pitched cry pierced the air. Mulan cast around for the source, but she saw nothing. Zhonglin waved her hand again, and a shimmering image appeared above the table. The image was in constant motion, as if things were speeding past. Mulan realised that she was seeing vast expanses of grassland race by from above.

"My bird is at the northern border," said Zhonglin.

"Bird?" asked Mulan. And then an image flashed through her mind of a hawk with red-tipped wings. Zhonglin had always had a way with animals.

"This is what she sees right now," said Zhonglin.

Dots came into view. A moment later, Mulan realised they were soldiers. Larger dots became horses and cavalrymen. As the bird flew, more and more of the army came into view. They were gathered near a round fortress with thick brick walls – the outpost they'd captured.

"Are they marching?" Mulan asked.

"Not yet. They are regrouping," said Zhonglin. "But they will march soon."

Mulan calculated frantically. The bulk of the imperial army was stationed near the Imperial City. It would take weeks for them to reach the northern borders.

"The Huns could march in uncontested." Images of burned villages flashed through Mulan's mind – smouldering ruins, a doll abandoned amid the ash.

"The imperial army will be a long time getting there," said Fu Hao. "But another force might be able to slow the Huns. They might be able to buy time."

"Even with a small number of soldiers, the right strategy can do significant damage," said Hongyu, the muscular woman who'd led a female militia. "I once ambushed an army of a hundred thousand with a force of eight thousand. The coordination must be precise. We used drums and flags to send messages between our troops."

"You're right." Mulan ran through possibilities in her head. "If we had a small force, a quick force, we could harry them and slow their progress. Attack and flee."

"The Huns are expert riders," said a woman wrapped in the light riding robes of the northern tribes. Mulan thought her name was Qacha. "They're not flat-footed troops. A guerrilla strategy might not work as well as you hope."

"All right, then…" said Mulan. "Maybe we can stop them at a bottleneck. It's too late to build extensive fortifications. We'd have to rely on terrain."

A map appeared on the table in front of her. Mulan threw a surprised glance at Zhonglin, who winked.

Mulan took a moment to get her bearings. The Imperial City was marked with a tiny picture of Mulan's palace. She scanned north, to the vast grasslands near the border, and found the round brick of the fallen fortress. "Here," she said, pointing south of the fortress. "They'd have to march through this pass."

"You can hold that pass with a few hundred soldiers," said Fu Hao. "Not forever, but it would buy time. Mistress Zhu might have some thoughts on how to strengthen your position."

A woman who looked more like a grandmother than a warrior nodded approvingly. "Fortify the area well. Dig trenches. Line them with sharpened stakes. Don't rely solely on the labour of your soldiers. I am no warrior, but I led a hundred civilian women in fixing our city's fortifications in a time of war. It was what saved us in the end."

"That's a good point, Mistress Zhu," said Mulan. "But I would still need trained troops to fight on the front lines." Mulan looked to Zhonglin. "Do you know what Shang is doing? Can your bird bring a message to him?"

Zhonglin shook her head. "My bird can only fly and see as a normal bird would. If we don't know where Shang is, she would not be able to find him."

That wouldn't work, then, especially if Shang was trying to stay hidden.

Were there outposts nearby? Pockets of troops she could tap? Mulan scanned the map. "Here's an outpost two days' ride to our south," she said, trying to remember the number of troops stationed there. "I can ride there myself and see if the troops are still loyal."

Could those troops make it to the pass in time? That was

272

assuming they would follow her in the first place.

Zhonglin cleared her throat. "You have loyal troops closer to the border than that."

Mulan scanned the map. "Is there another outpost?"

"Not an outpost," said Zhonglin.

Instead, she pointed to a village to the north. There was something vaguely familiar about the surrounding terrain, and it took Mulan a moment to realise why.

"That's my home village," she said. Slowly, Zhonglin's meaning dawned on her. "My militia."

"They're trained, and their loyalty can't be questioned," said Zhonglin. "It's time to stop being overprotective of them. Let them come to China's aid."

And there it was again, Zhonglin pushing Mulan to let her militia fight, just as she had from the very beginning. "You've been telling me to stop protecting them for a while."

Zhonglin's eyes sparked with the wisdom of centuries. "Because I knew this day would come. Will you send them to fight?"

Mulan thought of the women in her militia. Fu Ning, whose leg still bothered her, but who trained hard to regain her strength. Wenling, always the jokester, whose aim with an arrow never failed. Ruolan, drilling endlessly while her son played at the edge of the field.

"You're right," said Mulan. "They are good soldiers. And they will fight."

CHAPTER SEVENTEEN

M ulan didn't know how many hours she spent around that table, poring over the map, learning what she could from that bird's-eye view of the enemy. The light never seemed to change in the forest. Mulan wasn't even sure there was a sun above that misty canopy. She also didn't grow hungry or thirsty as she worked, so work she did.

Finally, she stood back from the table, rubbing her neck. "I think that's all we can discuss for now." From around the table came long exhales of agreement.

One by one, the women of Mulan's war council stood. They headed for the portal that had magically reappeared, some taking Mulan's hands or giving her encouraging pats on the shoulder before they left. Then the trees themselves dissolved, and Mulan found herself back in the forest she'd left either hours or ages ago. The fire where she'd burned the tortoise shell had died to embers. She realised with a jolt that Grandmother and her other ancestors were no longer there.

"Your relatives have left," said Zhonglin. The girl stood a few paces behind her, wearing the same clothes as before, but somehow looking more mortal. "They'll be back, though."

"But you're still here?"

"The rules that govern our existence are complicated. I have more freedom to stay and move in your world."

Talk of her world reminded Mulan of Guozhi's caravan. Had they noticed she was gone? She turned towards the campsite.

"They're still sleeping," said Zhonglin. "But not for long."

"I should say goodbye to them," said Mulan. "They've helped me greatly, and it wouldn't feel right to simply disappear."

Zhonglin nodded. "Say your goodbyes. Once you're on your way, I'll find you on the main road."

She stepped off into the shadows as Mulan returned to her camp. The scout stared blankly past Mulan as she walked by and stayed oblivious to her movements as she climbed into her bedroll. Mulan didn't think there was any way she'd be able to sleep, but when she next opened her eyes, the sun was well above the horizon. All of the others were already packing the wagons.

"A late morning for you, Ping," said Guozhi as he walked by with a bale of hay.

She groaned and climbed to her feet. The events of the night before were much harder to believe, now that the sun was bright between the branches. Was Zhonglin really waiting for her by the main road?

She stumbled to the edge of the camp, ignoring the puzzled stares directed at her back as she weaved through the trees. Mulan stopped when she saw the remains of an extremely large fire. When she nudged the charcoal aside with her toes, she uncovered an upside-down tortoise shell carapace. The ashes, when she sifted them through her fingers, were still warm.

Guozhi looked at her with mild curiosity when she returned. "Something on your mind?" he asked.

"I was up late last night," said Mulan, blinking away her memory of the flames.

"What troubles you?" said Guozhi.

"The invasion," said Mulan. "The army coming in and the damage they've already done. I'm afraid I can't continue on with you to the Imperial City. I must return to my home village and help however I can." It wasn't even a lie.

Guozhi looked at her, thoughtfully rubbing the knuckles of his right hand with his thumb. There was no aggression in his gaze, only appraisal, and Mulan found she could return his gaze easily. "I fear we all have tough times ahead." The way Guozhi spoke made Mulan wonder what he was leaving unsaid. "Will you leave immediately?"

She nodded. "I can't overstate my gratitude for the help you've lent me. If it is within my power, I will do my best to repay you."

"You've been a welcome help to my caravan, and I wish you the best. Perhaps I shall hear of you again."

•••

Mulan had been travelling the road for several li when Zhonglin rode up from behind.

"He was generous with supplies," said Zhonglin, eyeing the packs of dried foodstuffs loaded on Mulan's horse.

"I wonder if he suspected who I was," said Mulan. "Either way, I'll have to find him after the war and thank him properly."

They rode quickly, stopping only to eat and grab a few hours of sleep. At times, Zhonglin told her more about herself and those who sent her.

"We're a sisterhood, a circle of women who hold power," said Zhonglin.

"Women who hold power?"

"Queens, empresses, duchesses... there are many throughout time and history, even if it might not seem it."

"How did this circle come about?"

A pheasant ran across the road ahead of them, flashing iridescent blue, green and orange feathers. Zhonglin watched it disappear, and then drew breath to speak. "There was one queen that came first. One not unlike you actually, though she was born into a royal family. Her parents died before their time, and she took the throne at a young age, surrounded by men who sought to control her."

Zhonglin's words reminded Mulan of her ministers and touched off an unpleasant twinge in her chest. "What happened?"

"The young queen's uncle pressured her to hold a contest for her hand in marriage." Zhonglin's eyes flickered slyly toward Mulan. "She didn't feel she was a prize to be won, but what did she know? She was young and inexperienced. Her uncle surely had her best interests and the good of her realm in mind."

Zhonglin's storytelling had settled into a rhythm now, and her voice took on a singsong tone. "The tourney lasted for days, and many young princes sought to win her for his own. The victor was a prince from a distant land, handsome and strong, a mighty warrior. He had to be the latter, since his homeland was locked in perpetual war. And when he ascended the throne alongside his new queen, he saw enemies everywhere, even suspecting those who had always been friends. Always, he expected to be betrayed. Little by little, he began to poison her mind as well.

"When the king declared war against the queen's old allies, the queen's advisers begged her to stop him. Even her old uncle, the one who'd married her off to him, regretted his mistake. But the queen was too caught in her husband's web by now, and she trusted him to do what was right. Only after war had ravaged her country and killed her husband, only when her former allies closed in for revenge, did she realise how far she'd fallen."

"What happened?" asked Mulan with some trepidation. The queen's story resonated with her more than she would have liked. She knew too well that feeling of doubt when confronted with confidence, the assumption that anyone who sounded so sure of himself must know better than her.

Zhonglin glanced at Mulan, aware of her nerves, and continued. "It was too late by then to win a war by the usual means. The queen's armies had been decimated. Relying on the soldiers that remained would have doomed her people to certain destruction. But this queen had one last source of power – the magic that flowed in her veins."

"Magic?" Mulan supposed that if ancient spirits could show up in her militia, magic could exist as well.

"Yes. Her mother was descended from sorcerers. The queen had true power, but she'd long hidden it from her people because she knew they feared such things. Now the queen had no choice. She summoned her magic and had the earth do her bidding. Chasms formed in front of her enemies. Boulders came out of the ground and formed a wall around her kingdom. The invaders could not get in."

"I... don't suppose you could do that for me?"

Zhonglin smiled, but not without pity. "I can't fight your battles for you."

Somehow Mulan had expected that. "Did the queen save her kingdom?" She was invested in the story now. Perhaps part of her felt that the queen's fate would predict her own.

"The queen did save her kingdom, but she paid a price. When her subjects saw her magic, they became afraid of her power. Once their fear of the invading enemy faded, they began to fear her instead. They rose up against her and burned her at the stake."

Mulan's gut clenched at Zhonglin's words. After the fire last night, it didn't take much imagination to once again feel flames against her skin. Hear the queen's raw screams. "Was this supposed to be an encouraging story?"

The corner of Zhonglin's mouth curved up. "I'm sorry," she said. "I've told this story many times and grown used to it in the telling. This is not a story of triumph, but it did give rise to something good. As the queen awaited her death atop the pyre, she reflected on all that had brought her to that point. She realised that she'd left her fate to those who didn't love her or care about her, those who sought only to use her for their own ends. She hadn't trusted her instincts about whom to trust, and that had been her downfall. As she died, she wished that other queens like her would not make the same mistake. Her magic effected one last spell, and her soul transformed."

A flock of birds flew out of a tree and scattered. Mulan wondered what a transformed soul looked like.

"The echo of that queen's power lives on," said Zhonglin. "It takes different forms, and it encompasses the lives, experiences and wisdom of all the queens that power has helped. I am part of it, as will you be."

It was a lot to take in. And despite what she'd seen of Zhonglin's powers, it was still hard to see her as part of something that ancient and powerful. "I don't understand. Are you a spirit? A ghost? Were you ever mortal?"

"I've lived my life on earth already."

"Did you live your life in China?"

"I mustn't give up too many of my secrets, must I?"

Days passed in a blur. The terrain gradually became more familiar. One day at high noon, the edges of Mulan's village appeared on the horizon. Mulan pulled back on her horse's reins, nervous despite the urgency of her mission. She scanned the black-tiled rooftops, the whitewashed walls. Had anything changed in the time she was gone?

"There they are," said Zhonglin, pointing across a field.

Mulan squinted in that direction, expecting to see soldiers training, but the field was empty. Finally, her gaze fell on a crowd of women under a tree.

Zhonglin dismounted. "Come on."

As they walked closer, they could see someone talking. A few steps later, they could hear that the speaker was constantly being interrupted. Not a single person turned from the discussion as Mulan drew closer. With a start, Mulan recognized Liwen's voice.

"I've heard nothing about her on the roads," Liwen was saying.

"Could she have gone west? Did either you or Shang go in that direction?" asked someone from the side.

"No, but those at the Imperial City spoke of a wagon going east."

"Maybe you heard wrong."

"Maybe you'd like to ride west yourself," Liwen snapped.

"She has to be alive," moaned someone else.

Mulan hurried closer, ecstatic to see Liwen safe and well. A clod of dirt crunched under her foot. One woman glanced around and stared, her mouth slack. The woman next to her followed suit, and then more and more. Liwen stopped speaking mid-sentence.

"Commander," came a voice from the crowd, just as someone else said, "Mulan," and a third said, "Empress."

Mulan looked down at her tattered men's clothes and mud-crusted shoes. Her face must be smudged with dirt as well. "I don't look very much like an empress, do I?" she said.

The crowd dissolved and re-formed around her, like a swarm of bees converging on a tree branch. Long-necked Jiayi threw her arms around Mulan, cackling. Wenling giggled and hugged Ruolan, her childish face alight. Mousy

Mingxia stood silently at the edge, gazing at Mulan and smiling. Everybody spoke on top of one another.

"It's really you!"

"What happened?"

"We searched for you, we really did."

"We've failed you," said Fu Ning, leaning on her cane.

Mulan hushed Fu Ning. "Many things have happened, but my loyal militia failing me is not one of them."

Liwen joined the crowd, staring at Mulan as if she couldn't make sense of her. Mulan caught her eye. "Shang found me. He told me what happened. Thank you."

Frustration flashed across Liwen's face, though Mulan could tell it was directed at Liwen herself. "I didn't see them trailing me to the astrologer's house. They caught me unawares—"

She stopped then, her eyes landing on Zhonglin, who'd quietly moved to the side as everyone swarmed Mulan. Liwen's eyes opened wide in disbelief and then hardened into rage.

"What are you doing here?"

Zhonglin appeared unfazed by the dangerous undercurrent in Liwen's voice. She brushed the dirt off her sleeves. "There's work to be done."

Liwen strode towards Zhonglin, pushing aside the women in her way. "You cowardly, traitorous..."

"Liwen, stop," said Mulan as her friend drew her sword.

Cries of confusion sounded all around as Liwen bore down on Zhonglin. "Stop!" Mulan shouted again. She pushed closer, but too many people stood in her way.

There was a flash of metal and a metallic clang. Mulan's heart seized, and she weaved through bodies to get a better look. She saw, with relief, that both Zhonglin and Liwen were still standing. Zhonglin held a short sword in her hand. Liwen's blade lay on the ground several paces away. Liwen stared at it, slack-jawed.

"Liwen," said Mulan. "There's been a misunderstanding. Zhonglin is a friend. I will explain everything later."

Murmurs sounded. Surprised exclamations. More than one woman pointed towards Liwen's sword. Mulan rushed to take control before everything dissolved into pandemonium.

"Quiet, everyone," she shouted. "Much has happened, and we do not have a lot of time. You must listen to me."

The voices died down.

"I've been betrayed by my ministers," said Mulan. "They wanted power for themselves, and in their attempt to grab that power, they've let our country fall into disarray. The Huns saw the turmoil and attacked, and my ministers were not able to mount a proper defence. The enemy is marching in from our borders now, unhindered."

Mulan took a moment to let that sink in. By the utter silence in the crowd, she could tell it had. She met each of their eyes as she continued. "Many of you have wanted to put your martial skills to the test. You've wanted a fight. Now I have a fight for you. It pains me to lead those I love into danger, but the truth is, there is no safety to be had. If the Huns breach the pass, they will march unopposed into China. Then there will be no escaping the bloodshed that will ensue. We must stop them. We *will* stop them, because I know your training, and I know you are able."

Mulan looked around at the faces in front of her. Some were drawn with worry, and others mirrored confusion, but she also saw excitement.

She caught Liwen's eye. Her second-in-command stood a few paces from Zhonglin in a tense truce. "Liwen, you are still the day-to-day commander of these troops. You have kept them battle-ready, and for that I thank you. I need you to dispatch our fastest rider to the Imperial City with a message for General Shang. He is to gather as many loyal troops as he can and come aid us at the border."

Hopefully before the Huns cut their way through us.

Liwen straightened, and a measure of pride lit up her beautiful face. "It will be done."

Mulan looked around. "I also need several volunteers who are good with embroidery."

A few hands came up.

"Ruolan and Wenling," said Mulan. "Make me a banner of gold and red. I want an emblem of a dragon and a phoenix, and it must be completed tonight." Dragon for emperor, phoenix for empress. Dragon for power and authority. Phoenix, that symbol of yin-yang harmony, because she was a woman and unashamed to be one.

As the embroiderers ran off, Mulan checked the sun. They had half a day for preparations. "Tonight, say goodbye to your loved ones and tend to your weapons. We leave tomorrow morning."

She stayed a while as the crowd scattered, clasping hands and embracing those of her militia who greeted her. It wasn't long, though, before Mulan made her excuses and left. There was one more place she wanted to go, and she wanted to go there alone.

It was high noon, and a good number of people worked the millet fields, pulling weeds and ushering water through the irrigation channels. Mulan tried to take the less visible paths, but heads raised as she passed and murmurs followed in her wake. Mulan didn't stop, even when she sensed a small crowd following behind her. She would address the crowd eventually, but not yet.

The walls to her parents' house gleamed white as always, shining despite the marks left by everyday wind and weather. The front gate was unlocked. As Mulan stepped inside, she was aware of someone stepping into place behind her. Liwen, keeping back the crowd.

In the garden, the stream burbled as if nothing had changed, and the wind stirred leaves overhead. There was no one in view. Mulan walked around to the back, anticipation uncurling in her stomach as she rounded the corner. Her heart jumped at the sight of her mother and father on a bench, heads bent in conversation. It was her mother who first glanced up briefly, and then looked again, eyes wide with shock.

Warmth flooded through Mulan, and her mouth widened into the first genuine smile she'd given in days.

"Mama, Baba," she said, and she flew into their arms.

•••

The next morning was punctuated by quiet footsteps, louder hoofbeats, and the occasional whinny as Mulan's troops prepared to leave. Mulan stood to the side with her father and mother, watching as those who had horses loaded them with supplies, and those who didn't adjusted packs on their backs and tended to last-minute gear maintenance. The entire militia was going, even Fu Ning, whose injured leg was now well enough that she could ride slowly.

"Quite a different sight from my coronation parade, isn't it?" said Mulan. Instead of fine gowns with embroidered flowers, they wore travel tunics embroidered with the names of warrior women. The only music was the occasional chirp of morning birds. Despite the knowledge of what they marched towards, Mulan found the trappings of this parade far more familiar and comforting than her coronation.

"Not the same," said her father. "But no less honourable."

Mulan was proud of these women. Proud of their calm preparations, proud of the ease with which they strapped on their weapons, their gentle yet firm touch with their horses. And she was proud, most of all, of the banner that flew over their heads. It was mud yellow rather than the rich gold of palace silks, since mud yellow was the only shade Ruolan could manage with the herbs at hand. The dragon and phoenix pictured on it were bare outlines. But Ruolan and Wenling had stayed up all night to embroider them, and Mulan could see the heart that had gone into every stitch. Now they would put down their needles and wield their swords with no less skill.

"Grandmother sends her love," said Mulan to her parents. She'd told them the night before about her dreams and visions, and they had marvelled at her words.

"She will no doubt watch over you," said Mama. "And you shall surely prevail."

Liwen came by with her equipment checklist. "We're almost ready." Her gaze flickered to Zhonglin as she spoke, as it had all morning.

"You don't trust her," said Mulan. She'd relayed the whole story to Liwen the night before. And while her second-in-command hadn't challenged Mulan's judgment outright, Mulan could tell that Liwen was still on edge where Zhonglin was concerned. It didn't help that the spirit had disarmed Liwen in front of all the other women.

"Time will tell," Liwen said, before turning and checking the last items off her list. Whatever Liwen's personal feelings about Zhonglin, it didn't interfere with her efficiency. "When we get going, do you want to stick to the main roads or avoid them?"

"The main roads," said Mulan. She'd been thinking about how best to do this. "I want to pass through all the villages. In fact…"

Like yesterday, a crowd had gathered to see the new empress. Mulan stepped out now to address them. She took only a few steps, but the crowd quietened immediately. As all eyes turned to her, Mulan couldn't help but inventory her own appearance once more. She was dressed as a soldier, in tunic, trousers and armour Liwen had found for her. Her hair was tucked underneath a plain iron helmet. There wasn't much to differentiate Mulan from a common foot soldier, but she found that this didn't bother her or make her feel less worthy of power.

She drew a breath. "I am Mulan, daughter of Fa Hsu. I grew up among you, I've fought to protect you, and now I am your empress." Her voice echoed in the now quiet morning. A hawk shrieked in the distance. "Today, I stand here before you because our country faces a grave threat. The Huns march on us from the north. Treachery has slowed our armies, but I am still here. My warriors and I march to battle, and we need more to fill our ranks. If you can wield a sword or bow, come fight alongside us. If you are untrained but able-bodied, help us prepare fortifications, tend to the wounded, and feed the troops. We won't let China fall without a fight."

Her words were met with silence, but it was the silence of thunderclouds before a rainstorm. Mulan surveyed the faces around her. She saw fear, but she also saw hope, and most terrifyingly, she saw trust.

"I will go," said a man from the back of the crowd.

"I can cook," said a woman in an apron.

"I have wagons to carry supplies," said someone else.

As more voices chimed in, Mulan exchanged a look with Liwen. Perhaps they might have a chance after all.

"Pack your things quickly," said Mulan to the crowd, "and follow us."

She paid her last respects to her mother and father, and then joined Liwen at the front of the procession. As they began the slow march up the road, a handful of villagers ran to join them, bearing large bundles. Mulan wondered if they'd packed beforehand and had simply been awaiting her invitation.

"More will come," said Liwen. "I saw many run back to their homes to get their things. They will follow as quickly as they can."

Mulan hoped it would be enough.

...

They marched village to village, stopping at each one for Mulan to call for recruits. They didn't tarry after each call, but told the recruits to catch up. Slowly, their numbers grew.

Mulan wondered how long it would take for news of her reappearance to reach her ministers. More than once, she saw people resembling imperial messengers watching her, and she made no effort to hide from them. Let them confront her, if they had a better way to defend the nation. A few times, she passed by small imperial outposts, where she called to the soldiers stationed within. They came, and her ranks swelled.

Since they marched morning until night, the militia no longer trained at dawn. But Mulan noticed that Zhonglin still woke up early to do sword exercises. These were exercises Mulan had never seen her do before, long, intricate routines that bent the body into all kinds of postures. They required a level of skill Zhonglin hadn't displayed when she'd been disguised as a common soldier.

One morning, Mulan grabbed her own sword and joined her. Zhonglin didn't say anything, but she did slow her movements to make them easier to follow.

"What are these exercises?" Mulan asked when they finished.

"I made them up, when I was teaching myself the art of swordcraft," she said. "There's a balance here of yin and yang, a dance between aggression and gentleness that creates real strength in any warrior. Attack, and fall back. Thrust and parry. It's beautiful, really."

Mulan thrust her sword forward and then skipped back. "A balance of yin and yang," she repeated. "I don't have to turn myself into a man to fight or rule. And I don't have to be a docile woman like my ministers expect me to be. I can be gentle and strong as circumstance requires."

She stopped talking then, because she'd noticed Liwen standing to the side, watching.

Mulan's second-in-command strode up slowly. "You have a distinctive approach to swordplay." She spoke to Zhonglin with the same deliberate attention that Mulan's mother might use to measure out a bowl of medicine.

Zhonglin inclined her head graciously. "I made a study of it in my day."

A ray of light glanced off Zhonglin's sword, and Mulan took closer notice of it. The pommel showed signs of age, but the blade itself was still bright and pliant.

"Is that a new sword?" Mulan asked.

"It's the one I prefer," said Zhonglin, a hint of pride in her voice. "I forged it myself."

Liwen stretched out her hands. "May I?"

Zhonglin laid the weapon across her palms and offered it to Liwen. Mulan held her breath as Liwen ran her finger over the flat of the blade and then hefted the weapon to test its weight. She sliced a zigzag line through the air before striking a stance on one leg, with her other knee pointed up and the sword thrust out at shoulder level. Liwen sighted down the quivering blade as an archer might sight down an arrow shaft.

Abruptly, Liwen retracted the sword and presented it with two hands back to Zhonglin. "It's a work of art," she said.

"Thank you," said Zhonglin.

Liwen sucked in her cheeks, a movement that made her cheekbones look even sharper than usual. "The nuns who raised me had a library of treatises on fencing. I spent hours poring over them when I was younger." It seemed to Mulan that there was hidden meaning behind Liwen's words, which Zhonglin's half smile acknowledged.

"Did you find them useful?" asked Zhonglin.

"Greatly," said Liwen, and she smiled her own half smile in return before leaving to tend the troops.

•••

The forests became sparse as they marched north, eventually turning to stretches of rolling, half-brown grass. Zhonglin gave Mulan daily updates about the enemy's movements.

"They're moving down through the northern plains," she told Mulan one night as they bent over a map.

"It's dry and flat all through here," said Mulan. "There aren't many places where we can stop them." She looked again at the map, tracing the mountain range on which they pinned their hopes. "Do you think we can beat them to the pass?"

"If we hurry," said Zhonglin.

There was another worry on her mind that grew as the days passed. Though Mulan inquired at every village and outpost, no one had any news of Shang. Had he made it back to the Imperial City? Had he received her message? Was he still alive? China was large, and it could simply be that his messengers hadn't reached her. She hoped that was all it was.

They increased their marching hours. The plains gave way to foothills, which grew taller and more jagged. Mulan eyed the tall sandstone cliffs, imagining how the dirt would slip beneath her feet, wondering how long it would take for troops to scramble up the steep slopes. She counted the sparse green bushes scattered over the flatter portions, and calculated how much cover they could provide. Below the cliffs, a river meandered, low and lazy in the summer heat, its water not quite brown enough to hide the sandbars just below the surface.

Finally, they came to a spot where the cliffs formed a funnel.

"This is it," Mulan said. "Unless the Huns have decided to take a different way."

"They haven't," Zhonglin said. "But they'll be here within a day."

Mulan turned to Liwen. "Can you organise the building of fortifications?"

Liwen shouted orders as she walked away. "I need a crew of able-bodied young people to dig ditches at the front lines.

Another crew to take the dirt out and build an earthen wall. A third crew to search for anything that can be sharpened into stakes. And a fourth crew to gather and store water." Liwen didn't say out loud that the river would not be drinkable by the battle's end.

Mulan called all the soldiers to her, a mix of the women of her militia, imperial soldiers who'd left their outposts, and villagers with weapons training. She divided them into new divisions and sent the archers to find vantage points on the hills. The valley air grew brown with dust kicked up by hundreds of feet.

They worked until the sun went down and were up again at dawn. Midmorning, as Mulan walked through the half-dug trenches, Zhonglin came to her side.

"The Huns will come into view soon," she said quietly.

Mulan acknowledged Zhonglin's news with a curt nod. "Keep digging!" she called. "I want the trenches smooth and steep. We are the only obstacle standing between China and the invaders."

An hour later, Mingxia from Mulan's militia shouted from atop a cliff. "Empress, I see them!"

Tiny Mingxia pointed north. Mulan stopped speaking mid-phrase.

"Now's the time for courage," she said to the workers she'd been addressing. With one last look at their stunned faces, she turned and scrambled up the cliff face.

Mingxia waited for her, gazing intently towards the horizon. "There," she said.

A dust cloud stretched across half the horizon. Tiny black figures emerged from it like a swarm of ants.

Below her, all movement had stopped. Mulan's troops stared up at her. "Keep working!" Mulan shouted. "They are not here yet."

Shovels hit the dirt with renewed vigour. Mallets drove the first stakes into the ground. Dirt flew. Workers coughed and kept going. Even from high up on the cliff, Mulan could smell the sweat and fear.

Mulan stayed at her perch, trying to estimate the Huns' numbers. Ten thousand? Twenty? She couldn't see the end of their line. The ants grew into people and horses with coloured banners. Sunlight glinted off spear points and swords. Birds flew overhead. At first, Mulan thought they were hawks, but then she realised they were vultures.

"Fill the gaps in the walls!" Mulan shouted. "Faster!"

Finally, when Mulan could make out the back-and-forth of individual horse legs, she ordered all preparations to a stop and arranged the troops to look as imposing as possible. Uniformed soldiers lined the first trench and the wall. Her militia had sewn dragons and phoenixes on the sleeves of their tunics, and it warmed Mulan's heart. As she walked the ranks, she was surprised to see Fu Ning in full armour, standing as to favour her good leg.

"You're supposed to be helping with the support crew," Mulan said.

"I'm standing with my sisters," said Fu Ning.

"But your leg," said Mulan. "You can't fight if you can't walk."

Fu Ning's chin lifted. "I can shoot arrows from the wall. I shot a target at three hundred paces last week."

"You'll be off-balance." Mulan had no patience for an argumentative soldier right now, even one who was trying to be brave. The image of Fu Ning on the floor of the teahouse came into her mind, the girl's blood forming a growing puddle around her. "If something goes wrong, you won't be able to react as quickly as your sisters."

"By that point in the battle," Zhonglin said at Mulan's shoulder, "she'll hardly be the only one with injuries."

Mulan hadn't even realised that the spirit was there. Fu Ning's face brightened at Zhonglin's words, which frustrated Mulan even more. Now that Zhonglin no longer played the rebellious recruit, Mulan had thought the spirit would stop contradicting her in front of her troops. Apparently not. But the Huns were at her doorstep, and she couldn't spare the time or the resources needed to deal properly with insubordination.

"Fine." Mulan jerked her head towards the highest reaches of the wall.

Fu Ning's wide mouth split into a smile. "Thank you, Commander."

Mulan turned so she wouldn't see the young woman limp to her position.

After all the troops were placed, the fortifications still looked sparse, so Mulan filled in their ranks with unarmed civilians, giving them strict instructions to pull back when the fighting started. They had no armour or weapons, but Mulan hoped the Huns would not be able to tell from a distance.

The Huns, on the other hand, were an imposing sight as they drew close. The majority of their army consisted of cavalry mounted upon strong, beautiful horses. The fighters atop the horses, both men and women, held their weapons with assurance. And there were many of them. All Mulan's people combined did not match a fifth of the enemy's numbers.

"Hold formation," Mulan called as the army marched closer. The Huns stopped safely out of archery range, as Mulan had suspected they would. She turned to Zhonglin and Liwen. "Come with me."

The three women rode out under Mulan's dragon-and-phoenix banner. As they drew close, two riders detached themselves from the enemy troops. One was an unfamiliar warrior with two swords strapped to his waist and a spear hooked to his saddle. The other was shorter and carried fewer weapons, but still rode with confidence. As he neared, Mulan saw heavy black eyebrows and expressive lips

– Balambar, the ambassador who had been at her palace.

Mulan had the satisfaction of seeing surprise cross Balambar's face as he came closer. From far away she must have looked like any other soldier. "You're trespassing on Chinese land," she said. "I demand that you turn your armies around."

The ambassador stared a moment more before regaining the smooth demeanour she remembered from before. "Your Majesty. We heard you were taking time off in the countryside."

"So you took the opportunity to launch an invasion? Your sources were mistaken. Turn your armies around."

Balambar pursed his lips. "I'm afraid that would not be possible. We wished to form an alliance, but Your Majesty was not interested. Failing that, we are forced to alternate measures."

"Your marriage offer was not conducted in good faith. I know you courted my ministers behind my back."

"We conducted diplomacy," said Balambar, "as any sovereign nation would do."

Mulan waved to indicate the troops in front of her. "And this. Is this diplomacy as well?"

The man next to Balambar had listened with interest to this whole exchange. Now he finally spoke. "If this is the extent of your troops, Empress, then diplomacy may be your only hope. Let our armies through. Agree to rule by my side.

There is no point in delivering your soldiers to slaughter."

It took Mulan a moment to fully comprehend what the man had said. Balambar glimpsed her expression, and a sly smile formed on his lips.

"Your Majesty, may I present Prince Erban, younger son of King Ruga."

Mulan couldn't help but take a closer look at the man she would have married. He was close to her age, lean but muscled, with a sharp chin and high cheekbones. He was handsome in his own way, but the arrogance in his countenance ruined his looks. Erban gazed at Mulan possessively, as if she were a prize he'd lost, rather than a human being.

"Prince Erban, I wish we'd met under better circumstances," said Mulan. "Nevertheless, I cannot allow you to pass through."

Erban's lip curled. "Then let us conduct any further negotiations on the battlefield."

There was nothing left to say. Mulan and her escorts backed up their horses a safe distance, then turned towards their troops.

Liwen made constant glances towards the enemy as they rode back. "That one's taken things personally," she said. "It's a matter of pride for him."

Mulan suppressed a shudder. Her interaction with Erban had left a slimy feel on her skin. "An alliance would not have worked."

She surveyed their fortifications, knowing that thousands of attacks would descend on them before the day's end. Cliffs on either side of the pass came steeply down, boxing both armies into the narrow valley. Two trenches stretched from cliff to cliff. In front of the trenches stood a row of sharpened stakes, long and sturdy enough to stop horses. Behind the trenches was a wall made from excavated dirt. The river had been diverted to a deep, narrow channel at the very edge.

The construction had come together remarkably well in the time they'd had, but Mulan couldn't escape the reality of what they were – improvised fortifications built in a day. Still, this was their best chance at stopping the Huns, and she would rather die than surrender China to their mercy. Mulan could sense the same resolve in her soldiers – resolve and loyalty that weeks ago she wouldn't have believed she truly commanded.

Mulan walked her horse over the plank that served as a makeshift bridge over the first trench. "Take your positions!" she shouted. "Prepare for a charge."

As a civilian took her horse, Mulan ran for the highest point on the wall. Zhonglin followed, while Liwen took her post on the opposite side.

"They're getting ready," said Zhonglin.

Mulan didn't need reports from Zhonglin's hawk to interpret the stirrings in the Hun army. The attackers rearranged themselves, moving their horsemen to the front. Mulan imagined their warhorses pawing the ground, snorting in impatience. She drew her sword.

"Are you ready?" asked Zhonglin.

"Yes," answered Mulan.

"Good."

The wind picked up, sending a low howl through the canyon. And then the enemy charged.

CHAPTER EIGHTEEN

Mulan shouted, "Hold your positions!"

The thunder of a thousand hooves vibrated through her being. A ripple of suppressed energy swept through the defenders' ranks.

"Hold!"

Mulan sensed her troops straining against her words – archers with their bows drawn, arrows a fingertip away from flight. Spearmen and swordswomen at the walls, bracing for impact.

The enemy was almost in range.

"Archers!" she finally shouted.

A volley of arrows shot up from behind her. More arrows rained down from the cliffs. The first horse stumbled. A rider behind him fell, clutching his collarbone. The rest of the horsemen drew closer. A shock of fear travelled across

Mulan's skin as the Huns nocked their own arrows.

"Take cover!"

Mulan crouched and threw her shield over her head as Zhonglin did the same. There was a long, horrible moment of anticipation, and then an arrow buried itself in the ground between them. A women's scream pierced the air, choking off into a gurgle. Mulan couldn't tell who'd been hit. She could identify her militia's voices, but she didn't yet know their screams.

A great shout sounded from the battlefield, and then the Hun infantry charged.

"Archers!" Mulan shouted again.

Another volley. Soldiers stumbled and fell as arrows found their mark, tripping their comrades. The attackers pressed on.

As the charge reached the first line of ditches, Mulan's defenders met them. Some Huns fell, impaled on the points of Chinese spears. Others dodged, dropping basketfuls of dirt and sand into the ditches before engaging with weapons. As both attackers and defenders fell, the Huns pushed the dead into the ditch, filling it up.

Mulan jumped down from her vantage point, grabbing a spear and raising it into the air. "Wall defenders, to me!"

She ran towards the trenches, taking care not to impale her own soldiers as she threaded her spear between them. Her spearpoint found an attacker. Mulan thrust it home, then dislodged the body to find another attacker, then another. The enemy kept coming. Her spear shaft felt slippery, and she realised her hand was bleeding.

The trench was already half-filled, and the invaders weren't slowing. Some defenders traded their spears for swords, the better to engage the Huns that made it across.

A shout sounded from across the valley. Mulan risked a glance and saw five horse-mounted invaders charge the ditch on the other side of the pass, where some stakes had collapsed. The Chinese defenders fell back, and then Liwen led a cluster of spear wielders in a countercharge. For a moment, all Mulan could make out was a clash of bodies. But then one enemy horseman fell, and then another, as Chinese soldiers plugged the hole in their defences. Still, the horsemen should not have made it that far.

"Retreat!" Mulan shouted. "Retreat to the first wall."

Archers laid down cover fire. Little by little, the defenders at the ditch fell back, running up wooden ramps that leaned against the wall.

Mulan took her place on the lookout again, watching, waiting as long as she dared.

"Raise the ramps!" she called. She still had troops who hadn't come across, and some of them looked up in shock. *I'm sorry.*

Guilt slashed at her heart. The attackers didn't slow.

Mulan scanned the walls, trying to get a sense of her

troops. At the other end of the valley, Liwen kicked a man off the wall as she parried another's sword. Zhonglin had joined her, her sword cutting silver arcs. Mulan had fighters along the entire length of the wall, but it was low, more a berm than a true structure, and too easy for the invaders to scale. Behind the front lines lay the newly injured. Civilians raced among them, carrying them in stretchers to be treated in the back. Some were so gravely wounded that Mulan doubted they'd survive the trip.

A Hun swordswoman breached the wall near Mulan, jumping down behind the defenders. Mulan shouted a war cry and ran to meet her. The warrior parried Mulan's first strike and her second, but Mulan's third attempt got through her defences and the soldier fell.

Mulan lost track of time after that. Fighting became mechanical – slash, parry, look for the next. The battle was a constant roar around her, a deafening mix of screams and clashing weapons. Somehow her ears sorted through the cacophony to warn her of enemies approaching. Somehow her eyes picked out the blades that meant her harm. Mulan's arms ached. Her throat burned. After a while, she stopped noticing the smell of death.

More Huns jumped over the wall. The defenders pushed them back, but the breaches happened more and more often. Their defences were crumbling. It was only a matter of time before the wall, like the ditches, became impossible to hold, but there was nothing left to fall back to.

Mulan dispatched another attacker, shoving him away from her sword. When she turned to find the next enemy, she realised that all the soldiers standing near her were Chinese. Stunned, she widened her search. More Chinese soldiers, some standing, some injured. There was a cluster of Huns halfway down the valley running back towards the main army. She saw no others.

The Huns had retreated.

That's when Mulan realised that the sky was rapidly growing grey. They'd been fighting all day. For a moment, the realisation stunned her. And then she collected her wits.

"Regroup!" she shouted. "Lookouts to the walls. Number the injured."

Everyone was covered in blood and dust, some so encrusted that they looked like human statues. Along the wall, those with strength left were collecting bodies from both sides. Others dug new trenches for burial.

Mulan found Liwen leaning against the cliff wall, nursing a bound arm and a water skin. Her shoulders were sloped, her hair a wild tangle around her shoulders.

"Just a scratch," she said when she saw Mulan draw near, though the tightness in her jaw belied her words.

"You're hurt," said Mulan.

"I'm fine." Liwen's voice was like worn steel. "Look to the others."

Mulan picked her way through the crowd. Some heads raised when she passed, but not many. She was too dirty to be recognisable. A soldier screamed as three men lifted him onto a pallet. Nearby, two other fighters leaned against each other, faces slack with exhaustion.

In the back of the camp, a long line of soldiers awaited rice rations.

"Empress." Though Mulan had been far from the line, a woman pushed a bowl into her hands.

She handed it back. "I've eaten."

The woman pushed it towards her again, more firmly. "Eat, Empress. We need your strength." She left before Mulan could refuse again.

The smell of the freshly cooked grains wafted up to her nose. Mulan's mouth ached in an attempt to produce saliva. She succumbed to temptation and scooped half the bowl into her mouth with her fingers, moistening it with a drink from her water skin. She handed the rest to a soldier in line and walked to the infirmary.

The sick tent was set up against the cliff wall. Blankets had been laid down on the dirt for the injured. The smell of blood was strong here, as were the odours of sweat and rot. A man whom Mulan recognised as a physician bowed to her.

"How are things?" Mulan asked. She looked around to see who else was tending the injured, and saw a handful of others. It seemed a small number, while the injured filled the tent.

"We've been keeping up as we can," said an elderly woman. "But there are many."

Someone moaned. A man in back cried out for his mother.

"That one is not doing well," said the physician. "We'll have to amputate his leg. Your Majesty may not want to be here for that."

Mulan's guilt grew heavier. "I've seen amputations. How can I help?"

"There are others who can run water and bandages," said the physician. Mulan opened her mouth to argue, thinking he was sending her away, when he continued. "But it would comfort the wounded to see you among them."

Comfort the wounded? It seemed both too easy and too daunting a task. If the doctor had told her to fetch water, she would have at least known how to do it.

Perhaps the physician sensed her hesitation. "Here's a bowl of water and some flannels, Your Majesty."

She took them, grateful to have something in her hands.

The first soldier she came across was an older man, probably a veteran from one of the garrisons. He lay on his blanket, mouthing words silently towards the top of the tent. At first, Mulan thought he was delirious, but his eyes were clear. His thigh was bandaged and splinted.

"Empress," he said as he caught sight of her. Mulan came to his side, feeling as if she'd been caught sneaking around.

"How do you fare, soldier?" she asked. She wondered if she

should try to sound more imperial, but she hardly had the energy to stand.

"I fare better than many in this tent."

Mulan couldn't argue with that. "I saw your lips moving earlier. Were you trying to get someone to help you? Do you need anything?"

The man's smile deepened the pain lines on his face. "Just my ancestors," he said. "We could all use their help."

The young man lying next to the veteran had a blood-soaked bandage around his chest. His eyes were closed, and his forehead was warm to the touch. He slept fitfully, shouting out occasionally about arrows and flames. When Mulan wiped his brow, speaking to him in low tones, he settled down.

The next patient was also asleep, though this one barely moved at all. The soldier was covered, as they all were, in the grime of battle. But as Mulan moved closer, she saw with dread that this was a woman. Holding her breath, she crept closer. Gradually she made out a stubborn chin and wide mouth beneath the dirt, and she stopped breathing entirely.

Fu Ning.

"Not again," she whispered. Images of the girl flashed through Mulan's mind – Fu Ning approaching the training field on her first day, nervous but determined, her wide shoulders back and her head held high. Fu Ning laughing after hitting a target with her arrow for the first time. Fu

Ning, confiding shyly about the young man who caught her fancy, the one who was now her betrothed. Fu Ning weak and bleeding after the teahouse battle, terrified that she'd failed her commander.

But of course, it wasn't Fu Ning who had failed Mulan. Mulan had failed her by allowing her onto the front lines with a lame leg.

What had happened to her? With trepidation, Mulan lifted the girl's blanket. There was a bandage wrapped around Fu Ning's middle, where a fist-sized spot of blood seeped through. An arrow to the gut.

As Mulan pulled the blanket back up, Fu Ning's hand closed around her wrist. Mulan gasped, instinctively pulling away, but the girl's grip was surprisingly strong. Ning's eyes had opened, and she stared at Mulan, seeing but not quite focusing.

Just as quickly, the girl's intensity faded. Her grip loosened, and her head sank back. "Thank you, Empress," she whispered. That stare... Mulan couldn't tell if Fu Ning was looking at her or some spirits she couldn't see.

"Ning," said Mulan, "I—"

But then she stopped, because Fu Ning let out a rattling breath that Mulan knew all too well. The girl's eyes closed, and she fell still.

"No," said Mulan. She took Fu Ning's hand again, feeling desperately for a pulse. It had to be there somewhere. She couldn't be...

The physician came to her side.

"She was just awake." Mulan's words collided and tumbled one over the other. "Just now, she was speaking—"

Gently, the physician took Fu Ning's hand and laid three fingers on her inner wrist. His expression told Mulan all that she needed to know.

Behind her, one caretaker told another that they were out of bandages.

The tent, stifling before, now became unbearable. Mulan fled, weaving between patients and caretakers, paying no mind to the eyes on her, aware only of the ache in her throat and the burning behind her eyes. Why had Fu Ning thanked her? It would have been better if she'd cursed Mulan for putting her on the front lines of an unwinnable battle.

"Where's Zhonglin?" she said. First to herself, and then to the soldiers around her. "Where is Zhonglin?"

She stormed through the camp, ignoring the stares. It didn't matter. She was beyond putting up appearances.

Someone pointed to a soldier near the wall. Mulan pivoted towards her, taking in the soldier's appearance as she neared. Like everyone else, Zhonglin was filthy, but she walked without heaviness. Mulan saw no wounds on her, and she carried herself the same way she did after any other day of training. Only now did Mulan realise how different this mystical being was from everyone else within these fortifications. Zhonglin didn't tire. She couldn't die. How had Mulan thought to entrust her with the lives of her most precious friends?

Zhonglin held three cups of water against her body. She distributed two of them to fellow soldiers, and then she looked up.

"She's dead," Mulan said, biting her words off like bits of dry tendon. "Is that what you wanted?"

The spirit straightened, blinking as if returning from a daydream.

"Fu Ning's dead," said Mulan. "An arrow wound to the gut. She thanked me before she died, even though she shouldn't have been fighting in the first place." Mulan's voice rose. She was attracting bystanders, but she didn't care. "You said I should trust my troops. You pushed me to send them into danger. Are you happy now?"

Zhonglin met her eyes, steady in the face of Mulan's approach. "Why do you think she thanked you?" she asked quietly. She didn't speak in anger, but neither did she show any guilt.

Mulan stopped.

"There were many shot today who went into battle with the use of both legs." Zhonglin spoke heavily, and Mulan saw now the weariness in the spirit's eyes, weariness that she hadn't noticed before in her anger. She saw also the shocked faces around them, the dirt, the blood, the desperation. She sensed the crowd's dismay at seeing Empress Mulan, their hero, behaving like a mere mortal.

Mulan's anger drained away, leaving only exhaustion.

"I need my war council," said Mulan. "Can you summon them?"

Zhonglin handed her final cup to a nearby soldier.

"To your tent," she said.

Stares followed Mulan as she and Zhonglin made their way through camp, each pair of eyes an additional reminder of Mulan's failure, both on the battlefield and off. Mulan moved past the gawkers with a dull awareness. Neither she nor Zhonglin spoke.

Mulan's tent was a large one, sewn out of cowhides and set up in the middle of camp. Though activity bustled all around, the fabric was heavy, and once the tent flap closed behind Zhonglin and Mulan, the sounds outside became muted. Inside, it was dark. Zhonglin raised her hand, and a light hovered over her fingers, which expanded into a door. One by one, the spirits of Mulan's council stepped out.

They crowded into her small tent, some sitting by the walls, others standing over a glowing parchment that had suddenly appeared on the ground. It was a diagram of the valley, with the positions of the armies marked by actual moving soldiers. Had Mulan seen it at any other time, she would have marvelled at it.

"A quarter of our company fell today," she said without

314

preamble. "A third of the remaining troops bear injuries serious enough to take them out of the fighting. All are exhausted. The Huns, on the other hand, will send fresh troops tomorrow, likely at dawn. If they do, we won't hold our position past the morning."

There was a silence as everyone contemplated her words.

"Any news of reinforcements?" General Fu Hao had a way of making even simple questions sound commanding.

"I sent my bird to scout shortly before sunset," Zhonglin said. "She saw nothing within two days' ride."

"Two days?" Mulan echoed.

Zhonglin looked gravely back. "Yes."

Mulan was afraid to ask the next question. "Do we know anything of Shang's whereabouts?"

"No." The answer itself was bad enough, but it was the tone of Zhonglin's voice that scared her. Maybe spirits didn't tire. Maybe spirits couldn't die. But she knew for certain now that they could fear.

"What can we do to hold our position longer?" asked Mulan.

"Heighten your walls here and here tonight," said Mistress Zhu, tucking a strand of grey hair behind her ear. "This is where they are more likely to fall. Do you have old stakes that have fallen? Dig up what you can and rebury them tonight at the base of your walls."

"Put your fresh fighters in the middle," said Siniang, her

beautiful features thoughtful. "The ones with moderate injuries can go atop the cliffs and throw rocks. Even small rocks can be deadly from that height. And they will serve to distract."

"Burning pitch as well, if you have any," said Fu Hao, tapping the pommel of her sword.

"Flames to frighten the horses..." said Xun Guan, her child's eyes fierce.

Mulan listened as the advice poured in, taking notes. Still, her advisers were leaving something unsaid. After a while, Mulan held up a hand.

"The advice you've given me is good. It could enable us to survive until the end of the day perhaps, or even into tomorrow. But how likely are we to hold out for more than two days?"

Nobody spoke. A muffled shout drifted through the tent walls.

Siniang was the one who broke the silence. "A soldier never gives up the fight. Even in death, an army can turn a war's tide."

The map flickered, causing the shadows in the room to waver. Mulan looked at the sombre faces around her and understood Siniang's words for what they were. Something about the layers of emotion in the concubine's throaty voice made Mulan wonder what sort of end Siniang's militia had met.

"Thank you," she said. "I am grateful for your counsel."

Her advisers disbanded silently, turning from the map one by one and processing through the portal. As Liang Hongyu passed by Mulan, she stopped and turned to her, her stance wide and confident, befitting the commanding officer she was.

"I was taken captive by the enemy once," she said softly, her sharp jaw turned to the side. "They were intrigued at my martial skills and made me entertain the court as a wrestler."

A wrestler. That would explain her strong shoulders. Mulan waited for Hongyu to continue.

"It was humiliating," said Hongyu, looking straight at Mulan. "But you overcome it. Eventually, you find a way to prevail."

"I see," said Mulan, though she didn't.

Hongyu turned and left through the portal.

After the spirits departed, Zhonglin's map darkened. She lifted the tent flap to let some torchlight in. "Would you like to speak more?" she asked.

"I'm sorry," said Mulan. "About earlier."

"War takes its toll on the best of us," said Zhonglin. The yellow torchlight gave her skin a warmer cast than usual.

And then she too took her leave.

Alone now, Mulan found herself far too restless to settle down. After a short while, she ducked outside and headed back towards the wall, climbing to her lookout point and staring out at the battlefield. Fires for the enemy army dotted the valley. Mulan started counting them, but stopped when she got to a hundred. She looked back to the sparse fires of her own camp, made by people who had come here to fight because she'd asked them to. How many of these fighters had family who depended on them? What kind of holes would their deaths leave?

She wasn't sure how much time passed before her thoughts returned to the present. Mulan took one last look at the Hun army before climbing down the wall. She asked the sentry outside her tent to wake her two hours before dawn. Once inside, Mulan removed her helmet but kept the rest of her armour on. The rough-edged scales caught on the fabric of her bedroll. Mulan thought it unfortunate that she had to dirty her blankets.

She lay with her eyes open for a long time.

•••

Mulan was in the middle of a fitful dream when Liwen called her name.

"It's two hours before dawn," she said.

Mulan sat up and rubbed her eyes. Liwen, standing by the tent flap, looked several years older than she had two days before. Her skin stretched tight across her cheekbones. Shadows darkened the skin beneath her eyes and gave her entire face a greyish cast. Mulan wondered if it was a trick of the torchlight. She hoped it was.

"Did you sleep at all?" asked Mulan.

"I just came from the sick tent. We lost ten to injuries overnight. About twice that number are battling infection."

Ten more women and men who would not go back to their families.

Mulan threw on a cloak and stepped outside. It was still dark, and colder now. The dust from the day before had settled, though the fields still smelled of blood. Most soldiers were asleep, huddled together under blankets and against the cliff walls. Only the scouts and those tending the ill still worked. A few people bowed to her as she passed.

Liwen trailed Mulan as she returned to her position on the wall. The enemy fires were dimmer this morning, but still as numerous.

"Has Zhonglin seen anything else?" Mulan asked Liwen.

"She went back to her tent a while ago and hasn't come out."

Mulan wondered if Zhonglin slept. But even if she didn't, her bird wouldn't have been able to see anything new in the dark.

The sky began to lighten. Soon Mulan could make out individual people in the enemy army, see the gradual uptick of activity. They were probably putting on their armour, preparing for another attack.

Mulan had gone to sleep the night before with a wisp of a plan in her mind, something that had felt out of the realm of the possible. But the plan had taken on weight as she slept. And now, as she woke to see things unchanged from the night before, it expanded until she had no other choice.

Mulan kept her eyes on the Huns. "Do you trust me to make good decisions?"

There was a moment of silence as Liwen searched her face. "You know I do."

"Wake Zhonglin, then. Saddle our horses, and ready a flag of parley."

To her credit, Liwen didn't argue. Mulan stood alone on the wall as she waited for them to return. The breeze raised goose bumps on her skin.

Footsteps sounded behind her. Zhonglin ran along the wall towards her, followed by Liwen. Much of Zhonglin's hair had come loose from her long night braid. Perhaps spirits did sleep.

"I'm surrendering," said Mulan as soon as the two women stopped in front of her. She looked at Zhonglin when she spoke, perhaps because she feared Liwen's reaction more.

Liwen's mouth dropped open. "Surrender? But—"

"We have no chance of prevailing," said Mulan. "Our army limps this morning, while their troops are still fresh. The Huns will breach the walls by the end of today, if not by high noon. When that happens, everyone under me will be slaughtered."

Liwen's eyes narrowed. "We're not afraid to die."

"I know you're not. But there's a difference between a worthwhile death and a pointless one."

Liwen's voice rose. "We could slow them down."

"For half a day." Mulan matched her energy. "A day at most. Your lives are worth more than that."

"Better a death on the battlefield than imprisonment, torture and execution," said Liwen.

"I've made my decision, soldier." Mulan's voice brooked no disagreement.

Liwen's eyes flashed with frustration and betrayal.

It pained Mulan to pull rank, but she didn't look away. "I've made my decision," she said again, more gently. "Now I need you to heed my orders. I want you to ride out with me."

Liwen opened her mouth and closed it again, turning accusing eyes to Zhonglin instead. "You're quiet."

"I advise. I don't dictate."

"That's why I don't trust spirits," said Liwen. "What reason do you have to fight if you're already dead?"

There was a flutter of wings, and Zhonglin reached up an arm to receive her hawk. "The living can close their eyes to the truth," she said as the raptor fixed Liwen with its yellow gaze. "The dead have no such luxury."

"Enough," said Mulan. All this was hard enough, even without their sniping. "You said you trusted me, did you not? Come, we must ride out before the Huns launch their next attack."

The surrounding soldiers watched with curiosity as Mulan readied her horse. Liwen saddled her own steed, her face a thundercloud, and anyone who ventured too close backed away upon seeing her expression. Mulan waited astride her horse until Liwen and Zhonglin took their positions on either side of her. A hush spread through the crowd as Zhonglin raised a white flag.

"Let's go," said Mulan.

Their horses' hooves beat a steady rhythm, the marching song of a forlorn drummer. As they drew closer to the enemy, Mulan's skin broke out in a cold sweat. Their flag was clearly raised above their heads, but would the enemy respect it? A stray arrow was all it would take. She breathed easier when she saw Erban and Balambar ride out, though only slightly.

"Empress Mulan," said Erban. "It has been a long day and night."

She'd never been in less of a mood to exchange pleasantries. "I'm willing to let you through the pass. But only if you allow my troops to go safely home. And you must give me your word that you will not loot the countryside."

Erban's mouth crinkled in amusement. "Offers from an army at the brink of extermination hold no temptation for me. Why should we spare you after you've caused us so much trouble?"

Mulan's jaw tightened. Though she'd prepared for this moment, she still found it hard to push out her next words.

There would be no undoing what followed.

"You will let my troops go safely home, because I'm offering myself as a hostage."

Erban's eyes widened in shock. Even Balambar's smug mask slipped for a moment. Next to Mulan, Liwen's hands tightened on her reins, her knuckles turning completely white. Zhonglin stayed still at Mulan's side, her porcelain face impassive.

"I will surrender myself to your custody," Mulan continued. "You can use my presence to ensure your safe passage to the Imperial City. We can negotiate the terms of our marriage there."

Erban exchanged a look with his ambassador.

"King Ruga was greatly disappointed when you refused his initial marriage proposal on behalf of his son," said Balambar. "It was a great insult to both of them. You've shown yourself to be hostile to us. What reassurance do we have that you will not go back on your word once we get to the Imperial City?"

"What reassurance do you need," Mulan retorted, "once you have your army in the Imperial City with no bloodshed or losses along the way? It would cost us greatly to dislodge you after you've come so far."

Erban and Balambar exchanged a long look. Finally, Erban nodded, directing his cutting gaze back to Mulan. "I will accept your offer if you turn over your sword and come immediately."

Liwen's breath hissed out. Mulan prayed she would not interfere.

"I will turn over my sword," said Mulan. "But I will keep my knife on my person until my troops have safely retreated. If you break your word and attack my troops, I will use the knife on myself."

"That's a rather dramatic threat," said Erban. His expression was vaguely amused, but Mulan could see exultation in his eyes, the way he gripped his horse's reins in jubilation. "Send your seconds back."

Mulan turned to Liwen and Zhonglin. Liwen looked as if she intended to leap off her horse and strangle Erban herself. Zhonglin watched everything, her expression distant.

"Supervise the retreat of our troops," said Mulan. "I will see you again at the Imperial City."

"Mulan, please..." began Liwen.

"You heard my orders."

Liwen flinched as if Mulan had inflicted physical pain, and Mulan's chest twisted in response. Stiffly, Liwen pulled her horse's head around, and Zhonglin followed her lead. Mulan gritted her teeth, forcing herself to take deep breaths as Liwen and Zhonglin grew smaller in her vision. She was hyperaware of Balambar and Erban watching her every reaction, and she was determined not to give them the satisfaction of seeing any crack in her composure.

There was a bustle of activity in the Chinese camp when

Liwen and Zhonglin reached the wall. Troops rushed to meet them, and the two riders disappeared behind the barricades. The camp went still.

"What's taking so long?" asked Erban. He spat on the ground.

"Give them time to absorb the news," said Mulan. The knife in her arm sheath pressed cold against her skin. "They will retreat soon enough."

The sun climbed higher in the sky. A bird flew overhead. Mulan glanced up, hoping to see red-tipped wings, but it was a vulture.

"How much longer?" said Erban, a note of impatience in his voice.

"It's a large camp," said Mulan tightly. She prayed they were not attempting anything foolhardy. "Give them time."

Finally, the troops started to move. Tent poles shifted and lowered. Horses came into view, bearing people and supplies southward. The exodus continued all morning, slow drips out of a cracked pot. Mulan's muscles ached from tension. The left side of her face burned from the sun.

Liwen was the last to leave. Even from this distance, Mulan recognised her astride her horse. Mulan's second-in-command turned one last time in Mulan's direction before kicking her horse into a gallop and disappearing from view.

"Your troops are safe, Your Majesty," said Erban. "Now hand over your knife."

Mulan shook herself, realising how long she'd stayed in one position without moving. The straps of her arm sheath felt tighter than usual, as if it knew it was about to be removed.

"No more excuses, Empress," said Erban, his voice hardening.

Mulan rolled up her sleeve, and unfastened the clasps of her sheath one by one. The blade dropped into her hand. As Erban and Balambar watched, she turned it hilt first and held it out.

Erban's lips spread into the faintest of smiles. "Thank you, Empress. Now come with us."

CHAPTER NINETEEN

Erban said to Mulan, "Ride in front."

Troops had already begun to gather at the edge of camp. Thousands of eyes followed her movements, and their combined hostility made it hard to move. Still, she gritted her teeth and urged her horse forward.

As she neared the Hun encampment, she heard the ambassador speak. "Keep a tight watch on your troops, Prince. The Chinese can be pushed, but they will not forgive easily if their empress is harmed or humiliated beyond reason."

"Beyond reason," echoed Erban. His tone dissipated any relief Balambar's warning might have brought. Mulan was beginning to realise just how deep Erban's grudge against her ran.

Jeers sounded from the camp as they rode closer.

"The great and mighty empress of China."

"Not much of one."

Erban led her to a large round tent of tanned horsehide. Stacked within were saddles, weapons and burlap sacks.

"Clear it out," he said. "Drive a stake into the ground."

As soldiers jumped into action, Erban patted Mulan down and affixed a shackle to her foot. The chain linked to it dragged at her feet. If she had enough slack on it, she could possibly use it as a weapon.

Erban took one end of the chain. "Come," he said, leading her towards the tent.

Every one of Mulan's muscles tensed. If the prince tried to lead her into the tent alone, she'd take out his eyes.

But he stopped at the doorway. "You'll behave like a proper prisoner," he said. "Don't expect to be treated like royalty. You'll march with the army. You'll stop when you're told, and you'll eat what you're given. If you show any signs of rebellion or attempt to escape, we'll make things worse for you. This tent can be taken away, as can your food. Your guards remain outside the tent for now, but they can be moved inside with you."

She stared back at him. Clamped down on her tongue and her anger.

"I don't know what you were thinking, trying to lead the country by yourself," he said. "You could have saved yourself a lot of trouble by simply accepting my father's offer, but perhaps you'll be more tractable now."

Erban took a few steps out of the tent and then looked back. "You know, Mulan, you're not bad-looking for a warrior woman. Perhaps if you washed off the grime, you'd be pleasing enough on our wedding night."

Mulan spat on the ground. Erban simply smirked and walked away.

•••

They left her alone for the afternoon, coming to her tent only to bring meals and a blanket at night. The next morning, she was awakened by guards shouting through the tent flap. "Get up! We march today."

One guard threw a piece of dry bread on the ground, along with a water skin. Mulan brushed the dust off the bread and took a bite. It was hard and unpalatable, but not mouldy.

Soldiers dismantled the tent around her, revealing a sky of bright blue. The air was crisp and would have been clear if not for the dust kicked up by ten thousand horses. Mulan found herself once again at the receiving end of scrutiny. She stared straight ahead, watching the horizon over the soldiers' heads as guards released her from the stake and chained her two feet together. Prince Erban shoved her rolled-up tent at her.

"Carry it."

They marched. Her chains dragged on the ground, catching on rocks and tufts of grass. Several times, she stumbled and fell, each time picking herself up to hoots and jeers. She soon learned the best way to hold her tent to cushion her landings.

"If she gets any dirtier," said Balambar from his horse, "her people won't recognise her, and she'll be useless as a hostage."

Prince Erban's laugh was sharp and savage.

As they neared the fortifications abandoned by Mulan's armies, the stench of decay grew stronger. Mulan's troops had done their best to bury the bodies, but this magnitude of death was impossible to erase. Vultures tore at lumps on the ground. Mulan averted her eyes.

Erban gave a command, and soldiers rushed forward with shovels. With no defenders to stop them, they quickly levelled a wide portion of the wall and filled the trenches in front of it. When it was all flat again, the army continued on its way. Mulan's chain caught on the tip of a sharpened stake, and she caught herself just in time. Better to trip over one, she thought, than to land on top of it.

They continued on. Though the march was no less gruelling after they passed the fortifications, Mulan found it easier to keep going. The further she could get from that blood-soaked battleground, the better. As the sun set, the army made camp as before, making no effort to keep their movements secret. The next day, they continued on.

Gradually, they came upon the road that Mulan's troops had taken on their way north. The army marched onto it, overflowing its sides like floodwaters overwhelming a riverbed. No one else travelled this stretch, and the few houses Mulan glimpsed had their doors closed and windows shuttered.

"A country of mice," said Balambar, chewing on a blade of dry grass. "They've all gone into hiding."

Balambar's words were calculated to anger her, and though they succeeded to some degree, Mulan was glad to see no further bloodshed. As they marched, she occasionally scanned the horizon, wondering what had become of Shang.

Late that afternoon, the Huns neared the first Chinese village on their route. Several hundred soldiers stood in formation across the road, waiting.

Stand down, Mulan thought. But the soldiers stood unmoving as the thousands-strong invading army neared. Who were these people? A local militia?

"Halt," said their leader in a clear voice. Mulan didn't recognise him. "We can't allow you to pass into Chinese lands."

Erban, who'd been riding in front of Mulan, kicked his horse closer. "On whose authority do you speak?"

"On the authority of China and our empress," said the man.

Erban tilted his sharp chin to the sky and laughed. "Your empress? Did you speak with her? Did she give you the command personally?"

The leader hesitated, aware that Erban mocked him but unsure of his meaning.

The Hun prince beckoned behind him. "Bring out

the empress."

Mulan's guards grabbed her by the shoulders and dragged her to the front. Mulan stared at a point on the horizon, every inch of her recoiling at what was about to happen.

"Your empress is our prisoner," said Erban. "She's granted us safe passage through to the capital. Do you go against her wishes?"

Mulan finally gathered the nerve to look at her soldiers' faces, bracing herself against their unbridled shock and horror. They recognised her, though she wasn't sure how. Word must have spread of her capture, though she could tell that these men hadn't truly believed the reports until now.

"These are your troops, are they not?" said Erban.

"Yes," said Mulan under her breath.

"Speak louder," he said.

"Yes." She channelled all her anger into that word.

"Order your troops down," said Erban with a smug smile. "Don't make me ask you twice."

Mulan clenched her jaw, staring at the ground. As much as she loathed Erban, she also didn't want to hear his arrogant voice say anything twice. "Stand down," she called clearly. "Let the Huns pass."

The Chinese troops shifted where they stood, exchanging unsure glances.

"You heard your empress," said Erban.

Gradually, in fits and spurts, the troops parted. Very few

of them looked directly at Mulan, but the few who did had such confusion and disappointment in their eyes as to evoke enough shame for all of them. After a while, Mulan averted her gaze.

Erban drew a deep, refreshing breath, as if he were touring a garden instead of leading an invasion. "There's one more thing," he said pleasantly. "Have them turn over their weapons."

Mulan rounded on him. "No," she hissed. "That leaves them defenceless."

"Don't be unreasonable." Erban's gaze hardened even as his voice stayed mild. "I won't lead my troops somewhere knowing their backs are vulnerable."

"Guess you'll have to send your troops back across the northern border, then," said Mulan.

"Watch your mouth, Empress." Erban spoke her title with the same disdain as he would have used to speak of rats or dogs. "We could crush these men."

His words had the jagged edge of truth. There was no doubt what would happen if the Huns decided to attack.

Mulan gritted her teeth. "You will let them go unharmed?"

"As according to our original agreement."

She looked down. Squeezed her eyes shut. Took a deep breath. *Humiliation is nothing. What they think of me is nothing. Their lives are what's important.*

"Surrender your arms," she commanded.

The men of the militia looked at her, mouths agape.

"You heard me," said Mulan. "Lay down your swords."

They didn't budge. Erban cleared his throat impatiently and moved one lean arm towards his sword.

Mulan caught the militia leader's eyes, mustering what last vestiges of authority remained to her. "Are you the leader?"

The man nodded warily.

"You will lay down your weapons first. I command it as your empress."

The militia leader looked at her, disillusionment and disbelief permeating every inch of his being. Mulan might as well have torn the sun from the sky and revealed it to be straw. Slowly, deliberately, he walked to the front and unstrapped his sword. It thudded dully on the ground.

One by one, the other men followed suit. No sound punctuated the process except heavy footsteps and the clink of dropped metal. The pile of weapons grew. After the last man surrendered his sword, Erban motioned to several of his soldiers, who scooped up the bounty and packed it onto their horses.

Then the Hun prince smiled at Mulan. "Now," he said with the self-satisfaction of one who knew he had absolute power over everyone within his sights, "let's resume our march."

•••

They passed more villages. Erban made sure Mulan was visible when they passed, moving her up front and giving her no chance to hide and spare her pride. At least there was no repeat of the humiliating surrender. Word must have spread. Mulan still scanned the horizon for Shang's troops, though she no longer hoped for them to appear.

Erban spoke to her sometimes as they marched, remarking on the weather and landscape, offering his opinion of army rations. Sometimes he complained about his father and being a second-born son, cut off from real power. Mulan never responded.

One afternoon he came to her again. "We don't have to be enemies."

Mulan didn't answer. Her legs chafed from her shackles, and every step hurt. Her badly bundled tent was unwieldy to hold.

"I'm not unreasonable," Erban said. He'd handed his horse off to his men in favour of walking, which disappointed Mulan, since Erban's grey mare was by far her favourite individual in this camp. Whenever Erban held forth on politics, Mulan amused herself by exchanging long-suffering glances with the animal. Every time Mulan's ration included a handful of sunflower seeds, she saved some to share with her.

Erban strolled easily at Mulan's side. It was much less difficult to walk when one's feet were not chained together. "We can learn to work together," he said. "You appear to have some talent on the war front, and I'm not one to let talent go to waste. You know that we have woman warriors among our riders, right? Not many, but we have a few. We're not as bigoted as your people."

They'd just passed a village and were heading into forested lands. Shade fell across Mulan's face as they walked under a cluster of trees. "There are some things that will be non-negotiable, of course," he said. "Tributes to the north, for one. We will co-operate with my father and my brother for the good of my people. In the northern grasslands, we lack for good resources. That's why we come south. You Chinese would do the same if our positions were switched."

Erban had a sword at his waist, as well as his dagger. The dagger looked well balanced, with a bone handle and narrow blade. Neither weapon was close enough for Mulan to grab.

"Earn my trust, and you can advise me on the battlefield," said Erban. "Life need not be unpleasant. We'll be living around each other for a very long time."

"I said I would conduct negotiations once we reached the Imperial City," said Mulan. "We are not at the Imperial City." She thought about her hands. They were chained together, but the chains were reasonably slack.

Erban laughed, his sharp chin lifting in amusement. "The sooner you face the truth, the better. Your government is in shambles. You can't even get an army together. I'm saving you from civil war. The longer you try to solve your problems on your own, the more grief you'll cause yourself. Accept my help, Mulan. Do it for your people."

Mulan stopped abruptly. "You're right that I can't rule on my own." As Erban cocked an eyebrow, Mulan let her tent drop. It fell, shapeless, at her feet as she looked him in the eye. "But you are not the help that I need."

Before Erban could react, Mulan snatched his knife from his belt and slashed at his face. When he stumbled back, she ran for the forests, ramming her shoulder into the soldier most directly in her way. The impact jarred her brain, but he stumbled back and she kept going. Running with her legs hobbled was harder than she expected. The raw skin of her ankles screamed at her with every step.

"Get her!"

Leaves and twigs whipped her face. Mulan stumbled over tree roots, wondering if she'd impale herself on Erban's knife if she fell. Footsteps thudded behind her.

Something jerked the chain around her ankle, yanking her feet back as the rest of her pitched forward. The knife went flying. Hard earth knocked the air from her lungs as razor-edged pebbles bruised her knees. Arms grabbed her shoulders and hauled her to her feet. Mulan spat leaves out of her mouth as she was half dragged, half carried back to Erban.

He held a cloth pressed to his sharp cheeks, and there were streaks of blood across his face. Raw fury lit his eyes.

As they dragged her closer to him, Mulan looked over Erban's shoulder to the mountains beyond. There were puffs of dark grey clouds floating above them, strangely out of place in the bright blue sky.

Then Erban's face filled her vision. He raised his fist, and everything went dark.

CHAPTER TWENTY

Once again, her problems followed her into her dreams. Mulan found herself wandering that strange silver old-growth forest, where she'd first met her spirit council. Thick fog hung in the air, like spider silk borne up by a non-existent breeze. There was magic in this place, but apparently the magic was not enough to keep her head from hurting.

Mulan felt gingerly for the knot on her temple, pulling her hand away with a hiss when she found it. Even the lightest touch sent a zing through her skull.

The mist grew thicker until she could hardly see beyond arm's reach. Mulan put out her hands as she walked, brushing away stray branches and leaves. On a whim, she plucked a leaf from an ancient tree and pressed it to her wound. The pain ebbed.

"That's an ingenious use of these plants," said Zhonglin. Somehow Mulan wasn't surprised to see her there.

"Is it actually healing me, or am I just imagining it?"

Zhonglin plucked a leaf for herself, tore it in half and smelled it. The fragrance that wafted towards Mulan was like mint smeared on the edge of a sword. "I don't know. You'll have to tell me when you wake up."

"I'm not exactly in a rush to go back to where I was," said Mulan.

Zhonglin tossed the leaf to the ground, pursing her rosebud lips. "You don't seem the type to give up so easily."

Mulan bit back a growl. "I've been trying to escape. That's what got me injured in the first place."

"Not a bad attempt, and you told him off quite well," Zhonglin conceded. "You're more confident these days about your marital choices, or whom you *won't* marry at least, which is progress. Though I wonder if your escape attempt was driven more by a desire to slash Erban across the face than any solid strategy. Next time, make sure you know where you'll go after you get away."

Mulan's headache started to creep back. "Thanks, I'll be sure to write out a full treatise before I try again."

"Your militia has regrouped," said Zhonglin, not acknowledging Mulan's sarcasm. "Liwen led them to a nearby village to tend to their wounds. You likely have twenty or thirty soldiers who could fight at a moment's notice."

Mulan snapped her head towards Zhonglin. "What are you saying? You want to send them here to rescue me? Thirty against an army of thousands?"

"Young Mistress Xun would be disappointed in your lack of faith."

Mistress Xun. Mulan remembered how the thirteen-year-old girl had led a small group of horsemen through enemy siege lines. "You think my militia could cut their way through to me?"

Zhonglin shrugged, dreamily studying the treetops. "I don't know. I'm not their commander. I didn't train them."

Mulan closed her eyes and tipped her head back, visualising the women at their morning drills. "I suppose their chances are as good as any well-trained cavalry against those odds. But they'd need to strike fast. There's very little room for mistakes. It's not simply a matter of getting me out. It would do no good if I were recaptured, or worse, if Erban took his fury out on the countryside."

"You're thinking now. That's a start. Now all you have to do is open your eyes. You have more resources than you think."

Mulan scanned the forest, half expecting an army to come out of the mists, but the forest stared back, as empty as ever. She supposed it would have been too easy for Zhonglin to lay a solution in front of her.

"A true warrior always looks for an advantage," said Zhonglin.

"All I've seen are Huns, day in and day out."

"Think harder," said Zhonglin.

A suspicion formed in the back of Mulan's mind, one that grew closer to certainty the more she thought of it. The moments before Erban had knocked her unconscious, the brilliant blue sky…

"Do you see now?" said Zhonglin. "Why there might be hope?"

"Yes, I see," said Mulan. It opened a door, albeit a narrow one. "Come get me. I'll do my best to be ready."

Zhonglin smiled brilliantly, her oval face lighting up. "That's the warrior empress I know."

"How quickly can you be here?"

Her smile widened. "We've been tracking you as you marched. If you throw your guards now, you won't have long to wait."

Zhonglin made it sound so easy, as if Mulan could simply drop her chains and send her guards away. But the Huns would likely be taking extra precautions to guard her now that she'd tried to escape once.

"Oh, I almost forgot," said Zhonglin. She held out her sword. "You might find this useful."

The weapon shone in the silver light of the forest. Mulan could see marks of wear along its length – scratches, dents and divots – but there was no doubt in her mind that the blade would hold true. She put two hands out to receive it.

"Be ready," Zhonglin said. And then she was gone.

•••

It was pitch-dark when Mulan opened her eyes. For a moment, she panicked, thinking she was buried or blind, but she stopped and forced herself to take a breath. As air filled her lungs, the darkness sorted itself into different shades of black. Mulan glimpsed a line of flickering light – torchlight through the seam of her tent. It was night-time. Her captors must have placed her inside after they knocked her out. If that was true, then she'd been unconscious for several hours.

She touched her hand to her head. The bump she found there didn't hurt. Had the dream plant healed her, or had her injury not been as bad as she thought? Mulan stretched out her legs and felt her chain drag along the ground. Cold shackles pressed against her wrists. She was just as much of a prisoner as she had been before, but perhaps...

Mulan explored the ground with her hands, patting rather than using sweeping motions that might slide along a sharpened edge. Her fingertips landed on a leather pommel.

Her heartbeat quickened. Holding her breath, she felt along the pommel's length until her fingers closed around a leather sheath. Working bit by bit – her wrists could only go so far apart – she slid it off the blade.

It was awkward holding Zhonglin's sword with her hands tied. Nevertheless, exultation swept through her. Mulan's shackles were heavy, adding weight to the otherwise light weapon. Even so, it was a weapon, and a better one than she'd dared hope for.

Mulan stilled and trained her senses outside. She couldn't hear anything, but she knew from previous nights that there would be a guard outside her door and another one on the opposite side of her tent. She probably shouldn't scream. A scream would bring both of them running, and she only wanted one at a time.

Instead, she moaned. "Water," she said. "My head."

There was a faint shuffling outside the door.

She raised her voice. "Help. Please. I can't..." She made the loudest retching sound she could muster. And then she did it again. The second attempt triggered a wave of genuine coughs. Bile burned the base of her throat.

Shadows shifted subtly outside her tent. One footstep sounded, and then another. The flap lifted. A soldier's backlit form appeared in the opening.

Mulan gripped her sword. He would be blind for a few moments until his eyes adjusted. She needed to get him within range by then.

"Help..." she rasped again, and doubled over, blocking the sword with her body. She didn't think the torchlight shone far enough inside to illuminate it, but better to be safe. "Help me."

When the soldier stepped closer, Mulan slashed him

across the throat. He went down with a thud.

How loud had that been? These tents let all manner of sounds through. Mulan felt urgently along the fallen guard's belt for keys.

Dirt crunched outside her tent.

Mulan sped up her search, trying to ignore the sound of her own panicked breathing. Finally, her fingers closed around jagged metal, and she sighed, light-headed with relief. Should she unlock her legs or arms first? Trembling, she reached for the shackles at her ankles, feeling desperately for a keyhole.

Someone called out in the Hun language.

Mulan found the keyhole. A click sounded, and the shackle around her right foot fell free. Now her arms…

The tent flap lifted again. Another soldier came into view. "What's going on?" he asked in heavily accented Chinese.

Mulan pushed herself to her feet, wobbling a split second before launching her foot towards his head. The soldier dropped. She tried to catch him, but between her bound hands and his weight, she barely managed to keep herself from tumbling down with him. Hurriedly, she unlocked the rest of her bindings.

She stopped then to listen. Silence. Had no one else noticed yet? Mulan felt along the second fallen soldier's body until she found the clasp of his cloak. It unfastened easily. His tunic didn't come off as readily, but she managed, then threw both on over her own clothes. She pulled her hair out of its tangled braid and let it fall around her shoulders. Then she smoothed down her uniform, fastened Zhonglin's sword to her belt, and lifted the tent flap. Soldiers slept on the ground all around her. A few snored, and one man talked in his sleep. Mulan saw several soldiers walking about, but none of them glanced her way.

Mulan wound her way around sleeping bodies as quickly as she could without looking like a fugitive. At one point, a soldier walked in her direction. She nodded a greeting, and he paid her no mind.

What now? She could see a ring of torches at the edge of the encampment. She could walk all the way there, but it would take more luck than she thought she had in order to make it without getting caught. Plus, scouts walked the entire perimeter.

A voice spoke behind her in the language of the Huns. Mulan turned. A squat man with sloped shoulders stood looking at her. He repeated the question. From his tone, she guessed he was asking her what she was doing.

As the silence lengthened, the suspicion in his posture increased. He said something else, more hostile this time, and then he stormed towards her and took hold of her arm. Mulan grabbed his wrist and bent it against the joint, leaning her body weight against it. He let out a yell of surprise and pain.

Too loud. Mulan had the bizarre urge to shush him. More

shouts sounded all around. Mulan looked wildly about, tensing for a fight, only to realise that the shouts were coming from outside the camp. The army's scouts were sounding an alarm. Mulan heard hooves pounding in the distance, and – dare she believe it? – female battle cries.

A horsewoman burst into view. Though Mulan couldn't see the rider's face in the darkness, she knew instantly that it was Liwen leading the charge, her sword held high. Liwen didn't slow an iota as the Huns rode to meet her. At her side was Zhonglin, and behind them, riding in a tight wedge formation, was the rest of her militia.

Blades clashed. Horses and warriors shouted as invaders and defenders met. Mulan glimpsed Liwen's blade sweeping down, Zhonglin's horse rearing and kicking, Ruolan the embroiderer throwing a javelin.

Then Mulan remembered the man in front of her. He also stared, slack-jawed, at the attackers. When she swung to cut him down, he was too slow to stop her.

A woman's exultant shout carried over the fray. "For China!" Jiayi always had a way of being heard in a crowd.

Another soldier charged Mulan. She parried, then snaked her sword past his guard. When he fell, she ran for a horse hitched outside a nearby tent. The dark grey mare tossed her head in confusion.

"Hello, beauty. Sorry about the commotion," Mulan said, untying the horse's rope. She leapt on the mare's back just as

Prince Erban stepped out of the tent.

Newly awakened soldiers jumped out of the way as Mulan kicked the horse into a run. At the edge of the camp, she could see her women cutting through the enemy lines. Small Mingxia crouched low in her saddle, the brown sleeves of her tunic contrasting with her pale skin as she parried an opponent's strike. Liwen came to her aid, slashing at the Hun's arm and drawing his attention until Mingxia struck him down.

Mulan needed to get to them. The further in they came, the harder it'd be to get out again. She urged her horse closer.

An enemy soldier shouted, pointing at her. Heads turned to look, and Mulan knew she'd lost her last shred of secrecy. She still had her guard's tunic over her old clothes, and now she tore it off. It wouldn't do to be shot down by one of her militia's arrows. Mulan raised Zhonglin's sword high. It glowed a faint blue in the darkness.

"To me!" she cried.

"To the empress!" Liwen yelled, her dual braids dancing around her face.

"To Mulan!" came the answering chorus.

Mulan's militia pushed forward with renewed determination. Eyes flashed. Blades sang. Mulan fought her way towards them, kicking at foot soldiers too slow with their swords, and parrying the strikes of those mounted. Little by little, the space between her and Liwen narrowed until they fought side by side.

"Turn around!" said Mulan. More enemy soldiers were joining the fray. It was only a matter of time before her militia would be overwhelmed. Out of the corner of her eye, she saw Erban riding up on a new horse, his still-bandaged face contorted with rage.

"Retreat!" Liwen yelled, flanking Mulan on one side. Zhonglin took her place on the other.

Mulan urged her steed forward, fighting, driving, never failing to push. Another rider charged her. Mulan blocked his attack and slashed at his arm. He faltered, and she rode past.

She passed the outer line of torches.

"Fast now." Mulan allowed herself a quick glance to see the women falling into formation behind her. "Did we lose anyone?"

"Ruolan and Jiayi," Liwen said. The wind whipped around their ears.

Mulan breathed a prayer that they had been captured alive. The best she could do for them now was to keep going.

"More horsemen coming behind us," said Zhonglin. "They're riding fast."

Mulan saw them, too. "How fresh are your horses?"

"We've been riding for an hour."

Mulan glanced over her shoulder. Could their pursuers be closer already? "We have to keep going." And pray that their mounts would last as long as she needed them to. She pointed to a set of cliffs in the distance. "Make for the rocks!"

Riding at a reasonable pace, it would take another hour to get there. But a reasonable pace would have them captured and killed before they were halfway there. Mulan stopped talking now and bent low over her horse. Rocks, sand and bushes blurred past her. Her parched throat hurt, and she wished she'd brought water with her.

Someone cried out behind her. Mulan glanced over her shoulder to see Mingxia clutching her side.

"Arrows!" Zhonglin cried.

Mulan cursed under her breath. "Can she ride?"

When Mulan looked back again, Mingxia was hunched over, clutching her horse's mane, her face a mask of pain.

And then she started sliding down.

No, not another one. Tears blurred Mulan's eyes, which she desperately blinked away. Riding blind at this speed would be a death sentence. Mulan could feel her horse slowing, see the strain in the beast's neck. If they pushed their steeds any harder, they would die. If they didn't push, Mulan and her warriors would die. She looked over her shoulder, past her militia this time. The Huns were catching up.

"Ride faster!" she yelled. But her strength ebbed even as she spoke. The cliffs stood unmoving.

A flash of motion caught her eye. A new rider raced alongside Mulan, weight perfectly balanced over her horse despite the breakneck pace. The rider was female, but she wasn't a member of Mulan's militia. Neither did she sport the fur-and-leather-lined tunics of the Huns. The rider wore no helmet, and her hair was tied up in two matching oval buns atop her head. Mulan found it hard to focus her eyes on the horsewoman, and she finally realised it was because the rider was slightly transparent. Dirt, rocks and the horizon beyond showed right through her body.

"Xun Guan," Mulan said under her breath.

The girl spirit turned towards her and grinned. Then she kicked her steed and pulled ahead. Behind her, more riders appeared. General Fu Hao, astride a giant war stallion. The nomad Qacha, dressed so similarly to the Huns that Mulan did a double take. Liang Hongyu followed with an entire contingent of female riders. Soon, Mulan's militia was surrounded by spirits, and she could tell from the gasps and exclamations behind her that the other women saw them, too.

"Find your strength," roared Fu Hao over the pounding hooves.

Mulan felt her mare's muscles bunch beneath her. With a leap, the horse found renewed speed. Next to her, Liwen gave an exultant cheer, and Zhonglin laughed in exhilaration. The cliffs loomed closer now. Though they'd seemed so small before, now they blocked out a larger and larger expanse of sky. "Just a little more!" she shouted.

The rocks came together to form a gap wide enough for fifty horses. As Mulan's militia entered, the spirit riders disappeared, leaving sheer rock walls in their place. The thud of horses' hooves echoed off the canyon walls. They were alone again. Mulan desperately hoped she was right to lead them here.

Finally, the cliffs opened up into a wide bowl with striped sandstone walls. Only then could she see what had been hidden from view. Shang sat astride his horse, face relaxing into relief as he caught sight of them. And on either side of him, lined up in disciplined rows with weapons at the ready, stretched the forces of the imperial army.

CHAPTER TWENTY-ONE

Mulan reined in her horse, sending rocks and pebbles scattering. Her legs gave way when she dismounted, and she grabbed the saddle to keep from crumpling to the ground. A hand reached out to steady her.

Shang.

His armour was clean. His grip was firm, his brow furrowed as he scanned her for injuries. "Are you hurt?" he asked, eyes going to her temple.

"Nothing serious," said Mulan. She scanned the terrain around her until she spotted the remains of a bonfire. "I saw your smoke signals." In the moments after her failed escape, as her captors dragged her to Prince Erban for punishment, Mulan hadn't recognised the grey clouds in a blue sky for what they were. It was only after Zhonglin came to her that Mulan put the pieces together.

People crowded around them, pressing food and water into her hands. Grooms helped the unwounded militia women off their horses, while riders with serious injuries were carried away. Mulan drank gratefully and allowed a woman to wipe her face, but she batted at a doctor who tried to lead her away from the pass.

"The Huns are coming," she said. "They'll be in view soon."

"My troops are ready," said Shang.

"Do you have archers on the cliffs?" Mulan asked.

"Fifty on each side." Now that he said it, Mulan could see the glint of helmets on the rocks.

"Tell them not to fire until the last of the pursuers are in the canyon. I don't want anyone fleeing back out."

"How many are there?" asked Shang.

"I'd guess about five hundred in pursuit. The main force didn't join in."

She looked to Zhonglin for confirmation. The spirit nodded, and then said with a wicked smile, "Prince Erban is leading the pursuers."

A hawk's shriek echoed down from the sky.

"They're nearing," said Zhonglin.

Mulan corked her water skin. "Take formation," she said. "I need a fresh horse."

"Are you well enough to fight?" asked Shang. "You could sit this one out."

Mulan weighed his words, taking inventory of her body.

Her limbs ached, but her exhaustion was gone, perhaps chased away in the excitement of the last ride. The pain in her head had not returned since the dream. "I'll be careful," she said. "But I need to see this through."

Shang nodded. A moment later, a familiar black stallion appeared at Mulan's side and nuzzled her ear.

"Good to see you, Khan." Mulan mounted her cheerful steed and followed Shang to the head of the army. Her army. The soldiers stood arranged in two wedges on either side of the canyon mouth, just out of sight, and ready to close in.

Mulan, Shang and Zhonglin rode to the centre-most corner of one wedge.

"They're almost here," said Zhonglin.

"Draw your weapons!" commanded Shang.

The slink of ten thousand drawn swords echoed off the canyon wall. A low rumble echoed along the rocks. Hoofbeats.

Mulan's blood thrummed in anticipation. The key now was patience. "Tell me when they've reached the halfway point of the bottleneck."

Zhonglin waited a moment, her eyes fixed on her hawk. "Now."

"Signal the archers," said Mulan.

A soldier raised a red flag. Mulan could just barely see the faint shift of bows lifting into position atop the cliff. Strings twanged. Screams sounded as arrows found their marks.

The first enemy riders came into view. By now they'd slowed, aware that they'd ridden into an ambush. A few turned their horses around, but arrows cut off their escape.

Mulan raised her sword. Shang blasted his horn. With a great roar, the imperial army charged, bearing down on the Hun riders. Mulan felt as if she were surging forward at the crest of a wave, strengthened by hoofbeats and battle cries behind her.

The Huns only had a moment to brace themselves before the Chinese crashed upon them. They fell back, overwhelmed by the imperial army's numbers. A few fought. Mulan blocked an enemy rider's attack as Shang dispatched him from the side. Other skirmishes ended just as quickly. The Huns were outnumbered, and they knew it. It wasn't long before they started dropping their weapons and raising their hands in surrender.

As the fighting quietened around her, Mulan surveyed the canyon. Most of the Hun soldiers around her had given up, though skirmishes still continued in places. One particular cluster of Huns caught her attention. They were skilled fighters, judging from the trouble they were giving the Chinese soldiers around them. Still, the Huns fell one by one, until one rider broke away from the rest and rode flat out for the canyon, trampling some of his wounded allies in the process.

"That's Prince Erban!" shouted Mulan. "Hold the archers.

I want him alive."

There was no time to see if her instructions were acknowledged. Mulan kicked Khan into a sprint as her troops hurriedly cleared out of her way. She flattened herself against Khan's neck. Khan was a fast horse, with plenty of life left after that short battle, but Erban had got a head start.

Hoofbeats rumbled behind her, but Mulan paid them no mind as her vision narrowed only to the prince. Erban looked to be uninjured, and he rode with the same desperation that Mulan had felt just an hour before. She was narrowing the gap between them, but too slowly. Mulan gritted her teeth as Erban neared the far mouth of the canyon. She wished she knew where the rest of his army was.

A red-brown streak dived out of the sky. Erban threw his arm over his face, desperately protecting his eyes as Zhonglin's hawk clawed at his face. The prince's horse reared and spun, and it was a credit to his horsemanship that he wasn't thrown.

As Mulan closed in, the bird lifted off. Erban reached for his sword, drawing it just in time to block Mulan's first blow. He was slower to counter her second. Mulan channelled all her anger from the past days into her attack, driving him further and further back, giving him no quarter. Finally, Erban's balance faltered. Mulan wrapped her blade around the prince's and flicked it to the side, sending his weapon skidding across the dirt. Zhonglin's hawk let out a defiant shriek and landed on the sword's pommel, wings spread wide.

"Prince Erban," said Mulan. The prince's eyes, so cold and cutting before, now regarded her with fear. "I'm ready to begin our negotiations."

CHAPTER TWENTY-TWO

The red-winged hawk flew low over Mulan's head and let out a high-pitched call.

Zhonglin glanced up. "They're lined up, waiting for you."

"Who?" asked Mulan.

"Your people," said Zhonglin, her wide eyes sparkling. "Word has spread that you're coming."

The road to the Imperial City was fairly clear except for Mulan's troops. But now that Zhonglin mentioned it, Mulan did hear something like a faint murmur around a bend up ahead.

The murmur turned into cheers as they rounded the curve. Before them, the path dropped down into a valley, and the Imperial City came into view. All along the side of the road, people were lined up several deep. Farmers with sun-browned faces, mothers with toddlers on their backs and infants in their arms, rich merchants in fine silk clothes, all lifted their voices.

"Long live Empress Mulan. May she live ten times ten thousand years!"

Mulan sensed a collective straightening in the troops flanking and following her. She couldn't help sitting taller as well. Shang, riding next to her, caught her eye, and they smiled at each other. Liwen rode behind them, holding the same phoenix-and-dragon banner they'd taken to war.

A flower arced through the air and fell on the path ahead of her. Mulan searched for the thrower and saw a peasant woman fanning her fingers across her face. As Mulan watched, the woman closed her hands into fists and stacked one on top of the other. The gesture – one that Mulan had so recently mistaken for a sign of rebellion – spread through the crowd. Mulan glanced at Zhonglin, who winked.

Negotiations with the Hun generals had proceeded quite smoothly once Mulan took Prince Erban prisoner. King Ruga was fond of his younger son and eager to have him returned in one piece. Two days after Erban's capture, the Hun army retreated north towards the border. Erban himself travelled back to the Imperial City with Mulan, where he would stay until a proper ransom was delivered.

As Mulan's army approached the city gates, the cheers grew to a deafening roar. Mulan waved and smiled until her arm ached.

"You don't look nearly as uncomfortable doing this compared to the last time we entered through these gates together," said Shang. Now that the dangers of battle had passed, he rode easily, his limbs loose and his smile quick to appear.

Mulan chuckled. That had been a lifetime ago, travelling into the city with no idea what the emperor had in store. Back then, she'd felt self-conscious, underserving of the attention lavished on her.

Shang watched her with interest. "What are you thinking?"

"That I probably shouldn't let this go to my head," she said. When he raised an eyebrow, she continued. "Mostly I feel grateful. For loyal friends."

"Just that?" said Shang.

Mulan thought about it. "No," she said. "There's more. I don't feel like a pretender to the throne any more. I'm grateful for the love my people are showing me, and beyond that, I'm ready for the responsibility that goes with it."

The palace gates opened for her. Inside the massive entrance courtyard, the entire staff had lined up to welcome the empress. Maids, eunuchs, gardeners, grooms and soldiers stood at attention, lining the path to the throne room. The troops behind her fell back as Mulan continued the final length of the procession with Shang, Liwen and Zhonglin at her side. While the crowds in the city had been raucous, it was completely quiet within the palace walls. The only sound came from Mulan's and her companions' boots on the courtyard flagstones. Mulan found the silence no less intense than the roaring celebration outside. If anything, there was more energy here, the sense of hundreds if not thousands of eyes on her, watching and waiting.

At the opposite end of the courtyard was a wide set of stairs leading up into the red-columned great hall. Ting and the rest of Mulan's personal maidservants stood at the top, eagerly awaiting her beneath lintels of red, blue and gold. The eunuchs that tended to Mulan and her advisers were there, too, but there were some conspicuous absences.

"Where are my ministers?"

Mulan's head eunuch stepped forward and bowed. "They have not been seen at the palace since last night."

Mulan's elation dissipated. Next to her, Shang's face darkened.

"They've fled," she said.

"It would appear so," said the eunuch. This time, he bowed as if to shield himself from her coming reaction.

Mulan shook her head, determined not to let this development cloud her return. She would deal with it later. Right now, her people needed her.

She made it to the top of the grand steps. From up here she could see the entire palace staff arrayed out before her in patches of blue, green and brown uniforms. Behind the palace staff stood a much less orderly crowd of commoners who'd squeezed in.

Mulan spoke as clearly and loudly as she could. "The past weeks have been difficult for our country. Treachery from within the palace and invaders from the north almost delivered us into the hands of our enemies. But you, my people, stayed true to China. You, my people, came to my aid when I rallied you to defend us. And today, because of your bravery, we are safe and poised to prosper."

The crowd erupted in cheers. As Mulan waited for the shouts to quiet down, a lone soldier moving through the throng caught her eye. He didn't look armed, but he was definitely headed for the stage. Shang left Mulan's side, moving quietly down the steps to meet him. The soldier bowed to the general and spoke in his ear.

Shang's mouth tightened. He came up the steps and spoke in low tones, for Mulan's ears alone. "Your ministers were caught trying to scale the city walls. My guards have them right outside the gate."

Though Mulan's stomach dropped at the news, her response came easily. "Bring them here," said Mulan.

It took a while for the occupants of the courtyard to realise what was happening. Little by little, the crowd made way for the sorry-looking procession now headed towards the empress. Mulan's ministers looked much less impressive when they weren't dressed in their finery. Minister Fang, usually so well put together, looked downright scraggly in ill-fitting peasant clothes, his owl eyes confused, instead of wise. Minister Wei, the physically imposing minister of justice, now resembled the criminals he dressed down in court. One by one, they were taken up the steps and made to kneel in front of Mulan. Most stared down at the ground. Only Minister Liu, the one who'd pretended to be her friend, looked up at her now. He'd seemed harmless before. Now, wrapped in commoner's clothes and sporting the same scholar's gaze, he was almost invisible to anyone not paying attention. But Mulan would no longer underestimate him or any of his associates. They'd almost succeeded in taking away her throne, but even more unnerving was how they'd made her doubt her own ability to rule, how they'd almost convinced her that she was useless.

Mulan spoke directly to them but made sure her voice was loud enough for all to hear. "The five of you are traitors in every possible way," she said. "You spat on the old emperor's wishes, and then you actively worked to give our country to our enemies. You did this for your own personal gain, because you did not want a woman to rule over you. Do you have anything to say for yourselves, before you are taken to await your trial?"

A long silence followed. Minister Fang lifted his head, and a trace of his old arrogance reappeared on his brow. "Hens should not announce the dawn," he said.

Mulan sucked in a breath, shocked that Fang would show such defiance even now. Next to her, Liwen hissed, and Shang took a step forward. Mulan motioned him back. But as she opened her mouth to speak, a great gust of wind blew through the palace courtyard. Instead of dying down, it grew stronger, until Mulan's clothes flapped against her, and she had to brace herself to keep her footing. The officials around her grabbed at their fu tous. As hats took flight all around them, a low thrum filled the air, growing louder and louder until it became the sound of thundering hooves.

Someone in the crowd screamed.

"Ghosts!"

"Riders from Heaven!"

Mulan craned her neck towards the sky. Wisps of what looked like clouds raced towards them from the horizon. For a moment, the remembered terror of her coronation night filled her again, the echo of her panic and dread at the shooting stars. But a moment later, the shapes resolved into female riders. General Fu Hao rode at their head, her sword raised high. At her heels, her arrow-like gaze fixed on Fu Hao, followed young Xun Guan. Behind Xun Guan came others – archers and nomad horsewomen, even old Mistress Zhu riding like a woman half her age. Lin Siniang led a contingent of women, each more beautiful than the last, and then came Liang Hongyu and her soldiers in tight formation. The riders were more ghost-like than Mulan had ever seen them – five times larger than any mortal, white as the clouds, their eyes lit with sun fire and their armour trailing rainbow light. The noise of their coming was that of an earthquake, and the people in the courtyard covered their ears. The riders rode until they encircled the palace rooftops. Then Fu Hao reined her horse to a stop. All around them, ghost riders gazed down at the openmouthed crowd.

Fu Hao raised her sword again in salute.

"All Hail Empress Mulan. May she live ten times ten thousand years."

As one, the spirits dismounted and bowed on one knee.

It was an awe-inspiring tableau, the motionless spirits united in their tribute. In the new silence, no one breathed. And then one by one, the people in the imperial courtyard followed suit.

As everyone around her fell to their knees, Mulan looked once again to her ministers. Liu, Huang and Kin were already bowing. Minister Wei turned his head this way and that, looking unexpectedly unsure for a man of his size. And Minister Fang, who had spoken so arrogantly, was now completely white. As Mulan's gaze fixed on both of them, they followed their fellow ministers and kowtowed.

Once again, Mulan was the only one standing, but this time, instead of rushing everyone back to their feet, she stood tall.

"You say that hens should not announce the dawn." She

spoke powerfully enough for all to hear. "And yet it has happened every morning since the day I was crowned. You presumed to know Heaven's will, claiming that the five falling stars at my coronation were Heaven's disapproval of me, rather than indictments of your own treachery. But the spirits have spoken. I am the rightful empress of China, chosen by my predecessor and given the Mandate of Heaven. And I will remain empress of China until the gods, not you, decide otherwise."

...

There was much work to be done over the next few weeks. It took a lot to keep a government running, and that work was infinitely multiplied when five of a country's six ministers were in prison. Mulan started the long process of vetting current staff and finding new candidates for empty positions. She also planned a tour of China to get to know her people and identify allies in other regions of the country.

Shang was constantly by her side – advising, helping, administering when needed. Mulan was glad to have him. As always, they worked together efficiently and agreeably, but there was an undercurrent of uncertainty when they were together. Mulan's ministers were gone. The Huns had withdrawn their marriage proposal. But Mulan was still Shang's empress. What did that mean for the two of them? Neither of them brought it up, and with all that needed to be done, there never seemed an appropriate time to have that conversation.

Still, Mulan sometimes caught him gazing at her, and the look in his eyes made it abundantly clear that his feelings had not changed. They shook her, those unguarded moments when Shang let his longing come to the surface. Invariably, something inside Mulan would yearn back. She thought often of the night they met secretly near Guozhi's caravan, and she would wonder.

A few weeks after their return, Liwen walked into Mulan's apartments.

"You need a new minister of justice," she said, snatching a loquat from Mulan's fruit bowl and popping it into her mouth.

Mulan grabbed a handful for herself, knowing that once Liwen got started, the loquats wouldn't last very long. "I need much more than that. Everyone except for Shang needs to be replaced."

Liwen spit out a pit. "I know. But your minister of justice should be me." She raised a perfectly sculpted eyebrow when Mulan stared. "What? I know the country. I've travelled all around it. And I've spent much of my life rounding up outlaws, I'll have you know."

Mulan finally found her voice. "I'm quite familiar with your qualifications. I just... I'd supposed you wouldn't want to be bound to the Imperial City."

Liwen shrugged. "I guess you're rubbing off on me, with

all your talk of honour and duty. I see now, how binding yourself to something bigger can move mountains."

It was strange, how nonchalant Liwen was being about all this. She seemed more interested in cutting the bruise off a loquat than discussing a course of action that went against everything she'd always claimed to be.

"Are you sure?" asked Mulan. "I wouldn't want you to give up your happiness just to help me out."

Liwen wiped juice from her chin with the back of her hand. "Don't flatter yourself, friend. I'm quite fond of you, but I'm doing this for China. And besides, you'd let me go off and have adventures once in a while, right?"

At this, Mulan finally smiled. "I suppose I could. But only if you get your job done."

...

Zhonglin also lingered in the Imperial City. Though she appeared every few days at court, she otherwise made herself scarce. Mulan wasn't sure where the spirit spent the rest of the time, or how long she planned to stay. Even when Zhonglin was around, she seemed more distracted and daydreamy than usual, as if her attention were already moving to another realm, time or place. There was much Mulan still didn't know about Zhonglin. She had her suspicions about who the young woman had been as a mortal, but she sensed that Zhonglin would not be willing to confirm or deny them.

One night, as Mulan took a rare break in her gardens before dinner, she found Zhonglin picking tea flowers and putting them into a basket. The guards hadn't notified Mulan of any guests, but then, it certainly wasn't the first time Zhonglin had trespassed into that space.

The girl didn't run this time as Mulan approached, instead smiling and waving her over. "Well met, Empress. How are you adjusting to your reign?"

"I'm still learning," said Mulan. "But it's much easier this time around."

"Things are simpler when one's advisers are not actively trying to undermine you."

It seemed as good a time as any to broach the question. "Speaking of advisers, I'd meant to ask—"

Zhonglin raised a long-fingered hand. "I can't stay. I wish I could, but there are other women who need our counsel. Now that you've established yourself, I must go help others."

Somehow Mulan had expected that. Curiosity won out. "When you go to them, will you appear as yourself? As Zhonglin?"

"No, the Queen's Council has no one true form. We have many faces and shapes. The next queen who needs our help may be in another time and place altogether, places far along and beyond the end of the silk road."

Mulan paused to imagine those great distances, feeling somewhat envious that Zhonglin had seen so much of the world. "When will you leave?" she asked.

"A few days," she said. "But don't look so glum. I'll be sure to visit."

"I'll be glad to see you when you do."

For a long moment, they smiled at each other. And then Zhonglin's smile brightened. "There's someone who wanted to take advantage of my talents one last time before I leave. She'd be very upset with me if I forgot."

"Who?" Mulan tried to remember if she had unfinished business with any members of her spirit council.

Raising her eyebrows enigmatically, Zhonglin waved her hand, and the familiar portal opened in the air of the garden. Mulan looked through, expecting to see the silver forest, but instead the door led to a very familiar garden, with a familiar red pagoda atop a hill.

Heart racing, Mulan stepped through. As she ascended the hill toward her ancestral temple, a figure beckoned from a bench by the door. Mulan broke into a run.

"Come, Mulan, my darling empress," said Grandmother, her crinkling eyes as warm as the summer breeze. "Let us make the most of our time."

• • •

Preparations continued at a swift pace for the empress's first grand tour of China. Messengers rode out daily with missives for provincial governors and returned with words of welcome and promises of hospitality. Mulan told her governors not to worry about lavish banquets or entertainments. She asked instead for meetings with leaders from all sectors and for tours of the major industries. Additionally, she made plans with Liwen to wander the countryside by themselves – in disguise.

Mulan also sent out messengers looking for the caravan led by a man named Guozhi. She hoped to hear from him before she left on her trip, for she greatly desired to sit down and have a long talk with him over tea. Part of it was simple curiosity at how much he'd known. Besides that, Guozhi was a trustworthy man who often saw great swaths of the country. He would be a valuable ally, if he were willing.

On a rare quiet evening before the trip, Mulan summoned Shang to her sitting room. It had been a day or two since they'd crossed paths, and she was glad to see his face.

"How are you faring?" she asked.

"Busy, of course," said Shang, "but well. I've finalised our escort unit. They're good, loyal soldiers and very capable. Also, the commander of the Chengdu militia has written me back. He's very eager to discuss co-ordinating defence duties with the imperial army."

"I'm glad." She still marvelled at how straightforward it was to accomplish things now, compared to the first time around.

"It's a good thing, this trip," said Shang. "The people will be happy to see you."

They sat down at her table, and Mulan poured them both a cup of tea. Shang took a moment to breathe in the chrysanthemum fragrance before raising the cup to his lips. For a moment, they sipped in companionable silence as they both enjoyed what she suspected was their first moment of peace all day.

"I see you're pouring your own tea now," Shang finally said.

Mulan chuckled. "I let the maids serve me when the occasion warrants, but I thought it better that they not be here for this conversation."

She'd said this in a light-hearted way, but the air changed after that. Mulan didn't speak, and Shang didn't speak. Mulan looked down at her teacup, where a lone chrysanthemum petal drifted in circles. Her heart beat lightly against her rib cage.

"I don't think," she said slowly, "I've ever properly thanked you for your loyalty during the coup. For coming to find me" – she was momentarily distracted by the thought of what else had happened the night he found he – "and for gathering the armies."

"You know there's no need to thank me," said Shang. He said it matter-of-factly. Not in the cloying way of her old ministers, but just as a statement of truth.

Mulan nodded. "I'm trying to surround myself with

trustworthy advisers, people who care about the country, who are honest and loyal. I'm also learning to trust my own judgement on the best way to rule." She looked at him. "Do you trust my judgement?"

Shang looked up, alert to her tone. "Of course I do."

Again, he spoke sincerely, and she felt a rush of gratitude for his presence. "I've been thinking about the dynamics of my reign, the unique challenges of being an empress instead of an emperor. Political marriages are especially dangerous for someone like me. The traditional office of the emperor commands too much power. The lure of it is too great. Any foreign prince who marries me would want to seize that power and make himself the de facto ruler. Even if my people love me, there will always be those who prefer a man to rule."

Shang nodded thoughtfully, though his expression betrayed nothing. "That sounds reasonable."

"There are ways to do diplomacy that don't involve loveless marriages. Treaties, trade, trustworthy ambassadors." Her pulse sped up, though she clung to an outward veneer of calm. "What I need," Mulan said quietly, "is someone who will stand by my side. Someone who will support me in my role." She looked at him, willing her heart into her eyes. "Someone who loves me, and whom I love in return."

As Shang gazed back at her, everything around them became blurred, muffled. Finally, she spoke the terrifying, hopeful words.

"I want you to marry me, Shang."

In that moment, Mulan could hear nothing but her heart beating in her ears. For what seemed like an eternity, silence hung between them.

Shang let out a shaky breath. His expression wasn't a clear yes, and Mulan's soul froze. "Mulan," he said. "Heavens know I want nothing more, but I worry I'll be holding you back."

Relief flooded through her at his words. She took his hands. "Shang, we've led China to victory now, not once but twice. You don't hold me back. Your love makes me stronger."

Shang looked down at their hands, furrowing his brow in deep concentration as if he couldn't figure out the lacing of their fingers. Abruptly, his expression softened. He chuckled softly. "You're hard to argue against, you know. Or perhaps I'm just eager to be convinced."

Mulan smiled. "Is that such a bad thing?"

Shang gave a self-deprecating grin. "No. It's just that when you want something... someone..." He stopped and tried again. "I've dreamed of being with you for so long. And now that it finally seems possible... I suppose I'm afraid of waking up and finding out that it's not real."

"We'll make it real." Mulan traced the edge of her teacup. "I don't mean that simply as pretty words, Shang. If there's one thing I learned these past months, it's that we can't expect to be carried by fate towards what is worthwhile and good. We have to reach for it."

Shang looked in her eyes, and perhaps he saw the certainty there, because it became reflected in his own. He sighed then. And his face shone with relief and deep joy. "In that case, may I have permission to kiss the empress?"

She beamed back, and even though the answer was clearly written over every inch of her being, she answered. Even though she and Shang already leaned for each other, bridging a distance that had been so impossibly far just days before, she reached for him. And even as Shang drew her close, their eyes drifting closed as their breath mingled, Mulan spoke the words a moment before their lips touched.

"Yes, General. Please do."

ACKNOWLEDGEMENTS

Writing my first Disney Princess novel was incredibly fun, thanks to the support of a great number of people.

Thank you to my agent, Jim McCarthy, for suggesting me as a candidate for this project and for being a guide and cheerleader throughout the process.

I'm grateful for Jocelyn Davies's guidance and genius throughout the entire process, from brainstorming to outlining to revisions. Thanks for being game when I suggested that more people needed to die. Thank you also to Kieran Viola for shepherding and fine-tuning the later stages of the manuscript. There are many other team members to thank as well, including Vannesa Moody, Cassidy Leyendecker, and numerous others who worked behind the scenes to make this book a reality.

I'm lucky to have my fellow Queen's Council authors, Emma Theriault and Alexandra Monir, who provided advice and comradery, and made this journey so much more fun. Alexandra also gave me some great advice on an early draft, including some excellent tips for strengthening the romance.

In preparing to write this book, I spent a good deal of time reading up on the culture and history of ancient China. This process was greatly streamlined thanks to my assistant, Birgit Saalfeld, who worked hard tracking down articles and books on everything from clothing to fortune-telling to biographies of female warriors.

As always, I'm grateful for my support networks. Much love to the writers of Courtyard Critiques and Fantasy on Friday for your friendship and encouragement. Thank you to my husband, Jeff, for picking up the slack in household duties when I was on deadline. My daughter's wonderful preschool teachers gave her a fun and nurturing place to play while I wrote. And after Covid shut down schools, Netflix's collection of Mandarin-language cartoons took over with some bilingual screen time. Thank you to my mom and dad for watching the kid when it was safe to do so, and for bragging to everyone that I was writing this book. And much gratitude to my mother- and father-in-law for reading everything I've written thus far.

The Covid lockdowns started a couple weeks after I finished the first draft of this novel. As I write these acknowledgments, the United States is hurtling into a deadly winter surge — its worst yet. I and countless others owe a great deal to the frontline and healthcare workers who risk their lives to keep the world running. Thank you. And here's hoping that by the time this book hits shelves, all this will be a memory.

LIVIA BLACKBURNE

wrote her first novel while researching the neuroscience of reading at the Massachusetts Institute of Technology. Since then, she's switched to writing full-time, which also involves getting into people's heads but without the help of a three-tesla MRI scanner. She is the author of the New York Times best-selling Midnight Thief series and the Rosemarked series, as well as the picture book I Dream of Popo.

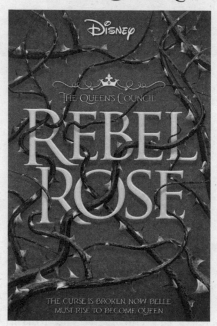

THE QUEEN'S COUNCIL

REBEL ROSE

THE CURSE IS BROKEN. NOW BELLE MUST RISE TO BECOME QUEEN

Written by Emma Theriault

Happily ever after is only the beginning...

It's 1789 and France is on the brink of revolution.
Belle has broken the Enchantress's curse, restoring the Beast to his human form and bringing life back to their castle in the principality of Aveyon. But in Paris, the fires of change are burning, and it's only a matter of time before the rebellion arrives on their doorstep.

Not so very long ago, Belle dreamed of leaving her provincial home for a life of adventure. Now she finds herself living in a castle, torn between her past as a commoner and her future as royalty. With violent factions looking to take control and a magic mirror that holds a dire warning, events threaten to overcome her. With everything she loves at risk, Belle must embrace her own strength and become the queen she is meant to be.